Sophie McCook started writing at an early age, completing her first novel aged ten. Her first radio drama, 'The Life Trainer' was aired on Radio 4 in 2003. She has written for the BBC, Channel 4, independent film productions, as well as national magazines and newspapers.

In 2010, Sophie began an Open University English Literature degree and a week later unwisely started writing a novel, one chapter per day. Failure in her course and a hilarious novel were the eventual outcomes. Sophie lives in Findhorn, Scotland. *Thinkless* is her first novel.

For more information visit:

sophiemccook.com

D1634396

THINKLESS

Sophie McCook

LIMEHOUSE
BOOKS

For Every Bod.

1. Chap 1

London, July 2003. Outside Temperature is 35°C.

Dogs are dying in hot cars, people are fighting for electric fans in Tottenham Court Road. Women with bikinis and umbrellas stalk Oxford Street. I'm being lapped by rising events and it's getting hard to breath. Wars and death yank protest behind them. People die in protest, people die in wars. It's a circle of strife and all the time, the spotless sun rolls across us from morning 'til night.

This room is windowless and chilled. It houses a collection of monumental stones; ornate slabs of limestone that originate in the Andhra region of India sometime during 1st Century BC. If you press a cheek to the surface, the chisel lines are visible. Rock of ages, cleft by someone. A someone who fretted the simple stuff; whether his toga was frayed or whether the grains he ate last night agreed with his stomach. Thinking of him anchors me. If I don't hold onto this stone, I'll be swept out in a deluge of history. The painted backdrop of my life is being torn. Invasion. Iraq. Bali. Chechnya. Blix. Kelly. Not in Our Name. Riot. Suicide. Drought. Flood. G8. SARS. WMD. 38 °C. I know I'm outside these events looking in, but from here they feel like extensions of me, the workings of my brain executed on the global stage, each popping synapse is a string puppet; a sniper on a hill, a child in a flood, a combatant behind a mosque. History is making connections like there's no tomorrow. I have to get away or risk being over-whelmed. But wherever I go, my mind goes too. There is no escape.

The attendant comes in and with him, unwelcome warm air.

'Hello.'

'Hello.'

'You're here again.'

'I know. Please don't ask me to leave.'

'Do you remember what I said yesterday?'

'If I keep coming and standing in this climate controlled environment, I'll send the humidity levels up and it's going to strip the stones like a chemical peel?'

'Well done, that was it word for word.'

And so, that's how I got barred from the British Museum.

*

If any weather can feel ridiculous, this is it. It's like swimming through ridiculousness. In this heat, blisters grow like potatoes on my feet as I squirm back to Bloomsbury to my brother's flat.

Like my brother, the flat is shady and cool. There's scaffolding running up the outside of the building so I am meant to keep the street windows SHUT AT ALL TIMES! But the builders have not been seen all week and what can be taken through a six inch gap in a dead-locked window?

This is where I'm living until my younger brother's stops throwing his BMX over cliffs in New Zealand. His other (fixed-wheel racing) bike is currently blocking the hallway in Huntley Street. When he's not on his bikes, he's up a snowy French mountain on twintip skis. In the few weeks left, he works for advertising agency ThWfctry (formerly known as the 'The Want Factory', before that, 'Ingongrua' and before that 'Hopkins & Stead'?). My brother was the guy who created all the funny adverts for that German supermarket, turning it from a budget warehouse into a middle-class secret deli. He still shops at Planet Organic.

My sister is seven years my senior and dislikes me. I am the embryo love spawn that stole her father and turned her mother into a hyper-protective Catholic. I in turn dislike my brother for similar reasons. He's the only one of us who seems happy. His own mother used smarts and legal foresight to keep Dad on side for most of Tom's upbringing. We all of us hope that Wife-to-be-Number-Four is post-menopausal. She doesn't look it.

I'm of no fixed salary, abode or career. I live in the moment, which I hear is very spiritual. The trouble is, the moments keep happening. I'm one long moment.

My ex-boyfriend maintains a holding pattern around my brain. Who knows when this obsession will end? Let's call him Chap 1. All communication between us stopped. I've developed the twitchy traits of a stay-at-home weasel; with one hand I'm texting friends to ask if Chap 1's been seen and with the other hand, I'm praying. What's the sound of one hand praying? All muffled promises to myself and scenarios and incantations and whatever mumbo-jumbo I think will make it better.

This black hole in my head is gradually growing. It's sucking in the horizon and all the time, the city heat increases. I stuff Kleenex down my bra to stop the sweat river. I don't have a fan. I have to get out of here.

2. Zombie Attack!

Tom's first pad in London was a squat with concrete floors and grey walls. Now he has concrete effect floors and slate-grey eco paint. There's one 10ft framed map of London on the wall and a racing bike in the hallway. I water the succulents. I skin my legs on his bike. I colour co-ordinate his bookshelf.

It would be a completely Yoko Ono existence if it wasn't happening at 31 degrees. The letterbox gives birth to rectangle placental sacks of magazine every few days, although Tom's only in the country eight weeks a year. I make glossy piles out of 'Cycle Sports', 'Gliding International' and the 'The Field'.

'The Field' hypnotizes me in both its randomness and its specialty. It's not just about what happens in the field, topics also cover everything between the field and up to the point of, but not including, real life. Questions of 'How to improve your Polo?' and 'Why ride sidesaddle?' are stabled alongside 'Working with worming'. The thorny issue of 'Hunting Wear' is flushed out. Many headlines benefit from my untrained eye. What I read as 'We assess potential lesbian' was in fact 'We assess potential lead ban.' The adverts aim for a demographic that, from the accompanying photos, seem to have been created by Gerry Anderson. You can almost see the strings. A balding, be-waxed guy gamely promotes 'Bettws, UK's leading Pheasant Shoot Provider'. There's a wan gleam in his eye and a dead pheasant in his fist. The bi-line should read 'Game Birds are Go!' The main issue for Fieldies is a general thinning of blond hair and lack of palate width. They seem completely at ease with this situation and all look vaguely similar, as if seeded one night during a short but productive alien fly-by. Field families are wax-wearing dead-thing holders. I have a jewfro and an on going puzzled-rabbit-on-stage expression.

Like any house with a trade entrance, 'The Field' sends workmen to the back. Classifieds is all jacket waxing, dog appliqué jumper selling and gun dealing. So many gun dealers. (Drug lords and pimps apply elsewhere.) Today I'm sitting on the sofa trying to tease the sweat beads on my forehead to join and form patterns. Drips build and eventually release on the glossy page of 'The Field'. They are forming a circle around a tiny advert:

"Wntd urgent. House sitter 3 month 1 bed lodge + cats. Wld suit sgle cat lover."

Most self-proclaimed cat-lovers are single.

A child without portfolio for ten years now, I squirmed responsibility so efficiently that my family gave up trying to hang a remit on my shoulders. The skills I bring to the table are bed-surfing and bigging-up my situation. But Chap 1 said I could be different, he said I could settle down and it would all be fine. I could have bet my weekly income on him so he in turn repaid me with a job-seeker's allowance worth of commitment. Even I find it hard to put a hopeful spin on this.

The argument started with me using all his socks and stealing his toothbrush. It grew until eventually every bit of orbiting bile had been opportunistically engineered to pad out our fight. I shouted, 'So do you want me to go?' and he said, 'Yes.' He changed his phone number but luckily not his address. If a grown women goes and stands outside their ex-lover's house in Streatham and just watches, watches the window blinds get lowered and the lights go on, and tracks the shadows as they flit around the house, that's ok isn't it? Is it? Isn't it?

A small voice in the back of my head tells me to stop, take stock. Sometimes I vaguely make out its despairing howls. Sometimes I hear it biting its nails. It's like mental tinnitus. The best cure is distraction, all the time from every direction.

Let's move to 'The Field'. Well, why not? There it is, being advertised as an option. Chap 1 would wonder perhaps a bit; he might even worry. Even if he doesn't I can imagine that he does and that's nearly as good. Suddenly the check-point between fantasy and reality swings opens again and before I can refer to my notes from before...

The ringtone at the other end doesn't just sound far away, it's from another age. A click and then a wall of large-dog barking.

I say 'Hello?'

I am talking to a dog. I loathe cats, I detest dogs. Bad feelings don't often hit within the first second of conversation.

'HAH-LAAH?'

A woman, her voice is crackling with dog-bark static, is yelling in a high-breasted gym mistress voice.

'It's about the house sit?'

Bark.

'Too late! Leaving tomorrow. Bugger the cat pound prices, I'm paying through the nose!'

'Oh that's a shame, I love cats.'

Bark bark.

'Rahly?'

'Obsess about them. My mum breeds Siamese.'

Bark bark

'Those other people didn't have the stomach for it. No good wasting time if you're not up to the mark. Are you single?'

Bark bark

(Only in real life.)

'Yes.'

'So what's this about loving Kit?'

(What?)

Bark

'It's for three months only, y'know.'

Bark bark bark

'Three months is my favourite length of time.'

'Well bloody get in the car and get around here with your references. Be here in an hour?'

'OK'

I put the phone down. I ring back.

Bark bark bark

'Sorry, what is your address?'

'Address? W'ja mean address? Where did you hear about this? I thought Kit told you?'

'Erm.' I can't do anything except tell the truth. Damn.

'I read about it in The Field.'

'Whose field?'

'My brother's?'

'Well, I'm on Beccles Road, by the back entrance. Stop at Toff Monks and ask for Marjory, if you get lost.'

It takes me an hour alone to discover that Toff Monks is indeed a place and not, as I was beginning to suspect, a Dominican Priory with a Gold Amex card. TofT Monks is a hamlet outside the tiny town of Beccles, near the unimpressive city of Norwich in the lesser-known county of Norfolk. You get there from the second shabbiest train station in London and the three hour journey takes you through locations that ring increasingly fewer bells until you arrive at the tiniest tinkle of a name. Ten stations later, 'Beccles'.

So I'm leaving London. Let's pretend I'm escaping Zombie Attack to speed things up a little. My belongings are packed within half an hour. The dishes get left in water, the milk in the fridge (who sweats that during zombie attack?) and the window OPEN a little.

I go. (Firstly moving Tom's bike away from the front door so I can exit safely.)

Train journeys can last forever, so to kill time I habitually make up bullshit for the consumption of fellow travelers. They're usually male and eager to believe. The most common ruse is that I'm French; I can do a brilliant accent and my curls and moley skin give it texture. After a couple of nasty episodes, I nowadays make sure that the person in question is not actually French and that my story doesn't become too outlandish (I won't be pretending I went to Cambridge anymore, not without learning what the colleges are called).

There is no-one near except a smirking blond lady (looking suspiciously alien-seeded) sitting diagonally across from me. At Chelmsford, Mark Cotterel est arrivé. Allors, moi, Monique is 'aving lots of fun avec Mark until il est descendu, à Halesworth. Then it's just me and The Smirking Lady who gets out at Beccles as well.

I ask her how to get to Toft Monks. She smirks and points towards the bus station.

3. Knee-Capped

The bus gets in at ten past six, after me nearly chewing my knee-caps off with it offering any destination in Norfolk but Toft Monks. It's all been going a little bit wrong since I left Beccles Bus station and realised my mobile hadn't saved Barking Ladies's phone number.

Toft Monks is a single street with houses stapled to one side. The road is called Beccles Road, just to remind the villagers that there are viable alternatives. I stumble down and back up again. No cafes, no shops. In fact, the village seems completely unmanned. The air is dusty. My hair is filling with matter.

I stand on the curb, in the centre of Toft Monks' commercial beating heart – a Fiat showroom and the pub.

Piss, stale beer and toilet duck. The Red Lion is an empty British bar. A shape pops out from a back room. Massively overweight and sweating a pink polo shirt purple. Imagine a nudist colony on a warm day, trying to break the world record for number of chubby naturists crammed into one elevator. He's carrying pint glasses on the end of his hands and that's what they look like.

'Awreigh-y?'

'I was wondering if you could tell me where Marjory lives?'

'Marjory who?'

'She has a lodge? She's going away?'

He shakes chins.

'Sary.'

'Cats. Lots of cats? And dogs?'

'Sary.'

He was supposed to know. Marjory said he would know.

So much piss, so much toilet duck.

At Liverpool Street Station, I refused the £1 price of a return ticket because I was enjoying the argument with the cute guy in the booth.

I've argued myself a long stretch Norfolk with no money, shelter or option to rewind or delete . No-one cares if I lie out in the middle of Beccles Road and pray for a Fiat test-driver.

Especially not Chap 1.

'She knows some guy called Kit?'

He blinks again. What is this? Morse code?

'Oh you mean KIT... at Taft 'all?' He removes his hand from the glass with a liquid squeak. 'You mean a big fat woman with a bunch of dogs?'

I smile sweetly.

'That's a good foive mile walk to Taft. JUMBO!?'

A skinny silhouette responds from the kitchen. Jumbo wears grease-stained blue overall emblazoned "FIAT". He tilts his ears. The hair on the back of my neck prickles. I am being sized up by a trainee mechanic from Norfolk.

During the journey of at least eight miles in his Fiat Punto, I make sure I don't ask why he's called 'Jumbo'. His grin froths. My heart thumps my eardrums. I'm sorry God – I was just mucking around. Please don't let me be a headline in next week's Beccles Gazette, headlined 'Decomposed. Found by Dog Walkers.'

But then I feel bad. Jumbo slams the door. I try to say 'Thank you' but he and the Punto spin away in a cloud of dust and a growl of diesel. He may have noticed my hand on the door handle all through the journey. I'm certain the frothing was just eagerness.

The tiny cottage he's dumped me at may or may not be Marjory's. A dark wood bear-hugs it on three sides and a blue- painted fence on four. I remember that Marjory thinks I've only come a short way so I hide my case under a bush.

'Ding -

Bark bark bark

-Dong.'

So, the right house. There's a stompstomp and then a scuffle and finally the door opens. I beam at Marjory and savour the experience of three red setters licking my jacket. Marjory is a woman of four parts – or two, depending on how you break it down. She has one enormous chest and one enormous arse. Or, two giant boobs and two prodigious hips.

'You took your time!'

Having lived in Tom's place for a few months, I'd forgotten what nick-nacks were. Every surface that can deal with gravity holds something of Marjory's. The kitchen has a sofa with a throw. On the throw are cushions and on the cushions is a dog blanket and on the blanket are hundreds and hundreds of dog hairs. On the dog hairs are slightly soiled newspapers. She invites me to sit down. I sit down. I smell dog in all its forms.

'The only thing you need to worry about are the cats.' Marjory is busy knitting a giant blue blanket. 'I have three. Two of them are Good Cats. They can go wherever they like except out of the front door. There's a fast road at the front. Please let them out of the back.'

I nod and wonder if her cats really are ignorant of the amazing world of front.

'The Bad Cat lives in the boot room. He can only go out when the two Good Cats are in.'

Everything in this room is blue. I nod again. 'Simple, Good Cats in, Bad Cat out.'

Blue. Blue curtains, blue rug, blue cushions. Blue plastic flowers. Even the pictures on the wall have faded blue in sympathy of the decor.

'There's not a lot to, I'm afraid. You can feed the cats and play with them. There's knitting if you're interested.'

There are piles of blue wool in baskets. She's a blue fundamentalist. If I wore pink sunglasses, this entire house would be in 3D.

'What about the dogs?'

'Didn't Kit tell you?' Marjory points with her knitting needles. 'I take the dogs everywhere.' She's even wearing blue herself. 'Whatever the dogs do, I do.'

(Really? I've seen dogs doing some pretty skanky things.) 'Well, if your stomach's holding up, I'll give you a go right away. Cat Kennels are beastly.'

Then I find myself outside her blue front door, promising to return as soon as I'd decided. The trees are ganging up on the sunlight.

This is awkward.

I collect my bag. I trundle it up and down the road a bit. I'm not the perfect candidate for peace, quiet and self-sufficiency. My ego likes blinkers, background noise and constant distraction to see it through the periods when my eyes are open. The woods have claustrophobic black holes and low whoopy sounds. My bladder tightens. Then my knuckles start rapping at Marjory's barking door. Her square silhouette fills the light.

'That was quick.'

4. Malevolent Ginger

I've woken up to a face covered in dog-hair and my cheek stuck to the couch. I'm not sure about this sleeping bag either. I think I met a cat in the night. Something purred on me in the pitch dark and dug its claws in my chest.

I lie and look at the ceiling which has a crack shaped like the River Nile. Outside, a bird is being so bird-like, I become convinced that someone is playing a swannee whistle. This gets me out of bed and out of the front door. I can't see anyone or anything – but the novelty in standing half naked in the open feels good.

Things look up later. After feeding her dogs what looked like an entire diced deer gut, Marjory insures me for her car! Her car – now my car! I have never owned my own car since my parents bought a Vauxhall estate for me (for them). My step-dad drove it into the ground until, during a lesson, it fell off its axle and the door came off in my driving instructor's hand. Now I have a cute little yellow Clio ('sorry about the colour but it was cheaper.' Yellow. Cheap by price, cheap by nature.) The back window is completely obscured by crusted gloop. I'm going to clean it, get rid of those blue seat covers and give it a name.

I lie low while Marjory thuds around the house, talking to everything – her dogs, her cats, her plants, her suitcases. At ten she lugs her bags out to the car and then watches me drive her, white knuckled, to Beccles train station. I never perform well in front of an audience but the trip is made trickier by Marjory's dogs who are taken by surprise whenever a car goes by. They throw themselves across the back seat and hit the rear window, barking in close harmony like the Andrews Sisters of saliva.

I leave Marjory at the train station, fussing dogs and suitcases into a straight line.

It's another blue-sky day. My yellow Clio winks at me. I, Miriam, am a Lady of Independent Means! Beccles is a cute town with an interminable one-way system. I pass butchers, bakers and teddy-bear makers. There's a little town square in one direction and a riverside in another. Everything in between is Trumpton in maze-form.

Over the bridge at Beccles (going from Suffolk to Norfolk) takes you straight onto the bypass that leads to Toft Monks. Between the village and the cottage, I pass an old yokel; the kind that staggers along the verge of any main road in the country. The local loon. They are whip-thin, have ravaged faces, ten-mile stares and a limp. They are often in wellie-boots and have a stupidly heavy shopping bag in each hand. This old guy has all of the above plus a dirty tweed jacket and silver feathery hair that waves with the passing of every speeding car. He is doing a mix of walking (ten steps) and running (five). He looks like he feet are attached to differing gears. I look at him and wonder if that'll be me in fifty years?

Back at the cottage, I decide not to park my car at the back but at the front where the main road intersects with what I guess was once a drive to the Big House and is now a farm-track with an avenue of chestnuts.

Back in the house, there's an uncanine silence. I take an exploratory creep around the house. The walls are splattered with framed images of dogs; oil paintings, tapestries, prints, etchings, faded studio photos, dogs in perspex. Dogs are definitely top...er...dog around here. Have the cats noticed? The two Good Cats are identical browny-black things. If you attached one to a stick you would have a duster. The furniture is entirely covered with blue throws. There's a matted blue sheepskin in front of Marjory's bedroom fire. There's a blue and white quilt on her narrow bed. Marjory's single and means to stay that way.

A boot room holds onto the room that attaches the back door to the kitchen. Inside this high space, with mouldering paint, frosted window and a washing machine for company is a malevolent curled ginger sphere. I close the door quietly. It's so hot outside I will not be getting the Good Cats in for hours. No wonder the Bad Cat is pissed off.

I go outside for a walk and straight away see that some tosser has parked a rusty Volvo estate on the track, completely blocking my exit. Arses! This is the kind of treatment I left London for! I pop home and return with a polite but firm note that I leave under the wiper.

The drive that leads up to the house looks like Pride and Prejudice but smells of silage. Green beech hedges lead to clipped yew. I've reached what may be a kitchen garden or some other outdated thing. By an opening I spot a wax-wearing man! My first Fieldie! But he has brown wavy hair so can't have been seeded, he's an interloper like me. I approach, ready to make contact, when he slips through the hedge and disappears. I speed up and follow and see him hurrying down the inner path and turn the next hedge corner. The top of his head bobs down the next hedged alleyway so I back up a little and cut him off at the next opening, but he carries on through the next gap. So do I.

This is madness – he's the White bloody Rabbit. I can see he's seen me and I feel my cheeks starting to burn, I at least want to tell him what I'm doing here; an explanation is becoming increasingly essential. I see his head lift momentarily, his eyebrows knit imperceptibly. He turns left through an arched gateway and is gone.

I stop. I am now purple with a strange indefinable shame, that I know is instinctive and feels vaguely Freudian.

5. Crack Den

I completely buy into the idea of cleanliness. My younger brother is tidy but he only owns twenty outrageously overpriced things. Marjory's place looks like someone lobbed a tatt-grenade through the window.

I pull the blue throws from the seats. So many throws. The fur's not coming off. Did she actually weave these rugs out of doghair?

I sit and look at the naked seats for a while. It's Friday. I've not spoken to Chap 1 in person for fifty-three days. He hasn't texted me for forty-nine . I miss him. I know I can stop thinking about him. I haven't thought about him all day. Until just now.

Marjory has a number of loudly-ticking clocks. She has a TV with one and a half channels. There's a lot of wool to knit with.

I get the urge to move furniture around. It's really heavy, lumpy and the fabric is the kind you don't want to look at up-close or have your face against. I find unspeakable things down the back of cushions – Marjory doesn't know it but her cats have tried really hard to impress her. At ten, I'm stuck. I've created a log-jam at the sitting-room door.

At ten-thirty there's excitement. Both the Good Cats want in and that means I can let Bad Cat out. I open the boot room door a crack. He's waiting for me. He is an ugly cat. He has weeping eyes, dandruff and a tail that sticks up to better display his unattractive cat-arse. He looks up at me while simultaneously looking down on me, and leaves, mooning, into the night.

I go back into the sitting room and realise I'm in near darkness. I don't know where the lights are so spend a full ten minutes feeling around the walls, climbing over seats and standing on things better seen than felt.

With the overhead light on, this room now looks like a crack den. What have I done?

Nearly eleven. It's still boiling. Will this summer never end?

The doorbell rings. What? Now? If this was London I would have the burglar-bashing stick ready. I have no peep hole, no chain-guard. What if it's green estate person from earlier, the one who I told 'There's acres of free-space to park your Volvo in. If you're still stuck, I'll show you where else you can park it!'? I grab hold of Marjory's cordless phone.

Opening the door a tiny bit, there's a guy standing in the mosquito-attracting beam of light.

He says 'Hah, I thought not!'

This sounds vaguely threatening so I close the door quickly. A pause and then the man knocks again. He shouts 'Sorry. Marjory said....well. I can't really explain through a door.'

They say that don't they, murderers? I'm alone in a house on a deserted country lane. The kettledrum theme tune to *Crimewatch* starts playing in my ears. I look at the cordless phone and try to work out how long it would take for the police to find me, especially as I'm none too sure of the directions myself. Then with a lurch, I realise I've opened the sitting-room windows. I have to keep him talking at the front door.

He says 'Your lights were on. I saw you moving furniture.' Oh God. He's been peeping in on me.

'Who are you?'

'I'm Kit.'

Oh, Kit.

'I was jogging down the lane. The furniture looks heavy.'

It is heavy. The Victorians have all the back strain of the twentieth century to answer for but have yet to pay a single osteopathy bill. I glance back at my idiot-pile of furniture.

It takes us two hours to move it. He is shortish, not much taller then me, but very strong. He has wavy dark hair and I wondered if he was White Rabbit guy from today, but WRG ran away. This guy Kit ran towards me, or at least jogged. He moves all the seats and I manage to hoover. The dog hair that comes up could insulate the roofs of half a council estate. Kit also explains why the kettle isn't boiling on the AGA. For an oven, it's kind-of stuck up.

Kit sits there in his tiny running shorts and vest. I make sure the kitchen table is in between him and me at all times. We drink tea in the very hot kitchen.

'When I opened the door, why did you say 'I thought not!'

'Marjory said...she had the impression we were friends.'

'Ah.'

'She thought we were in a relationship.'

My face heats.

'She's deaf,' he smiles. 'Breeding red setters does that. She doesn't process human speech anymore.' He has a grin that spreads across his face like Sellotape.

I hunt around for a new subject. 'I went for a walk today. I saw a guy at the end of the track. He took one look at me and ran away behind some hedges!'

'Oh. Do men normally run when they see you?' He meant this as a joke I think. 'What did he look like, this guy?'

'Like you but not in running shorts.'

Kit sits back a little.

'Oh right. That's my brother. Don't take it too seriously, he's not good at making small talk. Or any talk.'

'I chased him right around a garden.'

'Ah. Well, he wouldn't have liked that.'

Kit stands up and makes for the door. 'Night then. Enjoy your house!'

I watch him jog off into the dark. My plan to turn off every single male aged between 16 and 66 in the world continues, one man at a time.

6. Little Sweaters

Morning answers on my mobile – Beeep. 'Miriam, it's Lizzie. What's this about you moving to Norfolk? Your mum doesn't seem to know.'

Beeep. 'Good-morning Miriam, it's your mother. Haven't heard from you for over a week. I'm sending you flowers for your birthday so make sure you're in, Thursday morning. Where are you? Tom says he's tried calling the flat and had no reply'

Beeep. 'Miriam – where are you? I've tried calling the flat and had no reply'.

I return one of those calls. My step-sister Lizzie is my step-dad George's only child and is as different to me as any person completely unrelated to me could be. She's light-boned, honey-haired and constantly level-headed; the gorgeous NATO peace-keeper of the combined Short-Bosun family.

'So is this new place better than Tom's?'

'Yes, mainly because it's not Tom's place.'

'Oh give Tom a break. You know he's really generous...' Trouble with NATO peace-keepers, they treat all people equally. Yes, Tom is generous. He is aware that he's generous. He's also successful, popular, resourceful, handsome, significantly younger, do I have to continue? Isn't it clear why my relationship with him is complicated?

The sun. It's there again, bigger and better than before. Marjory's house is in the shade for eight hours a day and is mercifully cool but I have to go up to the 'offices' and pick up my sub-tenancy agreement. I am nervous. The outfit I go for is festival wear (denim cut-offs, O sunglasses, floppy hat and liberty top), which as a concept combines the best of 'rustic', 'flower child' and 'summer'.

My toes flip and flop along the chestnut track, dust rising to my knees. I eye the hedged White Rabbit garden and arrive at a more formal area, with a lawn – short and yellow in the middle, green and long at the edges.

At the fringe of the lawn, where trees and round bushes clump together to look artful, I see a tweedy figure cutting across to the back of the house, moving with knees ossified in the bent position and arms longer than his cuffs. With swinging carrier bags and black wellies, I realise in surprise that it's the run/walk crazy guy I passed yesterday on the A143. Perhaps if you're a loon everywhere's a right of way.

There is a flight of stone steps leading to a terrace and on the terrace is the house. Well, it's not Buckingham Palace but it's bigger than any sensible person would need. It has three floors plus windows in the attic. If you did a painting of the right-hand side only, then folded the sheet over and pressed it, you'd get an idea of what the whole house looks like. It is perfectly, stubbornly symmetrical.

I walk around a bit. The garden has lots of other gardens attached. If you get bored of one, just slip through a gap and here's another. There's a boules lawn and a croquet lawn. Quite the athletes then.

No sign of an office.

I discover a decaying building with a saggy roof; it's a stable with amazing blue tiles, mahogany dividers and brass hooks. No horses though; hopefully the luxury lock-up/thankless drudgery dichotomy caused an equine stampede and they broke out.

Still no offices.

Luckily at that moment, a Post Office van drives past. I flag him down and he lets me jog behind him to the offices as fast as my feet can flip. The offices are hidden behind a row of trees and a wall. It's a catalogue-built shed; basically a cheap ski-chalet. Dusty and toe-scrunched I stumble inside.

My Bridget Bardot attitude crumbles and rising from the debris is the star of my nightmares who finds herself embarrassingly half-naked in public situations. There are three desk females in neat little sweaters and shirts, all with collars up-turned. Their eyes snap over and they give me an up- and-down, typing all the while. I have no choice but to advance. 'Tenancy agreements?'

A woman indicates with her pen towards a back room.

The woman in the back room is blond, pale and angular.

Seeded. She's wearing a long-sleeved shirt, pearls and a sweater. She must be hot – boiling, but nothing gives that fact away. She's a cucumber dressed in Laura Ashley. She has a phone pushed to her ear. She turns to look at me and smirks.

I cross my legs and arms and wait. A chill creeps over me. She is familiar.

Phone call over, Cucumber seems to know why I'm here, the sub-let agreement is ready. I lean over to sign, showing as little cleavage as my pen will allow.

'Miriam Short.' She says, giving a cool smile. 'Funny, I thought you might be French. You were the other day.'

Oh God. Déja-vu, as Monique would say.

I get back home within ten minutes. Two cats come in, one cat goes out. At the front door, on the mat is a note. From Kit.

'Drinks tonight. You'll get to meet some of the staff, tenants and family. Be on the terrace at seven.'

I lie on the bed and analyze this. I have already met some of the staff, tenants and family. It might be safer for me to stay indoors for the rest of the lease.

At seven I walk up the dusty track, wearing the only below-the-knee dress I have, a red-spotted rockabilly number. There's not a single breath of wind to disperse the evening heat. Bird twitter backs up from miles around, the air smells of muggy, over-ripe flowers. At the climb to the terrace, every tread makes my breath become tighter and my mouth dries. I am suddenly aware of the weight and warmth of a vintage dress. Wine glasses clink, voices bray softly. I issue a little prayer to Buddha (because he and I have some history) and crest the final step.

7. Babysham

A mossy flagged terrace with carved stone balustrade. Groups of adults stand in defensive circles around wine glasses. As I currently appear to be invisible I take a moment to regroup. Warm air, my panic-sweat and pre-sputnik polyester are mixing together to give me a kind of muskiness that only small dogs go for. I should be OK as long as I keep my arms pinioned to my sides and no-one makes us do a mexican wave.

It's well after seven now. Craning around for Kit, there's no sign of him from where I am. Damn! Wish he was taller. There's no-one here I recognise. No, I lie. Smirking Blond is on the far side in a long linen dress. She's nodding at her male companion as if her seeded life depended on it. A wide set of French windows are open to the terrace. Decanting drinks sound from inside.

The drinks on offer are an organic pale ale, a local wine and, oddly enough, Babycham. I stand in the corner of the room with my Babycham, watching dynamics. It's like a dance. Everyone is very engaged with their partners, lots of eye contact. Then after a few minutes, everyone silently moves on and changes partners. Except for me.

There's a tiny spec of tin foil floating around the surface of my drink. I try to catch it with my finger and then chase it around the glass. Suddenly I become aware that someone is looking at me. I peek up and see it's White Rabbit Guy. He's huddled under a standard lamp with the face of a beagle in a cage. Oh no, our eyes have met. And they keep meeting. Shit, now we have to talk. He is drawn to me like the unwilling carp on the hook of a reticent fisherman.

He looks like Kit, but half a foot taller and with an anxious tension about him.

I open proceedings. 'Hello.'

He tries 'I don't believe we've met.'

He takes my hand and helpfully shakes the Babycham off for me.

'Oh we have!' says the woman with a flappping vent for a mouth. 'I chased you around the hedged garden yesterday.' There is a long pause. He stares through me for a second.

'I don't remember that.'

(Bloody liar!)

His mouth which is stretched so thin that when words come out, I'm surprised they're not squeaking like a paper comb. Quite incredible that evolution has made allowances for this level of handicap. He glances about, hoping for some crowd movement, then returns with 'So where are you staying?'

'At Marjory's. She's lent me her house. And her cats. And her car. A yellow Clio. And you?' I ask. (That's how it works isn't it? You just return the same question?)

'I run the estate.'

'Oh shit. Not the Volvo estate?' (I pretend I don't remember leaving the note under his windscreen.)

'Yes.' he mumbles. 'That too.'

Oh.

'Oh!' I take a huge swig of Babycham and suddenly get a whiff of my armpits. Chaos and fury raise my blood pressure not the slightest but place me in a normal social situation and my glands distill swamp oil and squeeze it through my pores. White Rabbit appears to be grinding his teeth? What do I do? What do I say?

'I've met your brother!' ses I.

He does something close to a complete juggling of his facial features but doesn't answer.

'He helped me move my stuff around last night.' I add.

This hasn't helped, I can tell. My cheeks begin to throb. I and my dress are becoming one. There is a throat-strangling silence.

'Well, nice to meet you. Sure we'll meet again.' White Rabbit bows a little and lollops away. I am alone again; me, my Babycham and my gingham polyester cheeks.

Maybe it's fine. Maybe that's as good a conversation you're ever going to have with a guy who hates talking. Like a nervous rodent, he's backed himself into the opposite corner of the room. He enters into close conversation with Smirking Lady. She looks up at him, nodding earnestly.

I stare at my drink. The bit of tin foil has gone.

Outside I sit on the balustrade and look over the garden. The groups have spilt out to sit or lie on the lawn. It's looking very idyllic. I wish for a second that Chap 1 was here or at least someone I could talk to. Just as I'm gloomy in the gloaming, I get a poke in the ribs.

'Hola Carmencita! Why so tragic?'

Kit is standing there grinning and necking champagne. I blame him for his brother and everyone else connected to this party.

'You're late!'

'Yes, I am.'

'I want to go home.'

'Oh.'

We amble down the track. Maybe it's because I'm lonely or maybe it's because I've drunk three glasses of Babycham. It could be because I'm perennially indiscreet. Anyway, in twenty minutes I have told Kit everything about Chap 1. How we met, a long segment about how happy I was and then how Chap 1 disappeared. I have cried like a baby a couple of times. I now have a runny nose, pink eyes, smudged mascara and streaky cheeks. In the dark, Kit can't see this. Usually a stranger would find this kind of content pretty hard to sit through but he's listening. When I start to blub again, he snakes his arm around my shoulder and gives it a squeeze.

'I met your brother tonight. Is he completely alright in the head?'

'He is. He just finds it hard to get what's in his head out of his mouth. Wym, by the way.'

'What?'

'Wym is his name.'

(That's not a proper name)

When we arrive at the house, the two Good Cats are frantically trying to claw their way out of the window and the Bad Cat is lolling on the warm doorstep. I do the cat exchange. Kit waits. Suddenly my stomach churns. Hold on, there appears to be something in the air, beyond mosquitos and clamminess. There is a kind of expectation and I'm not sure if it's me or him, or both of us. Are we both trying to say 'Goodnight' politely, or invite each other into Marjory's bed? I am feeling tender and bruised. I am ravenous for company. I would be a walkover but then, my dress smells like a monkey enclosure. I do the grown-up thing and say 'Well, night then'.

I see his Sellotape smile spread and he backs off into the woods. 'G'night Miriam!'

8. Product Placement

I wake up to find that my jewfro has bitten the dust.

My hair consumes frizz-ease, if it were a natural resource there would be EU summits and stock quotas. Tom and my older sister Signe also have curls. We are genetically manacled together by them. Signe and I don't have a relationship that encompasses hair-talk (apart from the horror we share when we meet at family functions and realise that, yet again, we have both chosen the same haircut, dress and accessories. We always sit as far apart as possible). Tom's curls are rarely washed. They hang over his face, sun-bleached at the ends. In a crowded room, you can always see where Tom is by the path he cuts as girls see him and swoon.

Clio and I go into town. I haven't quite got around to tackling the slime-encrusted rear window but her mirrors are fine. As tomorrow is my birthday, I'll celebrate by applying so much frizz-ease that John Frieda may call and offer me a contract. Everything about Beccles is cute and perfect. Apart from the people, who are wide, froggy and sunburnt. Boots has a rather limited range of Frieda products. I buy the lot.

On the drive home I spot Walk/Run man again, on the verge in his tweeds in the sun.

At home, in the ice-blue bathroom, my hair virtually wrestles the bottle out of my hand and applies it directly. I go out into the sunshine and hear my head crackle and fizz in the heat. Marjory's garden is wild and not in a Gertrude Jekyll way. The grass is dreadlocked with dog paths running through it. There are also dog toys, chewed bones and worse. White poos. There are some irises in the corner, not waving but drowning. If I can find a strimmer with a man attached, I will revive this lawn. The front grass is cut by the estate gardeners so I sunbathe there.

A dragging shug-shug-shug-shug. Suddenly a shadow, I sit up sharpish. It's Walk/Run guy.

'Well!' he says, with bouncy innuendo. He's in no state to impress. He's dusty and shabby and older than I thought. I stand up and try to lengthen my shorts.

'And you're Marjory's....niece?'

'I'm looking after her cats while she's away...somewhere.'

'Welcome and glad!' He extends a hand that I shake. His fingers feel like they've been constructed by a neanderthal out of leather, sinew and popcorn.

'I've passed you on the road,' I say. 'If you work here, I'll know to stop and pick you up next time.'

'You saw me? Damn! Didn't think anyone would notice.'

He leans in. 'I'm not meant to be here.'

'Oh!'

'They've taken the car keys. You know I've been driving since I was a boy! I could teach them to drive with my eyes closed. But...'

He shrugs his lumpy tweedy shoulders.

'They don't know I'm out and about.' He taps his nose and winks. 'Keep it to yourself? Long tall grasses, eh?'

He is a loon.

'So...' I think of something bland to say. 'Any advice for the new girl in town?'

'Yes! Don't for God's sake lie there. Ants everywhere. Growing wings and flying around, the blighters.'

I look down at the grass and if I adjust my focus, he's right – below the grass canopy, the ground is nearly black with annoyed ants. They're even climbing up my ankles.

'Bloody good dose of pesticide's what that place needs....' he nods at Marjory's cottage 'God know's how it's still standing. The woodlice must have joined hands.'

I zip my lip. He shuffles in the dust. He isn't moving on.

'Do you like hens?'

'Ahh, oh. Y'know, they aren't my thing. I was attacked by a chicken when I was small...'

'You haven't seen MY hens.'

He grabs me very tightly by the wrist, as if taking my pulse with a vice. I'm dragged across country through the trees – twigs whipping my legs. Luckily, it turns out that the hens are not too far from the cottage so I can punch and run if need be.

The hen house is creatively stacked timber held together with creosote. On a baking day like today, I am pie-eyed within a hundred feet of it. I love creosote. The hens live in a large wire cage run which they've made their own by digging holes in the dry soil and sitting in them, making 'hmmmm?' noises, not dissimilar to a teacher I used to have. There are thirty-something birds of many different feathers. Some are wearing flares. Some look like they've been through the tumble-drier. The Walk/Run man leans on the chicken wire, clicking. The hens rush at him, smitten. Then he calls me over the shed. It has boxes nailed onto the sides. When I peep in, there are real eggs sitting in real straw.

'Take 'em! Take as many as you want, They're free! Take 'em before the gyspies take 'em!'

I falter at this. 'I don't think I should. They might find out.'

'Who – them in the house? All heads on cockeyed! This place may as well be ploughed up - it may as well slide into the shitter. The staff are rum, no-one does a stitch of work. Sycamores seeding in the lawn and buttercups in the borders. Can't stand the climate either. I lived in Africa before.'

My heart softens.

'Is there anything here you like?'

'Yes. Hens.'

A distant yell. 'Prop! PROP!'

Walk/Run swings around. 'Damn!'

Into the clearing comes White Rabbit. He sees me and then ignores that he's seen me.

'Prop! I've been looking everywhere for you.'

Walk/Run grumbles a mumbly sound and slips an anxious look sideways. Oh dear – I don't like people being told off in front of me.

'He was with me, actually.' I say.

That lie needs some embroidery. Prop gives me a look that urges me to keep sewing.

'He was in my garden. He was looking at – the long tall grasses.'

Prop gives a big sigh and stares up at the blue sky. White Rabbit rocks on his boots with exasperation. 'Well. The Marchese wants to talk to you.' A petulant groan. Prop turns and drags his feet back through the trees. White Rabbit extends his hand and mumbles

'I don't think we've met.'

'Yes we did. Last night!'

He stares through me for a second.

'Oh yes, we did. You're over at Marjory's.'

A-ha. Progress!

'I'm Wym.' A brief handshake and then we're back side-by-side, arms folded. 'Could you do me a favour?' Wym shuffles. 'If you see Prop coming down that track, could you just spin him around and send him back again?'

9. Words and Hiccups

It's my birthday. I can cry if I want to...

I'm woken by a brace of messages on my mobile. My mother and Lizzie both cover the birthday subject vis-a-vis me and depression. A greeting comes from Capital One credit card, who then tell me that my account is still overdrawn. There's nothing from Chap 1. He still has time to send me a sign of some sort, the day is young. I often look on Friends Reunited, waiting for a cryptic clue. I haven't been on the internet for forty-eight hours, but that's only because I have no internet access.

I ring Tom on my mobile. He's in New Zealand. I only ring him if I have an issue that needs solving. It's the only civilised way we can carry on our relationship. Things are briskly sorted for me and he gets to exert control. Did I mention he's many years my junior?

'How's the flat?'

'The flat's fine Tom. How can I get the internet when I'm not in the flat?'

There's a long pause in New Zealand.

'You go find somewhere with internet access.'

'But what if there isn't anywhere? Let's say, theoretically, I'm in Borneo. How would I get internet access?'

'You would need a dial-up connection. Miriam. Where are you?'

'How do you get a dial-up connection?'

'You go into your provider account and add the number you're dialing up from.'

I give him a number starting with 01502.

'Where the fuck are you?!'

I make a partial confession.

'What about the flat? Is it locked?'

'Yes!'

'Are the windows shut?'

(Oh shit. I can't remember.)

'Yes!'

Tom takes my number and grumbles he'll sort it out. He doesn't mention my birthday.

One thing against me is a congenital handicap; for some reason, everyone I ever met dislikes me. For every ten people who meet Miriam, five are disenchanted immediately. The remaining four make valiant efforts with invitations to coffee mornings and girls' nights out. Gradually phone calls dry. The one remaining person takes me a bit of time, but usually so suspicious am I that this single stoic individual has not been a) weirded out or b) insulted by me that I start to wonder what their problem is. I become catty and judgmental. The lamb-like martyr's patience wears down. And there I am again, back in virgin territory.

So, for people who want to be my friend, just don't try. I will often say what I mean, and you've got to just take that. But I'll also say lots of things I don't mean. Then you've got to forgive and forget. Which things do I mean, and which don't I mean? I don't know, they swop around. And for those who find friend-making easy; who have all the sycophantic lines that sound like honey on fresh ears, who hand out smiles and nods like ambassadors with Ferrero Rocher, for whom a gambol to the nightclub is as easy as bouncing on a trampoline?

I hate you. Never be my friend.

I go outside and wash the windows but am quickly overcome with gloom. I'm cleaning windows on a day when people should be bringing me chocolates and surprise parties.

Weepy and exhausted. I go back in and step on a mouse head that's been left on the middle of the carpet for me. It's the only present I've had all day. My eyes well up again and I sit on the sofa, wiping mouse brain from between my toes.

I hear a shout. Oh God.

'Hello?' Kit comes in. 'You haven't seen an old guy wondering around? Looking a bit lost?... Oh!'

I've now met Kit three times. Two times I've been crying. He must think I'm a hormonal soup. In words and hiccups I try to explain but it all sounds very PMT, even to me. I'm just getting to the bit about my father never being there when Kit dashes to the window. 'There he is!'

Prop walks mechanically past my window.

'I've just got to grab him!' Kit exits and doesn't return.

So passes my birthday. I lie on the sofa and stare at the crack in the ceiling.

At four, my palms start to itch like crazy. I get excited because this has been proven to mean the arrival of money. But then I remember the cream-cleaner I've been using all day, and it actually means dermatitis. Still, a rash in the hand is better than two in the bush.

I go to the fridge and find a jar of crunchy peanut butter and turn on the radio for human company. Apparently old people are dying in France by the gîte-load, because their townie families have forgotten to check on them. I wonder how long I could lie here before my family started to worry? Chap 1's birthday is the twenty-first of June. I spent a year trying to find him the perfect present. I thought a sensual massage kit would bring us closer. It didn't.

At five, a locally bottled champagne with a spoon for a top comes into the kitchen and just behind it is Kit.

'So, how about a night on the town, Birthday Girl?

Parked beside the Clio is a rather snazzy Fiat convertible. The night on the town is in fact an evening in Toft Monks and the car is on a mates' rates test drive but... I'm going on a date!

Kit is looking very buff in a ripped lumber shirt. I slug back slightly flat champagne, watching the warm dusky countryside pass at sixty miles per hour and my birthday melancholy falls off in the slipstream. By the time we pull up at the Red Lion, I'm trying to work out if falling for another guy would be the best way to get over Chap 1. I started my relationship with Chap 1 to get over Chap Previous. It didn't work that time either.

There is a scattering of locals at the bar, and behind it the robustly built Landlord. I see his eyebrows and the attached jowls rise when he sees me. I give him a little wave.

'Awreighy.'

I settle with Kit at a sticky little corner table. An extension to my aforementioned social issues is that if I'm not attracted to a guy, I can be flippant, witty, naive, rude even. Guys love it. If I am interested in a person, my mouth acts like a ladder in a pair of tights. It starts and can't stop. The hole gets bigger and bigger and starts to implode. The men who like me, I'm disinterested in. The men I like avoid me because they think I have Tourettes.

In the space of five minutes with Kit, I cover topics as varied as 'denier and its meaning.' 'Squid, the cooking of.' 'Illnesses in foreign climes.' 'Camels, Iraq and Sainsburys.'

I have asked anything about Kit, not because I'm not curious but because I am fearful of what he might say if he gets a word in edgeways. Kit eventually breaks the conversation by going to the toilet. I decide my best option is to get him very drunk.

The landlord pours a pint of draught ale with his eyebrows raised.

'So, you foun' Kit then.'

'Yep, he seems really nice.'

'He does that. 'Til you 'ear the things ee got up to.'

I get a tilted jowl and a meaningful look.

'Why, what's he got up to?'

He leans in. This is my first piece of confidential local gossip.

'I woun loike to say ere'n'now. But you come back some toime midweek oi'll give you some noos. They hint got nuff cupboards for the skel'tons they got....'

10. Shock and Awe

I wake at seven, feel my red-wine head and opt for added sleep. At some time later, a total idiot knocks on my door. Then, minutes later some other (or the same) idiot starts a 125cc motorbike right beside my window. Now I'm neolithically furious. When I stand the whole room spins upwards. My brain, intestine and bladder are united under a banner saying 'Booze? Not in our name.' I grab Marjory's (blue) dressing gown. Whoever's out there, I'm planning to be sick in their boots.

The person is strimming my lawn! Someone's gifted me a gardening pixie. I stumble through the sunshine and he stops. 'Awreighy?'

I don't really want to go into whether I'm 'awreighy' or not.

'Jis doin your lawn. If you got a brew on, woun say no to whoite two sugar.'

The grass is suffering a shock-and-awe campaign. Oxygen gushes out of it. I slip into a nice dress and make a pile of scone mix. Yes, I can make scones. I also make pancakes. That's it. The scones go in the top oven of the AGA. This oven's on the whole time even when nothing's in it. I suffer AGA guilt - a sort of presbyteriyiddish post-war allergy to wastage.

I take the pixie his tea and he's less happy now.

'You could'a got rid of the dog shit.'

Ah.

Five minutes later, almost out of the blue, it starts to rain! I haven't seen rain for about three months. The guy comes into the kitchen and complains again. I accept partial blame for the garden poo. The rain has nothing to do with me.

It rains harder. The gardener goes. Then there's thunder and lightening that's quite scary. I turn off the laptop, radio and toaster and sit at the window. The storm goes on and on, really pelting. Then through the water spray comes a black shape. By the mechanical movement, I know it's Prop.

By the time I've sprung into Marjory's yellow wellie boots, sprung out of them again, emptied the mummified mice from the toes and edged my feet back in, Prop is already half-way up the lane. He is saturated and his skin grey and crinkly. For once he's chosen brogues instead of wellies. I chase and try to keep him from getting wetter under Marjory's tiny red umbrella. He blinks at me.

'Prop! You're soaking!'

He looks nervously about, as if this weather is a weapon of war; a climatic strafing. He doesn't stop so I follow. We squelch across the lawn to the terrace. Prop hasn't even acknowledged I'm here. He has a shopping bag on each side so I open the french windows. As soon as he's in, he transfers two bags to one hand, does the pincer-grip and leads me through a corridor with a sofa, through a door and up some narrow stairs. Then along a plush, carpeted corridor and into a bedroom. A very big bedroom with a big bed, a big desk, a big fireplace and big windows.

'Big.' I manage.

'Yes. This is Uncle Archie's bedroom. He had it before he went to Africa. Would you like some cake? I think I have a little cake. The sugar does buggery with my blood, but long tall grasses, eh?'

Prop gives each shopping bag a little prod whilst peeling off his clothes. I get ready to flee. He's safe now, though perhaps not sound. Luckily Prop preserves his modesty by wandering into a side room.

'Missing in Libya, poor chap. Caught it I suppose.'

A beam of sunlight crosses the garden and flies in through the windows. Summer's back.

'Archie was a champion cricketer and toad collector. True self-taught naturalist.'

Prop comes back through, top half changed. He is wearing huge shorts, elastic holders around his socks but still has his shoes on his feet. How did he get his trousers off?

'Archie taught me to clog dance. He was with the Lancashire Fusiliers – became their champion hoofer.'

Then Prop lifts his right leg in the air and brings it down with a thump, then his other foot does a little tip-tippity tap. Another thud and tiny heel-click. He swings his arms loosely. I'm impressed and also slightly scared.

Very soon a clipclipclip approaches the door. I move and it flies open. A short, front-leading woman strides in, all dress and necklace. She has a Boudicca thing going on.

'What are you doing?'

Prop freezes, one leg slightly lifted.

'You've left muddy footprints from here to the morning room.'

She becomes aware of me and snaps her head back towards Prop. He has dropped his leg and now fiddles with the frayed edge of a linen table cloth.

'Strangers in the house again. Edward.'

Prop's mouth falls open and then shuts.

Wym arrives. He sees me and his expression does not shift. The lady explains the situation to Wym.

'Your father is dancing half-naked in front of a women he has never met before.'

I have to agree, it doesn't look good.

The woman gazes on me. She has a little too much mascara, the effect makes her look as if she's constantly glaring. But at the moment I know I'm definitely being glared at.

'I've met her!' says Wym.

'So have I,' says Prop. 'She's living in Marjory's. She likes hens.'

A silent crowd cheers.

'Oh well, do please excuse my ignorance. It seems I'm the only person who hasn't been introduced.' She says this in a manner that could sheer an arctic ice wall. Then she turns on her heel and exits.

Wym leads me to an open staircase that winds and joins like two merging motorways. Down, down to a grand entrance hall, then back through the French window room. Wym treats this expanse as a perfectly normal family home. It's all tick-tock creak creak beeswax fireplace smell. In Basingstoke where I come from, a room is a terminus, not a place you walk through. In our house, a large framed 'canvas effect' photo of Lizzie in black robes and mortar board takes pride of place over the mock stone fireplace. Our clock is the video recorder, and the smell of home is of bacon, Mr Muscle and a glade plug-in. In Toft Hall, twelve generations avert their eyes as I pass. Even the miniatures are judging me.

We go out and back across a steaming lawn.

'I hope Prop's going to be OK!' I say in my kind voice.

'Thanks for bringing him in.' says Wym.

Heavy drops of water fall from the trees onto our heads.

'I didn't know he was your father.'

Wym's jaw clenches a bit. 'Did you get your lawn cut?'

It takes me a second to organise a response.

'Oh! So you got the gardener?'

'You said you had long grass – didn't you?'

I remember distantly that I did. Wym seems increasingly uncommitted to this walk and eventually he stops and turns and says 'Erm. Good-bye then.'

My new lawn is ragged but short. The fresh damp grass gives a heady scent of ... burning? I follow the smell to the AGA outlet in the wall and detect the whiff. Carbonised scone!

Running into the kitchen, I tear open the upper oven door and reach into its black maw. Then notice that my wrists are touching the edge of the metal. That can't be good.

After a good five minutes of running my wrists under the cold tap, I see I've burnt my way through a couple of layers of skin. The hole looks like a canyon. Creamy soft skin disappears first, then a bit of skin like hubba-bubba. Finally red raw, shiny stuff. The good news is it doesn't hurt. Bad news, it looks as if I've tried to top myself. No-one will believe the truth. Neither do I.

11. Cherry

I am standing on a ladder in my nice summer tea-dress and Marjory's yellow wellies. Holding the ladder enthusiastically is Kit. We are playing a little game where I pretend that I am completely unaware that he is looking up my dress and he is pretending that he is unaware that he knows that I'm aware he's looking up my dress. We are 'Carry On Cherry Picking.'

The orchard is big. If I knew how large an acre was I'd guess it was a few of those. You know how one punnet seems like a lot of cherries? Well think of ten thousand punnets, that's how many we've got here. And you know how cherries in Sainsbury's cost £3.99 a box? I am just looking around me and thinking 'money, money, tasty money'. Cherries are dripping off the trees, all velvety and almost exactly the same colour as 'Rouge-Noir' nail-polish by Chanel.

We're not alone. There's an old guy helping to pick as well. The cherries are being sold tomorrow at a car-boot sale. He is picking faster than we two combined and occasionally makes his feelings known. For those who like regional linguistical variety, the old guy says:

'Ah hint seen yew luvvers fill wun baaasket, corr oi hint minabbe doowin all on moiown. Us ulh mint tebe in Gillinham caaah boot morra un yew, blust as yew bahrnibees is gettin on moi wick, puttin on sappy paaarts loike thaat.'

This morning I had a phone call from my step-father George. He only calls when my mother is too upset to talk and needs a spokesman.

'You may not realise this, but your mother is too upset to talk to you.'

'What's wrong with her?'

'What's wrong? Well, you didn't return her message on your birthday, which has made her sad. And then she got a call yesterday from Sheila to say that apparently you've left Tom's flat and are now living somewhere near Norwich.'

Sheila is Tom's mum. My entire family communicates behind my back.

George and I never lived together smoothly from the outset, when he arrived bringing with him a copy of the Telegraph and his three-year old daughter Lizzie. I was eight. I made his life difficult by making his life difficult. He, in turn, was able to mortify me at the drop of a hat. One example:

I'm eleven. George has taken Lizzie and me out for lunch at Pizza Hut. I partake in what used to be my George-specific ritual, which is to not actually consume the food I'm given. I half-chew it, shove more in but never swallow. Eventually it squeezes out of my mouth like a play-dough machine. This drives George mad for putting everyone off their food and on grounds of money wasted. His face, inclusive of balding head, goes pink. He shouts at me:

'For God's sake Miriam, masticate! MASTICATE!'

There is no conversation from fellow diners for a good ten minutes.

On the phone, George continues:

'Sheila was very nice about it but Tom is quite angry. I'm afraid, Darling, it almost gives the impression that you're being self-centered again.' George calls me Darling when I've disappointed him.

The best way to ignore family reprimands is to pick cherries in the sunshine with Kit. We fill over eighty punnets, which go into three cardboard boxes. Kit takes two and I follow with the last. He is wearing his lumber shirt again. It has splotches of cherry juice on it.

I do what I often do, which is carry the box on my head. I do this because it's easier, because it shows I have an independent spirit and makes me look exotic. Then I realise I just look like a loon. Then I feel embarrassed. By the time I have gone through the 'take-it-off-you-look-like-a-nut/but-then-I'm-giving-into-the-constrained-expectations-of-society' argument in my head, I've usually reached wherever it is I'm going. Kit doesn't seem to mind though and we talk as we go.

'Did Wym tell you I found Prop wandering in the rain yesterday?'

'No, he didn't.'

'So Prop's your father too?'

'That's how it works.'

'I'd love to hear more about your family?' I pry. There's a pause.

'Two boys, a mother and a father. That's about it. Conventional.'

Hmmm. Him and Wym, neither of them tripping over themselves to lift the curtain.

Around the side of the Big House is a dank courtyard. It's north-facing and slightly green with damp. Kit says that's where the servants used to have their bedrooms. What I see is class stratification re-enforced with brick. The courtyard has windows, weeds and a door to what looks like a kitchen. I'm interested to see inside but we don't make it that far; he leads me to a tiny cold room with little holes in the wall and a skanky white chest freezer. Shelves hold boxes of root vegetables, dated condiments and dusty home-made bottled booze. There are white onions like giant pearl necklaces hanging on hooks. I feel a certain tension being in a close, dark, confined room with Kit. I have imagined kissing him, and it seemed to go fine in my head. Now that we're very close, my heart is going bumpbumpbump in my ribcage. I affect complete calm by tinkering with things. I open up the chest freezer for a nosy.

I scream!

The chest freezer is a nightmare – it's a scene directed by the Coen Brothers. So many dead animals lying frosted and glaze-eyed. They all look terror-filled, in set motions of 'running away.' Kit hardly seems to care, pulling out a frozen popsicle rodent and holding it by its long rear leg so it points to the ceiling.

'Hare!' he says.

The romance has gone from me. I turn down Kit's offer of company and trudge home. I think about the skeletons in Kit's cupboard.

12. Kirsch

A week ago, I was lying in a cold bath in my brother's flat, wearing frozen pants on my head and wondering why my life was going down the plughole. Now I'm in a parched field in Norfolk, selling fruit and veg from a trestle table.

Gillingham is the commuter satellite-village of Beccles. Its car-boot sale is surprisingly big, about one-quarter the size of the entire village. A crowd of Norfolkians talking has a kind of farmyard thing going on. There's lots of coo-ing and o-arring. The cherries look 'quoite noice' but the clientele are picky. We're selling punnets much cheaper than Sainsbury's but not as cheaply, apparently, as Old Barbara Fitch From Up The Road.

I've got the old guy for company. He's called Mr Perry. Mr Perry tells me:

'Bah-rah Fitch jus picks a poile uh cherries an leaves a honesty bux. That hint gaht no overeads.' He's right. Honesty boxes are everywhere. Flowers/fruit/veg/honey/eggs/household items crop up randomly at front gates. If that happened in London, you'd lose your produce, the money and your front gate. Mr Perry says the honesty box is completely wrecking the local economy for legitimate cherry traders like him and Sainsbury's.

I offered to help at the car boot because I thought Kit would be there but he's not appeared yet, much to the huffing of Mr Perry. At eight a.m. Wym arrives with a trailer full of vegetables. He sets up beside us. I help him and he's very patient at being repeatedly asked 'What's this?' 'It's a squash,' 'What's this?' 'It's an artichoke.' 'What's this?' 'It's a potato.'

Wym has a wide range of mystery vegetables but no sales technique. He doesn't like calling, or making eye-contact or even talking. I've seen enough car-boot sales to know you have to create a crowd, not for nothing do I have a brother in advertising. I stand on the far side of the trestle making noises about 'How Good This Squash Looks.'

Mr Perry is less than impressed. He thinks I should only be on Kit's stall.

'Oym ony givin warnin. Yew shud be inarrr camp, nat sellin fir the henemy.'

'Enemy?!'

'As good as theys two be henemies. The laast few year anyow.'

'But why? Kit and Wym are brothers!'

Mr Perry rolls his eyes and looks up at the sky. If his false teeth fitted better, he'd be whistling.

'Caan't roightly tell yew, seein as it's proivit.'

Just then, Kit turns up. He looks bleary and rumpled. My heart gives a leap. I see him clock his brother as he comes over. He gives me a big kiss on the cheek and a squeeze of the bottom!

'How'r we doing?'

My head is spinning from the squeeze but not so much that I don't notice him flicking another look at Wym.

Kit draws flocks of ladies around the table. This makes me feel prickly and annoyed. Wym's stall is definitely quieter but when I point this out to Mr Perry, he only shakes his head ominously.

At about eleven we have sold out of cherries except the squashed ones. For a while we sit on the grass, Kit shows me how to spit cherry stones. Eventually we leave Mr Perry to pack up the boxes and table. Kit takes me by the waist and guides me to The Swan.

The bar is packed. The sun-parched pub garden is full of drinkers who look less like the patrons of a car-boot sale and more like refugees from a natural disaster. There is a little shady step by a shed so Kit sits with his pint and I my southern comfort. He is really generous – he eventually buys me another five! In the heat, and having had nothing to eat except cherries, I am very light headed. Soon all my blood has been replaced by kirsch. I ask direct, drunken questions.

'Tell me about your childhood!'

'No.'

'Have you got any skerrytons in your cupboard?'

'None that I want to tell you about!'

'Rhy doesn't Vym I mean Wym like gew?'

Kit wants to shut me up. He turns, tilts my head and kisses me. He kisses me again. It gets sore on my neck kissing at this angle so we stand up and lean against the side of the shed. I am still sober enough to note how different fantasy kissing is from the real thing. Dry and heavenly in my dreams, beery and sloppy in reality. We then kiss like this for the next hour until Kit pauses. He has just been tapped on the shoulder by Wym.

'Herr-o Vym.' I say

Wym doesn't seem to notice me.

'Kit. I just want a quick word with you.'

If I was less drunk I would be better able to describe the dynamics, but from where I'm standing, the two seem to be having an amicable, brotherly discussion. Kit puts his face close to his brother in a friendly way and pokes his finger in his chest. Wym brushes the hand down in a light-hearted slap. Kit gives a cheerful one-fingered salute and leaves the pub garden. I try to follow but stumble against Wym.

Then I remember being in Wym's car. He doesn't say much. Five minutes later, we stop and he holds my hair out of my face while I'm sick beside Barbara Fitch's honesty box.

The rest of the afternoon I remember in flashes. I recall being helped in through my back-door. I remember being tucked up in my bed. Someone held a basin for me to be sick in and then gave me a towel. Much later, when the room was darker, I vaguely recall someone waking me to say 'I've got to go now.'

Blank.

13. Mercenary Cow

Oh the degradation. I've lain immobile all night and all morning. Eventually I get out of bed and fall on the floor. What I think is a stroke turns out to be the deadest leg you can get before the doctor amputates. Then pins and needles follow me as I drag my leg around the room via furniture and the night-storage heaters. In the icy glare of the blue bathroom I see that in the space of one night I have lost my youth. I'll never touch another cherry.

A whole tray of carbs with melting butter is what I need. I decide to make scones. I cannot find the mixing bowl. I give up. The two good cats are going crazy to get out but the bad one has not yet materialised. Their meowing travels straight through my brittle brain so I lock them in the boot room. That should keep them busy. I find the mixing bowl. I clean the sick out of it. As the scones go in the oven, my phone goes off. It's Tom. Normally I wouldn't answer but listen to his message instead. But I do need to talk to him. The phone trips onto answer. Damn! There's a word I once heard that perfectly describes Tom, and I keep meaning to remember it for when I'm talking to him. Occasionally I'll read it again in a newspaper and think 'Aah, that was the word!' I return the phone-call and try to remember.

'Miriam?'

'Hi Tom.'

'I keep leaving answers on your phone – you never call back.'

'You know, it's New Zealand. Pretty expensive.'

'I heard George's still paying your mobile?'

'That's none of your business.'

'No, I suppose not. Well let's keep this short, for George's sake. Ok – internet access. You need to buy a specific lead to attach your landline to your computer. I'll text you the name of the lead. You're best to keep the connection time very short or you'll be paying outrageous prices on your landline. No browsing.'

'Marjory's agreed to pay all phone bills.'

There's a pause.

'Right.'

'Tom, how much is this cable going to cost? Cos I haven't got any money.'

'You want me to pay for the cable too?'

'I haven't got any money.'

'ARRRRRRGHHHHH!! Fucksake!'

I pull the phone back from my ear. Has Tom just stepped on an upturned plug?

'Miriam – you're the most self-centered person I know! You use people and you never stop and when they eventually get tired of it, you complain. You need to sort your life out!'

'And you...!' I try to muster my recall 'you're a ... there's a word for you, Tom!'

'Words? I've got some words for you, Miriam. Undependable. Inconsistent. Capricious. Fickle. Mercenary. You.'

Ooo. Those are good. Tom goes on for another ten minutes like this. I lay the phone on its back and quietly drink a pint of water while Tom's munchkin voice fits ten thousand miles away. He says he will not buy me the cable.

I am not the juvenile Tom thinks I am – I live in a dainty cottage. I have an AGA. I have knitting. I have china and silverware in the cupboard and a yellow Clio in the drive.

I change the sheets, open the windows and take a deep breath. This is me, the new cautious, wise, thoughtful me, powered by will. I will not give my younger brother the satisfaction of another lecture.

My hair is globby and my skin papery so have a deep bath to re-hydrate myself inside and out. After about forty minutes, when the water is tepid and I'm starting to freeze, there's a voice at the back door.

'I'm in the bath!' I stupidly shout.

'You are?!'

'Hold on!'

The footsteps are still moving. I leap out, taking most of the water with me. I grab the nearest blue towel just in time to see Kit peep around the door. That's a nasty abusive invasion of privacy and just a bit kinky. He's waiting to see my reaction. I can't quite work out what my reaction is.

My reaction is that I invite him to share my towel. The bedroom is just a hop, skip and a jump away.

An hour later we are nose to nose in Marjory's narrow bed. It has not been designed for athletics, being very springy and off-puttingly squeaky. Up close, Kit is quite beautiful. He has blue eyes set in a dark but freckly face. Even his lips have freckles. I stamp down my nerves by making inane conversation.

'I'm sorry you saw that show-down between me and Wym yesterday.'

'I can't really remember it.' I say truthfully. 'Do you not get on?'

'We never really got on but it's been worse the last few years. You know I'm the elder brother?'

'No, I didn't.'

'By two years. Well, our dad...'

'Prop?'

'Yes, Prop has given Wym the running of the estate. He's going to leave it all to him when he dies.'

'Oh. That's not fair.'

'It suits Wym just fine – and I don't mind. I'm not really a farmer. I admit he's good at what he does but he uses this as an excuse to tell me what to do all the time. He's my younger brother. It was me that gave him his name. I couldn't pronounce William when he arrived on the scene, so I called him Wym.' (Interesting. When I appeared, my sister pronounced my name 'Most-Hated Zygote.')

'And Wym's got all the money?'

'Some control over it, but I get to keep the title.'

'What title?'

'Lord Hebbindon.'

'Prop?' I say (The crazy clog-dancing loon in wellies? is what I think.)

'He's Lord Hebbindon, Baron Toft. My mother is Lady Hebbindon, Marchese of Toli. She calls herself 'Marchese' because it's a few notches higher than 'Lady'. It's a continental title, so....'

'But why is Prop Prop?'

'Oh his name deserves a blue plaque. When he was seven, Prop and his father went hill-walking in North Wales with Lloyd George. Young Prop was the right height for the former Prime Minister to lean his elbow on, and he was leant on all the way up the mountain. From then on, he was a Prop.'

Aww

I lie in his arms and shuffle through my brain index card and find this situation amazing. If sex were top-trumps, I feel I've scored well.

'So in general, is it better being rich or being a Lord?'

Kit jumps on me.

'You mercenary little cow!'

14. Chap 2

Kit is now Chap 2. We spend all day in Marjory's bed. By six pm we think it would be a good idea to transfer to a king-size. He goes back to go back to the Big House and I pad around on a cloud knitted from post-coital endorphins. What's interesting is that I've discerned that Kit has no interest in deeper feelings, mine or his.

I have a very unhealthy relationship with Love, being someone who craves attention; when it appears, I mainline. I toss swatches of impossible reality into the air while swallowing whatever stupid song lyrics I become convinced soundtrack my life. Meanwhile, detachment, balance and self-awareness melt like spit on a griddle. I am a tail-chasing puppy, unable to stop until someone hits me with a figurative (or literal) frying pan.

In terms of phobias, you're meant to hug the monster. If the monster is a relationship, I don't just hug it; I smother, flee, return, pinch, tease, fret and flip-flop the monster to death.

Kit does not want anything from me beyond my pelvic region and several G-spots. For once, maybe I have found the lover in me who does not need someone else for sanity and validation. Maybe I can be a tart, without a heart. This opens a door of perception in my head. A semen-al moment, as it were.

At ten, as instructed, I tip-toe around the back of the Big House, through the drippy, scary, dank courtyard to the kitchen door.

Kit leans out and grabs me, muffling my squeak. Then there's kitchen kissing on a table. It lasts so long that when it stops I ask for a drink and can only squeak 'Water!' Kit dashes away like it's an SAS mission. While waiting, I have a little wander. This kitchen's only one of five kitchens. Where we would have individual white goods (oven, dishwasher, washing machine, fridge freezer) they have rooms. This room is 'The Oven.' There's a ten-foot wooden table, some utility-ware kitchen units, thick pipes and an AGA twice the size of mine. The walls are lined up to eye-level with rectangle cream tiles – the thick Victorian kind that you can smash your servant's head into without cracking the glaze. It's very dark and quiet. Outside the kitchen door is a pantry with a black glass panel box on the wall. The glass has gold writing listing every room in the house. Drawing Room. Dining Room. Billiard Room. Conservatory. It's a life-sized game of Cluedo.

Kit comes back with a glass of water.

'The coast's clear, let's go!'

'Clear of what?'

'The Marchese. She's at a fund-raiser in Aldeburgh, she definitely won't be back for ages. She's the only one who'd check up on me.'

This is a grown-man talking.

We push through a swing door muffled by green felt (for added servitude, I expect) and then we're out by the huge open staircase. Everything seems noisy, about twenty clocks are ticking themselves off their faces. Up, up, padpadpad, creakcreak, along a carpeted corridor either the same or similar to the one that Prop lives in. Kit opens his door with a flourish.

Kit's room is a modern bachelor pad in an 18th century container. The king-sized bed is modern. So is the heap of dirty washing and so is the weights bench in the corner. There are candles lit above the fireplace. It's a room for having all-over-the-place sex and Kit gives me a tour of the room in twenty minute bursts of jack russell-style enthusiasm. I've never previously been on the receiving end of such self-centered love-making. There is no two in this tango, just one feverish performer athletically doing it for both of us. As satisfying as it is to be the cause of animal lust I can tell that if my conscience gets in the way, it may start moaning on about emotional commitment and sexual equality. Eventually Kit collapses and falls snoring to one side. I also dose off, only to be woken regularly by the clocks that chime every quarter hour. Which would be fine if they rang at the same time but they each like a solo gig.

Things are just kicking off again when a squeak is heard in the corridor. Kit freezes. So do I.

'I thought you said she wouldn't be back for ages?'

'She shouldn't be.'

'What about Prop?'

'His rooms are on the other side.'

'Do you have a ghost?'

'Yes but not here.'

At last he takes a candle from the mantelpiece and we set off for an explore. Shadows swing around the walls – the ceilings are vault high. I remember how much I used to need to pee when I was a scared little kid.

Passing across the top of the staircase landing and into somewhere that leads into a long, wide, tall, high room with portraits of people who almost seem to be stepping out from the frames in this half-light. Kit shows me how to do cartoon-skidding on the wooden floorboards. This leads to whooping. Just then, the door opens and a long shadow fills the room. I melt behind a sofa.

'Who's there!?'

'It's me, Mother.'

'What are you doing up at this time? And why are you indecent?'

Kit shoves me with his foot and nods towards a corner door. Then he slopes carelessly towards his mother's cenotaph silhouette.

I'm alone. It's very dark and cold. I edge my way along the walls, trying to visualise my position within the house. My kneecaps bounce. This treatment by Kit is quite perfectly ungallant.

A narrow staircase has to be gone down. Panic shoots through my bladder. This is the point in a slasher movie where I've screamed to the victim 'Don't go down there!' And sure enough, the bottom of the stairs is a dadaist nightmare. There's enough bleached dawn light to reveal shelves of bone-white tennis racquets, dead cross-country skis and stuffed animals; glass-eyed, dusty and behind glass. I think I can hear them whimpering. It's horrible.

I note by the smell that this is a kitcheny area – ten minutes of trying every door and wanting to cry, pee and be sick ends with my staggering free into the courtyard.

Gamboling down the lawn, I'm gloriously relieved and – as my panties are inside the house, at liberty to pee whenever I like. Free! Alive! Joy! I'm here to face a newly minted day and I'm full of trippy-trappy-happy-smiley-rosy-puke-inducing-love. Love has been discovered to be a mental disorder apparently. So many endorphins get pumped into your brain, your hypothalamus goes on a rampage and holds your cortex hostage. The cortex becomes a gibbering Stockholm-Syndrome victim for two years until your hypothalamus gives up and hands itself in, drained and contrite. But by that time you're married! Hah! Now you've got to do the next 40 years without the endorphins.

For here and now, I glory in the experience; in the grass and trees, which are a strange luminous lettuce green against graphite sky. Dawn breezes blow. Dawn birds sing. Damp moss bubbles between my toes.

BANG!

I dive behind a rhododendron bush!

BANG!

Which is badly equipped to deflect bullets.

The echo flies across the garden, bouncing off the face of Toft Hall. Below the smutty line of trees, the shooter emerges from the undergrowth. From what I can see, he is wearing a open tartan dressing-gown and little else. He approaches the center of the lawn lifting his knees high, tip-toeing with the comic drama of a stage villain.

In the smudged fluorescent light I see it's Prop, Lord Hebbindon, Baron Toft; a praying mantis, naked but for tartan toweling. Then at last he stops. He pauses, his knees brace, he points his rifle into a molehill.

BANG!

The mound of earth explodes, rises and dissipates. Two distant pheasants scream. Then hunter turns and creaks away with knees a-crook towards the terrace steps. The blanket of bird-twitter resumes.

I go home. I think on.

15. Pepper Spray

I don't like animals much but that doesn't mean I like them being killed for fun. My early morning dreams are full of giants popping thunderous bubble wrap as distant animals meet their maker. Inside my house wildlife is free to roam. The amount of dog/cat food that's been trampled into the floorboards means we have a mouse colony the size of Djakarta. I tried setting the Bad Cat on them, he spent a lot of time sniffing around then walked backwards towards the wall, and pee'd on it.

I'm going to buy a humane trap.

I get up. I still have no computer lead. I still have no money or food. I start going through Marjory's pockets in her wardrobe. She's big on used tissues, doggie-bags and crumbled biscuit. My thieving is interrupted by the bell. Kit! I'm so pleased. My conscience was already fledging tiny paranoid doubts about him. He's very secretive about what he does all day and he hasn't given me his mobile number yet. Maybe he'll lend me some money?

I open the front door.

It's not Kit, it's Lizzie! A taxi pulls away and she's standing there, in real life.

'I thought I'd come and check you're still alive, seeing as your mum's convinced you've joined the Moonies.'

Lizzie knows me better than anyone else. I taught her every disgusting thing she knows. Touching tongues. Trapping farts. Race-licking chocolate off digestive biscuits. She says she's starving. I say I am too. I take her to Prop's hen house to steal eggs. After pancakes, she's sussed my situation and offers me petrol-money in exchange for a trip to Norwich.

'So, how are you feeling about Chap 1?'

'Better. I've just found myself a Chap 2.'

'I thought you were in love with Chap 1?'

'I am. I was a complete addict but then he dumped me. With Chap 2 in place, I don't have to do cold turkey.'

'So, Chap 2 is your methadone? Isn't that what you said about Chap 1? You went out with him to get over Chap Previous. You can't do this forever, one day you're going to have to fall out of love.'

Ugh. Lizzie is a civil servant. Like Tom, she's usually right. But unlike Tom, she's likable.

Norwich is twenty miles and a fashion era away. The Victorian covered lanes are cute and contain all those shops that only sell one thing at eye-gouging prices – they have names like 'String!' 'Brushes!' 'Porridge!'. Once I've found the shops called 'Computer Leads!' and 'Mousetraps!' my little list is done.

Then we're free to roam.

The Norwich street plan is designed on the Golden Ratio. You corner at increasingly desperately angles until eventually you have to stop or risk entering a worm-hole. The town's look is akin to a fading film starlet, in that it has really historic wrinkly bits joined on to badly thought-through facelifts that were tacked on in the seventies. East Anglia is currently at the center of a cultural high-point. Some local lads with bad teeth and long greasy hair have made good. Their first album is being piped out of shop fronts, giving the effect of a hundred car alarms going off at once.

The poshest shop in Norwich, we're told, is Bonds Department Store. Lizzie is fun to play with because she enjoys messing but tries to fight the urge. We go to the make-up counter and let Lizzie have her 'pre-wedding make-up tester session' done; blow by blow evidence of how a beautiful girl can be transformed into the mask of a footballer's wife, through the simple application of block colours on an orange matt base.

This naturally leads to the perfume counter. While there, I annoy a woman. She rudely leans over me to pick a bottle of Chanel Mademoiselle and takes her time doing it too. I happen to have a bottle of 'Parfume Celine Dion' in my hand. I give her chest three squirts; like Celine, it has some very shrill top notes.

The women leans back. She glares at me. There's something of the reptile about her in that she's sleek, angular and doesn't blink. She has the longest eye-lashes I have ever seen and from here they look like they're her own.

The bitch is stare-fighting me. I can do that. I could stare-fight George for days at a time. This woman has pupils the size of bb pellets and straw-green irises. I am unaccountably reminded of those brands of lizards that lick their own eyeballs to keep them moist.

We are causing a jam in the aisle, this could go on until closing time but for a man's voice that calls 'Jonty!'

Jonty blinks at last, tosses her head and marches away. Seeded.

She is head-to-head with a man who I expect is her husband, he looks hen-pecked. The woman points at me. I grab Lizzie and leap us into the Ladies' Sanitary Wear aisle. That was Kit.

'Chap 2!'

They're on the move, Kit and 'Jonty'. I take Lizzie by the arm and follow their bobbing heads.

'What? Where?'

'With the lady, that's Chap 2. Look, she's walking with him!'

Lizzie thwacks her head at me. 'You've got a married man! I thought you said this wasn't going to happen again?'

They go out onto the street, cross and go down a quieter lane. Lizzie is starting to complain.

'Look, Miriam – stealing someone's husband is thick but not illegal. Stalking them is.'

'We don't know they're married. Maybe they're....work colleagues or something.' I know in my heart that Kit doesn't work. The two of them pause, talking closely. Intimately. We duck by a litter bin. Look at him; chunky, square, edible. Look at the woman; her hair so conditioned it appears to have been enameled. Her nose is short and her eye-lashes long.

They turn and go into an office. I run up and name-check the sign. A solicitor's office. That means something. I'm not sure what it means, but I'm really really hurt. I want to make him pay for whatever unknown thing he's done to me. I notice the sample bottle of Celine Dion is still with me. I will keep this like some people keep pepper spray. I'm going to secretly spray Kit and Jonty whenever I see them. Because, as far as I know, that's not illegal.

16. Death of the Innocents

I've decided I'm going to go back to London with Lizzie.

Lizzie follows me around as I stuff clothes in a bin bag.

'You can't go, you've just got here!'

'I've been debased.'

'Well maybe if you asked a few questions before you sleep with someone, you wouldn't keep doing this. But you can't move house every time your heart gets a knock. It's impractical.'

Frustration starts to windmill my arms around.

'Tell me, Lizzie, because I want to know! People sleep with people, right? It's a big social scene as far as I've heard. So why is it so impossible for me to find one balanced, sensitive, loving, man attached to his gonads and not attached to a woman? JUST.'(I point my finger upwards for Lizzie. She's seen this before. She's unimpressed). 'ONE!'

There's a tiny tap on the door frame. It's Kit and he's staring at my moves. I go into defensive pattern.

'When are you going to stop coming in to my house? I have a right to privacy in my own space.'

Considering he's been invited into most of my spaces, this is probably a moral cause lost. And in terms of my house, if he doesn't own it now, he probably will one day.

Kit is trying to effect 'calm' while scanning my reactions. This must be the moral high ground I'm on.

'I guess you're trying to work out if that was me in Norwich?' I say.

'Was that you in Norwich?'

I want to make this linger in the air but Lizzie blurts 'Yes!'

Lizzie's poker technique was never that good. I continue to pack.

Now Kit's in the kitchen, looking in my fridge. Why can't he just keep to his own space? But, oh yes, he'll own my kitchen too one day. Unless the revolution gets him first.

I slam the fridge closed. 'So, you going to tell me who it was?'

'Why have you no food apart from eggs?'

'Who was the woman?'

'Have you got no money?'

'WHO'

'My wife!'

'Uh-oh!' squeaks Lizzie.

I take Kit by his stupid, sweaty checked-shirted chest and push him to the front door.

'Right. Go away. Leave my fridge and my finances and my life alone. I won't mention your rancid sex-life, your nutcase family and your special-needs brother who can't spell beyond three letters to invent a name.'

In the final sentence. I open the door to throw Kit out only to find Wym standing at it with his knuckles raised, about to knock and now frozen. The two twerps stare at each other.

Then it's just me and Wym.

'Hi.'

'Hi.'

'I came to see if you wanted your lawn finishing. I heard the gardener stopped half-way.'

Outside it's sunny but I have ice running through my veins – I'm the human fridge. As I take Wym to the shed to pick up the strimmer, he says

'You know, Kit's wife left him last year.'

Oh.

'But I saw him with her. They went to a solicitors together.'

Now he knows I'm a stalker as well.

Wym does the thing with his mouth where it swops from side to side.

'They were meeting to negotiate the divorce settlement.'

Oh no.

From the shed I drag out the strimmer. Wym doesn't look me in the eye when he takes it. I pause, have a sniff of creosote for some light relief. There is a tiny scrabbling noise – like a minuscule elf-dance. I look down. The rear end of a mouse is doing a jig of death, his head is stuck in the crack of the door, into which I have viced him tight simply by opening it. Oh Shit! I quickly close the door. Too late. The outside of the crack frames a tiny squashed mouse face, with two popping, bleeding, fading, questioning eyes.

I have killed a mouse. I have abused the man I have fallen in love with. I have bad-mouthed his family.

Lizzie rings up Tom to 'sort my internet' but in reality to update him on my antics. She takes herself into the kitchen and I hear the muttering of two moral people having a conclave. I passive aggressive knit when she comes back in. When I've knitted my panic room, I'm going to lock myself in it and ignore everyone.

As much as I love my sister, her attachment to Tom has always set my teeth on edge. During my father's fiftieth birthday party I caught her and Tom snogging in the utility room. They've never really got over it and neither have I. I consider them brother and sister, even if blood tests refuse to back me up. I hope they never get it together. The world is not ready for the glorious deity that their union would produce.

At about seven, the strimming stops. I put down my knitting and peep out of the kitchen window. Wym is pulling his shirt back on. Oh gosh. He's very buff! I avert my eyes, Kit looks like a doughy loaf of bread in comparison. It's a shame Wym's such an up-tight collection of psychosis.

The lawn's looking flat and clean. All the dog toys have been shredded. Wym puts the strimmer back in the shed and is about to go, without saying good-bye.

'Hey!' I call.

Still he won't look at me.

'Hey, I'm sorry I said you had special needs. I know you don't. I was just angry at your brother'

He half-turns as he steps out of the garden. He actually looks hurt. 'Yes well. You and everyone else.' The gate is slammed shut.

17. The Aberration

Lizzie says the couch wasn't all it could have been in terms of comfort last night.

I'm bright and clear-headed. Yesterday felt like déja-vu. I know I'm not seeded. They know I'm not seeded. I will stop trying to assimilate. I'm going to go feral.

As a parting gesture, my dad gave all of the 'left wives' a blank cheque for Any School Anywhere. My sister Signe went to a posh Catholic boarding school in Stoke, and maxed-out in the subject of climbing over the wall and giving the local boys holy communion. She blames her falling from the straight and narrow on my arrival. My brother Tom went to Bedales where, I'm lead to believe, they show you how to roll a very tight joint.

My mum picked 'St Philip's School for Girls', a scraping-by boarding school, filled with angry army kids and children whose parents lived too far away to spot the fungus in the sports hall.

By thirteen I'd just about accepted stunted growth, luxuriant body hair and ethnic quiff. But St Phil's took body-image and shoved it into social order so nuanced that any freckle out of place could set you back years. I slunk around with the primordial bottom-feeders, by turn hating my looks and then thanking God I wasn't the acne-covered, flat-footed victim in the study beside me. I have melted the enamel off entire bathrooms with bottles of sun-in. I faked 'ski-holidays' by painting goggle marks on my face. I caused five separate fire-drills by overworking my straightening irons. But the more I relaxed my hair, the more I stressed. In sixth-form, I got paralytically drunk with my friend Webby. We woke up the next morning to find we had shaved our heads. We were made to wear bobble hats for eight weeks. As 'fitting-in' was no longer an option, we stopped trying, and as if by magic, the tall blondes left us alone. We became happy lepers.

So I'm a socially-needy recidivist. It's not that I don't learn, I just have to revise sometimes. As a first step, I decide to go and liberate some eggs from the chicken coop; a chicken coup, as it were.

On a bench, tilted back against the boiling black hen house in a sleeping Prop. The mis-buttoned shirt gapes open, the tweed jacket rides up over his bony shoulders. As his jaw has fallen open, his top row of false teeth is resting on his lower lip. I don't know what to make of it. If I found a child looking as unloved as this, I would send a message to social services, but apparently elderly adults can drown in squalor.

I reach in quietly to remove two eggs but the chickens of the run are now tutting violently. Prop leans forward and as I scamper for the trees, he calls 'Lovelace?' I don't reply but the name 'Lovelace' and the hopeful way he said it follows me all the way home.

Lizzie is scheduled to take the afternoon train back to London so I stop at the Red Lion to buy her a drink and to wait for some kind of postmortem on the skeletons of Hebbindon.

'Awreighy.' Says the landlord. In a stringy vest, he is sporting a fine pair of man boobs. I often wonder why Marks & Spencer's haven't cashed in on the male chest, which in this super-hot summer of 2003, seems to be on-trend wherever I go.

Lizzie and I are not the only mid-day boozers; old Mr Perry is there too. I never knew what a family retainer was, turns out Mr Perry is one. You have to leave school at fourteen and turn up for work in rags. Then the whole upper-class guilt kicks in and you get to do your job as slowly and as shabbily as you like. Forever. Once you're over eighty, the roles reverse and the Family run around doing whatever senile shenanigans you dream up and demand.

Mr Perry is as old as Prop almost to the year. I have lots of questions I want to ask him, or at least, I would but Mr Perry is managing to deflect me. I can't work out if it's discretion or just his marbles-in-mouth yokel accent.

The barman, 'Fat Terry' is almost quivering in his desire to share juicy information but Mr Perry keeps clearing his throat or shaking his head. Kit and Wym are 'out of bounds'. I load my left-of-field question and fire.

'So, what about Prop?'

'Oiy naat wun to maardal but, what urs call Prop, hint his roight noime, see. 'Is Laardship's an Edwoid.'

'And who is this Lovelace person?'

Mr Perry sucks in his lips like a drawstring purse then puffs until all his broken veins stand out. 'It hint commun noos, see. Yew hint mint to know.'

This is definitely classified information We all lean in, even Lizzie who has no idea what we're talking about. Mr Perry the showman clears his throat.

'Prop's, ee lived twenty year in Kenya. Afor. He'd raather be back there, see. Well, ee got a woife. Thaat be 'is Lovelace for yew. Ee left a fa'amly too.'

'A family?!' gasps Lizzie.

'Big faamly' says Mr Perry. 'But, loike, she were native n'is own family, and, well they dun loik it. They call im back n'made im marry a whoite guhl.'

'Ahh, that be the mar-koi-zarrrr,' says Terry.

'Ee were told to maarry n she was the best of the bunch, reckon ee.'

'She fram Iharly'

'Iharly?' I ask.

'I-harly, I-harly. She's IT-AHR-LIAN.' Terry clarifies.

Ahhh. That explains her incredible bad manners.

'But what about Prop's family in Africa?' whispers the ever-sympathetic Lizzie.

'Ne'er saw'rem agin.' Mr Perry shakes his head. 'Four girls ad ee. Cor dunnit fair broik an art still.'

'Why didn't he just go back?'

'The n'eritance. You'd better'ope your daddy dun leave you a n'eritance.'

'It cause noht but bad blood twixt fork.' nods Terry. 'See them two boys. One going roihght off the roils, tuppin every oggit standin'an th'other, old afor 'is toime.'

Lizzie and I have lost the thread. Listening to Mr Perry and Fat Terry is like hearing two very long ropes made of vowels being bound together by the occasional consonant.

'Well whatis Laardship do say is, 'is real woife is an n'aborigine, an the Mar-koi-zar's an n'aberration.' Mr Perry mouths the words carefully.

'So sad for Prop' persists Lizzie.

'Now just think on, 'ow that'd feel fur a daddy niver see 'is kiddies', says Terry.

I think about it too. My dad doesn't seem to mind never seeing his kiddies in the slightest.

18. Later the Same Day

Lizzie is safely on the train and I weave home perhaps, but not definitely, over the limit. Back at the ranch, I find a mouse sitting on the couch so I break-out the humane mouse trap.

I am tipsy and light-headed and fall on the couch for a ten minute snooze.

Two hours later, *knocknocknock!*

Grizzly and bed-shaped, I open the door to Wym. Hi eyes flit up to the top of my head. I know that my hair resembles a semi-felted soldier's busby.

'It's the Marchese's birthday tomorrow. We're having our first driven shoot of the season and I wondered if you wanted to come? We'll all be there and some friends of Jonty too, picking-up. And Mr Perry and his men are beating.'

It's alien language. No matter what my mind boggles, every image I come up with is wrong. The only thing I do understand is that I'm being included, almost as if I was seeded, which I'm not. But Wym doesn't stop there. He attempts eye-contact before muttering:

'There's going to be a little preparation and some serving.'

'Uh-huh?'

A silent metaphorical canapé tray appears between us.

'I heard that you could use funds.'

My jaw sways. If Wym, the most discrete member of the Big House, is happy to talk about my finances, then the news has been figuratively been stuck down a howitzer and fired across a wide space.

'It'll be cash in hand, if you like.'

I tell him I'll think about it and close the door. I pace around a bit. I check the empty mousetrap. I sit on the couch. Why do I feel grubby? Normally I love making easy money but Wym is treating me like someone you expect to hire, cash in hand. I'm not plusfours, I'm petits-fours.

Inevitably, the next morning, I find myself up at the Big House. Land Rovers, with engines running, fill up the weedy courtyard with smog and people in olive-green. There's a middle-aged lady shaped like an onion in wellington boots. She sees me and croons some orders. I say 'croon' because her accent is as thick as tar. I discover she's the 'Young Miss Perry.'

I've never seen Wym being 'in charge' – he's quite manly with it. I'm realising the courtyard has no end of unsettling rooms. The gun room is behind a protected, locked and bolted door. The walls are lined with locked and bolted cupboards. It looks like a secret military retreat (quite different from a buddhist retreat).

He is the center of all action so I want to get in the van with him but there's a strict gender divide. I end with hampers and rolled-up awnings and the Young Miss Perry.

Bumping along on a canvas roll-bag, watching the dry lane turn into rock-hard rutted field. The soundtrack is skylarks versus diesel engine. I get a sudden lurch of 'not-fitting-in' – the paranoid self-awareness that radiates from my belly button and makes me want to head for the hills. Or the city. Or the hills.

Then we get to our destination and it's far worse than even my imagination could conjure. The hillock is speckled with people, mainly men – looking as green and as leafy as I recall in all those photographs in *The Field*. I blame that magazine for my current situation. I see Smug Seeded woman talking to Kit's long-eyelashed wife. In front of her are three small children. I can see from here the kids are mini-Kits. Kit's there already. My chest is suddenly flapping; nerve butterflies. Or it could be my exclusively ovine diet that has made me lose about a stone in weight but has caused unmentionable problems in the bathroom.

Kit pretends that the ladies and I have never met. He turns to Smug. 'Anna – Miriam Short.'

He looks at me. 'Miriam – Anna Sievewright-Stevens.' 'And this is my...may I introduce the...er, Jonty.'

The lizard queen looks on me.

'The mother of his children.'

I have no choice but to return her look. I know that for every dog-eared, exhausted Croyden shop assistant, there is someone somewhere who shook the magic eight ball and got everything. Jonty has an excessive slagheap of attributes, with her Betty Davis eyes, Mona Lisa smile, Cleopatra nose and the highest follicle area of any one eye-lid. Meanwhile, have a peek inside any mini-Boden catalogue to get an idea of the kids. They are nut-brown, freckle-splattered and sun-bleached. They are called 'Tibby' (a boy) 'Robsie' (smaller boy) and 'Min' (very small girl.)

For God's sake! When the aliens did their spawning, did they not hand out one usable baby-naming book?

This is a Show and Tell session for Kit. The idea is that I find out he has kids in a safe, public environment where he has control of all the weapons.

Some way back, Jonty has started issuing commands to two circling spaniels. They reel in the distance, they sniff the ground by the fence, and yet, for all these visiting dogs, not a single lead. Posh people don't own leads, they just bellow. If only Jonty could make her own spawn 'sit' and 'hold' but at the moment, the two sons are enjoying themselves by filling Prop's tweed deer-stalker with rabbit poo. Kit tells me that Jonty and her friends are 'picking up' today. I become aware that the term 'picking up' must be different to the one that would apply if I was a lady standing at the corner of Denvale Trade Park, Basingstoke just around midnight. All Jonty and Co are up to is staring intently at the hillside like meerkats in tweed.

From across the field, there's some kind of small advancing army. Mr Perry is swishing the long grass and he's accompanied by a mob and more bouncing dogs. A partridge family who, only minutes before, had been planning their futures, are now facing life without a pension, scattering and screaming as their home is ransacked.

The soundtrack to this scene starts, and goes something like this; 'POSY DON'T EAT THAT' *driiiiillllll* clickclickclick BANG! BANG! *SQUAWK* thud 'SADIE DROP!' *driiiiillll* clickclickclick BANG! BANG! *SQUAWK* thud

This ridge sits above a lower hill and during the beats the birds are flushed out from the long grass below. It's like shooting fish in a barrel. Except with no fish. Or a barrel. To my mind, the scene is ghastly. Birds soar from the woods then plummet the forty or so feet to the ground with a hollow thud. They are never dead, they are nearly all alive. Many are still able to run, limp or roll like bloody rags. These birds are called 'pricked', after the blind pricks who shoot them in the least humane way possible. Staggering birds drag wings behind them. I scream and jump and hop as the flapping semi-dead pass; staring, broken and upside down in the mouths of dogs. All horror leads back to the ladies who have sticks. The ladies hold the flapping ones by their reed-thin necks. There's chat as they slowly bring out their sticks and beat them dead. The birds' wings and legs carry on peddling the air for a minute, a last sign of how much they want to live.

I tell Kit that shooting is hateful. Kit strokes his gun like the Freudian metaphor it is and informs me that the game is killed as quickly as possible. But looking around me, all I see are dribbling, blood-thirsty grins and cave grunts. The Marchese is the only woman shooting, aiming wildly like James Cagney just before the coppers get him. Prop leans on a shooting stick with his arms crossed, speaking through the side of his mouth, Popeye-style.

'Game should be high and wide. If a gun can't kill a bird within four cartridges, they're not up to it.' Grizzle grizzle. 'Wrong guns, not enough choke.'

Wym is all the while orchestrating the whole shooting match with a walkie-walkie. He's taking it really seriously, even though his ear-protectors are sat on the top of his head, making him looking like a blinky-eyed six-foot teddy.

I retire to the marquee, itchy with doubt. If I see an injured bird, I always try to help it. I will attempt to nurture fallen fledglings or window-trashed blackbirds. Vet Miriam will feed them, warm them, clean them and watch as their eyes fade, their necks go limp and their tweets wither. I kill birds with kindness. Am I any better or worse than the tit heads shooting birds who were bred for just that end?

Young Miss Perry is making Eton Mess, a dish heavily combining dairy products, summer fruits and sugar to vomit consistency. I'm given dishes to lay out; handmade spring rolls and sushi. There must be something of the Eastern mystic about Miss Perry that goes further than East Anglia.

I don't know much about guns but I do know a bit about people. Prop is as spruce as a goose but not joining in with the shoot. I put it to Miss Perry.

'I saw Prop with a gun the other day. He was stalking a mole hill at dawn.'

'Oh I bet ee was. Ee keeps a twelve bore in 'is bedroom for jis thaat. An ee shoots wasp nests too. Hint been stung yet!'

'But why is he not shooting today?'

'Oh thaat. 'Ees on stroike, it's the same every year. 'Er Ladyship wants to shoot cos where she come fram, there's no rules. But ere, we dun shoot til September. The season hint started an his Lardship won't shot til the season.'

'So, August is no good. Not even the thirty-first?'

Miss Perry shakes her cheeks.

'But the first of September is just fine?'

'Oh ye-es, that would be quoite alroight.'

A morning peppered with gunfire is a long one. The shoot moves around and volleys echo from different directions and distances. Eventually it subsides and the slow peaking tide of nasal voices reaches the tent. Rich types speak in superlatives that they confuse for effect. For example, if one cuts off a finger, they are liable to say 'Oh just a scratch, a simple plaster will do.' But offer them a plate of Eton Mess and suddenly, 'it's quite WONDERFUL, simply the MOST INCREDIBLY RAVISHING pudding ever encountered in their ENTIRE benighted life....' and so it goes on for the next ten minutes.

Kit's two boys chug coke, stamp on people's feet, throw their rubbish in a trail and shoulder butt their younger sister who picks her nose joylessly. I sidle up to Min and offer her an alternative to bogeys – cream and meringue.

She gives me a Medusa stare. Uh-oh, tough crowd. I bob down to chat her up.

'So are you at school yet?'

She glowers through me.

'Teach me something you've learnt.'

Suddenly the little squirt pulls some kind of crazy pose, with her arms across her body. I'm not sure it this is a self-defense move. Then she barks... 'F...F...F!'

Then she does 'Jesus on the cross' pose. '...T...T...T!'

Ah. Full body phonetics.

C...C...C is for contorted, M... is for making no sense. It's not much of a conversation, but it keeps us going. Kit comes over. I'm expecting him to reveal her position on the autistic spectrum.

'You like kids then?'

'Oh yes,' I lie.

The only kid I've ever dealt with is my own sister and my influence on her was to her detriment. 'I worked as a nanny once.'

'Really?'

'In Switzerland.'

Why do I always say Switzerland? I've never even been there. We stare down at Min, sitting on the ground with her legs straight and her arms up, as if about to dive skywards.

'...L...L...L!'

'She's a smart kid.' I dutifully say.

'I think so', says Kit. 'We pay the school enough anyway.'

After an hour, they've either run out of birds, bullets or inclination. The shooting stops. Kit sidles up and lays a hand on me. He has a very sparkly look in his eye that could either be love or post- killing frenzy. He leans in.

'Jonty's going tomorrow.'

'Oh?'

'I have the children for the next two weeks.'

'Lucky you.'

'Do you still need work? Is it true you were a nanny?'

19. Cat Food

Early morning. I have reached my egg event horizon. There's a good chance my sweat smells of Victoria sponge. But I'm hungry and no money continues apace. Clio has a little petrol so I prepare for a harrying of Norfolk. I bid farewell to my only companion, but the Bad Cat hates me. He blames me somehow for his being locked in twenty hours a day in the hottest summer Norfolk has experienced since since 1976.

It truly is another pan-fried day in the increasingly arid Broadlands. The webbed-toe thing is a joke but Norfolk is a place where people are still psychologically standing knee-deep in water. Some ambitious iron-age guys decided it would be a good place to drain so that one day their heirs could build Great Yarmouth and Lowestoft and install slot machines. If they didn't keep pumping out all day long, Norfolk would return to the swamp it's long been trying not to be.

Lowestoft Safeway is the shop that I will be working today.

Here are my tips. Firstly, don't allow yourself to look as if you're down to your last bean. Dress up, wear make-up. Two. Go early, before the staff are alert and while they still see the day as fresh and full of hope.

You stand at the exit. You talk loudly on your silent phone, perhaps discussing the 'pre-production meeting' or the 'wrap party'. You watch the bin and wait. Eventually, someone will drop a very long till receipt in it. Check the receipt. Does it have the kind of produce you want? No? Then wait for an alternative. If you think you can work with it, grab some carrier bags from recycling and go shop.

It's a fab game of hunt the item – you have to hope your receipt has the essentials but sometimes there are bonuses. I once did once end up with a huge steel kitchen knife. That was the day Chap Previous left me. Nothing happened of course, it just seemed as if fate was trying to enthusiastically shove me towards revenge. As you wander the aisles, you start to judge a person by what's landing in the trolly. Gin? Paracetamol? *Heat Magazine*? Uh-huh?

Anyway, this is Lowestoft so it's a mixed bag, (or bags, I have five).

Here comes the coup de grace. You grab something very useful; 4 litres of milk for example. You run to the check out, all flushed and anxious and say;

'Hello! Your colleague just served me as you can see...' (wave long receipt around) 'But stupidly, I forgot the milk, which was the one thing

I came in for haha...' etc.

You pay for the milk. You leave. They cannot prove you didn't buy this shopping without lots of detective work.

I don't know how I stand on karma. I'm very kind as a person. I do know this is probably an immoral thing to do but then, it's not as if a missing bag, or five, of shopping is going to bankrupt Safeway.

On the way home, I get a call from Lizzie.

'How are you getting to the wedding?'

'What wedding?'

'Carmen's wedding, tomorrow.'

Oh. Shit. I had completely forgotten.

'Yes yes yes. I'm taking Clio.'

'Ok, I'll see you there.'

'Lizzie?'

'Yes?'

'You know that silver velvet jacket?'

'You want to borrow it again right?'

'And tights and shoes. And some cash please?'

I hear Lizzie writing this down. 'Ok. Miriam?'

'Yes?'

'Oh,' she sighs. 'Nothing. Never mind.'

I walk into my kitchen to discover a grinning Kit alongside three freckled, grumpy faces. I quickly have to do two things:

1) Ask for my pay up front and
2) Tell him that I'm going away for two days.

Kit takes this double blow moderately well. I agree to keep the kids this morning and deliver them to their mother for an emotional good-bye in the afternoon. They help me to enforce the cat exchange (one kid per struggling cat). Then I have sheets to dry, so send children into the woods to collect giant branches. They will need saws and knives so I give them each a tool kit, adding scissors, string and a handy firing staple gun. The remit is that each of them have to built a stick shelter in my garden that I can lay a damp sheet over. It's fun, practical fun but the kids don't play nice. Robsie bites Tibby and pokes him in the eye with a pinecone. Min's branches are more of the twig variety, and she has to make do with a face cloth as a cover.

In terms of success it is a roaring one. I always start any project with Oscar-winning performances. Over the arc of any project, I usually time it so that the final half is mired by under-achievement. But for now, I am the Sir Larry Olivier of childcare.

Little Min notices I have a mouse in the trap. I promise her we will release it on the way back to her mother.

With great ceremony, I have brought the mouse in its box. It is filling up the remaining space with little mice poo, so I have to let it loose soon.

The kids succumb to the 'Awww a mouse' sentiment. I open the trap on the track. The mouse slides out, gets its bearings and takes one step. Then from out of a bush jumps the Bad Cat. He picks up the mouse, sweeps us all with a malicious, steely glare and springs away.

Six wide blue eyes look to me for answers.

We find Jonty and two friends sun-bathing on the slope in front of the tennis court. The ladies don't move, not to look at me or to greet the children. A friend turns her head away and clearly says.

'Is this Kit's latest?'

And Jonty clearly says, 'Yes, he screwed her first and turned her into a nanny second.'

20. Three-Day Binge (Part One)

When my family unite for celebration, it just hammers a wedge into our emotional fissures. Not a marriage or a funeral goes by that doesn't end in someone not talking to someone. All you have to do is turn up (or not) and join the queue on the shooting range.

Carmen is my double cousin through some clever brother/sister shenanigans a good while back. I am keen to attend her wedding because of all the free food and wine and also, in the hope that my family can exhibit some ties that aren't made of bile and repressed rage.

Kit has given me £100 for 'services rendered'. That makes me feel a bit grubby but I don't wait around long enough to analyse it. As a wedding gift, I take with me a nice Victorian bone-china loving cup that Marjory will later hear has been unfortunately knocked off the dresser by one of her good cats.

I've never driven Clio out of Norfolk. The local roads include regularly spaced death traps every few miles. You can tell by the number of decomposing bunches of flowers tied to roadside fence posts. And the driving challenges are almost predictable in their hicksville unpredictability. Maybe it's a couple of tractor drivers who have decided to stop mid-road for a chat or maybe you're negotiating 'Chicken Roundabout', the intersection in East Anglia where people go to dump cockerels and unlaying hens. The approach to the roundabout has something of a Super-Mario feel about it because chickens never cross roads without changing direction a few times.

The wedding is in Brighton, a place so achingly hip I develop arthritis during the five hour drive. I reach it just as the sun sets, the mist knitting itself a white blanket on the South Downs.

I did discreetly hint around but no-one has offered me a free bed. I've booked myself somewhere called 'The Urbane House and Spa Boutique Retreat.' According to its website, it's a classy joint but my room for three days is an amazing steal. Everyone else is staying at the Omi, a huge square thing of maple, marble and mocha.

The front of Urbane House seems fine. It has the whole Georgian white frontage thing going on. But from the moment I enter I know something's wrong. The carpet is sticky. The paintwork has the fingerprints of a hundred disappointed customers. There is a reception of sorts in a cubbyhole behind a staircase. The man behind the desk is very foreign and sweet. I feign surprise when my credit card is declined (when did it last work?! The good people of Capital One have stopped cold-calling me.) I promise it will work in the morning (no hotel likes cash) and he offers to carry my bag for me. A gentleman.

I see why he's carrying my bag. We go up the shabby, 100 watt bulb-lit staircase, then up another. At the fourth winder he says 'Mind your head' and we bend in towards the wobbly bannister. Through a fire-door. Then more stairs. We stop at the top – there's no more corridor, just three blank doors and one overhead bulb. He unlocks my room, gives an expansive wave and scarpers.

It's attic-shaped and roughly the size of a small double bed plus one foot. There's a wardrobe with no doors, one window with a water-marked blind and a corner chunk that is a tiny shower room. At least they haven't scrimped on the hair in the plug hole. The merkins I could weave ...

I've no choice but to bite my lip, having no money for anything better. The dreams of a spa retreat are blown out of the airlock in my head. I set phasers to slum.

Off to the Omi to see the rest of my family and lie to them about how great the Urbane House is. There they are, sitting like chums at leather couches in the huge bar/diner. Perhaps it's the jazz, perhaps it's the mood lighting but they all look mellow – maybe this will be a happy event after all. Mum is there with George in his silly Pringle jumper. Lizzie is chatting up a continental barman. There's my maternal grand-mother. A pioneer blue-stocking, she gained her medical degree in 1951, becoming a ground-breaking neurosurgeon before being forced back to the kitchen sink on marriage. Now she is a gin-tippling intellectually-bitter Machiavelli who has views as far as right-wing has horizon. She sits with her brother, Creepy Uncle Owen. He's also a doctor of high standing. You know how some people confuse paediatricians with paedophiles? So does he. He gave me a left leg overly-sensitive to knee grasping. Beside him, my father's first wife Inga and beside her my sister Signe and husband Samson; as far as I know, the only Samson-and-Signe combination in the world.

Signe has grown her hair. So have I. She is wearing emerald green. So am I. I do not sit down beside her – I am repelled by her force-field of resentment.

'Hello Darling,' says Mum.

'Hello Miriam' says George.

'Ooh my-oh-my' croons Uncle Owen. 'I have to say...' (I feel it coming). 'It's always a surprise' (Signe can feel it too) 'DON'T you and Signe look alike. Spitting image. Except....' (Don't say it, Uncle Owen.

Please, all those creepy beach snaps, I forgive you, really I do) '...You look a bit younger, Miriam, hurr hurr hurr.'

I don't even glance at Signe. I withdraw to the bar to join Lizzie mid euro-flirt.

'Hey, you're here!'

Euroman doesn't give me half a glance, but does give me half a cider.

'So where're you staying?' asks Lizzie

Lying to my favourite sister, I wax fantastical about the Urbane House and Spa. Lizzie is staying with Carmen. They are not actually related but happen to be best friends.

'So, you'll be wanting me to pay for that drink?' she says.

There was a time most of my family would have bought me a drink. Now they don't – perhaps I'm getting too old. The conversation at the table is the same brand that my family always have. Very reactionary, always incendiary. But I am sober. At midnight I decide to have an early night so toddle back to my luxury retreat.

21. Three-Day Binge (Part Two)

At about two in the morning, I wake up feeling itchy. In the glow of the bathroom I discover my whole pelvis is covered in red lumps. I have no idea what they are.

I wake at seven.

Oh. Dear. God. Now I look like one of the X-Men mid-transformation.

The hotel front desk is empty but I smell burning toast and hear a fight in the kitchen. A man appears. I show him my unattractively bitten hips. He stares as if I've just asked for my money back. He doesn't know I haven't yet paid. I ask for a different room. He says that insects are 'an unforeseen circumstance.' I can have a new room at full price. This tug-of-argument ends with me packing my bag, weeping it down four flights of stairs and outside while the manager yells 'scam artist!' to my rashy back.

Now standing with my bags on the pavement, I've no idea what to do. I ring Lizzie and cry with the righteous indignation of a toddler. By the end of the conversation, she promises to sort out a room at the Omi. By the time I reach her, I truly believe I'm succumbing to a heart-attack. Lizzie translates my snot-stained tear-filled panic to the polite desk staff. I am given a door-card and guided to a huge, mocha bedroom.

One hour to go until the wedding. I am woozy from hyper-ventilating.

Forty minutes to go. An audience has gathered at my bedroom door. My mother ships Uncle Owen in. I'd happily show my hips to any other person in Brighton but I am pressurized to let him inspect my thighs. He announces with satisfaction that I'm a bed-bug feast. My Aunty Leah, Uncle Owen's daughter, who is orchestrating this wedding, indirectly accuses me of hogging the limelight. My mother bristles. This is getting more like the family weddings I remember.

Thirty minutes to go. The doctors of my family berate me into believing I am not dying after all. Lizzie pops a dress over my head. My face and arms are clear, I'm winningly pale and interesting. I start to feel better.

At ten to eleven we are standing in Brighton Town Hall. Just before the bride arrives, there's a square shadow at the doorway and my father enters. Heads whip around, conversation lulls. This is our first real-life glimpse of Wife-to-be-Number-Four. My dad has thick curling hair, long black eyelashes around snake eyes and a general air of well-oiled ease.

The new wife is slightly taller than him and looks like she could crack walnuts with her cleavage.

Aunty Leah moves around the council chamber with the tension of a coiled-spring. She places the frog-like groom in his position and rattles instructions to the cowed Humanist Celebrant. My father and Wife-to-Be-Number-Four sit on the front row. We, the former children and wives stand behind, staring at the back of his head.

Carmen sails graciously down the room. She is slim, blond and consciously well-maintained. The most successful family-member of my generation, she wisely turned herself into her own business, scaling promotions in a media company until she found a way to seduce the CEO. When she was quite clear there was no-one above him, she cashed in her chips and here we are at the trophy presentation.

The civil ceremony is quick and painless. Now we have the party and everyone has to account for their own behaviour.

I take up the corner of a free table. 'Hello' says the Wine, 'You're an attractive-looking young lady.' Good. It's complementary wine, my favourite. Every fibre of my back hooks itself on my clothing. It feels like the sunburn I got in 1983. Although this wedding was a mission to eat, I don't feel hungry. Instead, I fill up the empty space with alcohol. The best man gives a speech that makes a virtue of how many luxury sports cars the groom has written off. My uncle makes a speech that is the verbal equivalent of showing everyone naked photos of Carmen as a baby.

On the far side of the room, Signe grips Samson tightly, drinking and handling cutlery despite this handicap. My mother snipes at Aunty Leah who is still in charge even as the red wine gets the better of her. My grandmother openly calls the Pope 'the Antichrist' in front of Catholic Inga. It's like being stuck in a audience participation farce. I sit beside my father who seems completely untouched. I ask his new-matic girlfriend what she makes of it.

'Don't sweat it, Honey! Where I come from if you make it out of a wedding clear of knife wounds, you're doing well.'

She gives a perfect American smile. I give a British one by return. Then I notice my father looking at me. He gives a little nod.

Towards the end of the evening, in front of friends and family, Uncle Owen violently spills a full glass of wine down the front of a teenaged waitress. Then apologises loudly and sloppily while 'drying her' (actively groping her chest) with a small tissue.

This will be the memory of the night; the painful thumb tack that the rest of the wedding will cling to. In the venue kitchen, while we are trying to replace the correct Victoria Wine glasses in the correct boxes, Aunty Leah loudly proclaims to my mother and everyone else, 'I was SO embarrassed by GEORGE dropping that wine on the poor waitress and then drying it off!'

Family jaws unhinge. Does she really believe what she's saying?

Yes she does! The incredible power of delusion and doublethink! In our family, history is always re-written by the most desperate. How come I know them so well and yet I don't know myself?

22. Three-Day Binge (part three)

I'm standing by the ladies' toilet. Lizzie is asking me to spell words of decreasing difficulty, beginning with 'epistle' and ending with 'you.'

It started so well.

Lizzie and I got a lift back to the Omi with my Dad and Wife-to-be-Number-Four-named-Vivien. I go up to my room to change. My body now looks like a map of the British Empire. I am red from knee to shining knee and acutely itchy. One scratch gives two seconds of bliss and an hour of teeth-searing pain. But with my clothes back on, I look fine. More than fine; my face is strangely luminous, probably because the blood is off dealing with issues elsewhere.

At the bar/diner Signe has my father beside her. She tosses her curls at me and passes her arm through his. Signe has all the psychoses of an only child but I have a slinky blond step-sister in my court. Lizzie comes wobbling over -

'I've found a dance floor!'

And she has! She's persuaded the continental barman to unlock the disco area. We are just one "Now That's What I Call Music! 52" away from a party. The barman reappears and starts dancing with Lizzie. Then Signe's husband Samson comes in. He's very good looking.; he's a black and white photo on the back of GQ magazine and he knows it. Two drunken songs later, he's dancing with me. Suddenly, jeopardy! Kelly Llorenna's "Tell it to my Heart" causes Samson to coil himself around me. I am too drunk to engage 'nun-mode'. I try to keep my elbows out but his fingers moon walk down my spine and clamp onto my buttocks. I shoot a look at the doorway, just in case Signe is standing there staring.

Signe is standing there, staring.

I make the worst move possible, which is to jump back guiltily. Signe and I freeze like two lions vying for the same caribou. The hatred that exists between us has never been voiced. Signe doesn't need to, she made her views known when I was four.

I'd often heard about the presence of a mystery sister so when she eventually turns up, I treat her like a visiting foreign dignitary. From my position as a mud, snot and pee-stained toddler, she has Princess Leia poise and regency. That she never looks at me or seems deaf when I speak, only makes me need her attention more. One day I'm out making feeble attempts to rock the swing that is attached to a tree in our rambling garden. Through the copse comes dainty, curly-topped Signe. She's struggling with a huge metal bucket that crashes against her kneecaps.

'Hello Signe!' I hear myself pipe. 'That looks heavy!'

She has the empty eyes of a ghost child. She carries on towards me, now closer than she's ever been – I can see the print on her little cloth-kit dress. In one move she heaves the pail onto her shoulder and tips the contents on my head. The freezing, shocking water has two effects. 1. I abruptly learn that people are unpredictable and 2. That Signe loathes me for reasons that are far bigger and wider than I can fathom as a four-year old.

Outside the hotel I breathe hard. The ground is periscoping, I feel strangely alien. My father strides up and down the pedestrianised Brighton street on his mobile. Vivian smokes a cigarette and twirls it towards me.

'You still being troubled by the parasite?' she asks.

I glance back inside. If she means Samson, I can see my older sister delivering what I expect is a poised hairdryer telling-off.

Dad is on the phone to Tom, his attention is entirely focused on his blue-eyed boy.

'Well that's very generous, Tom. Carmen's lucky you've got friends in Barbados – she'll enjoy that I'm sure.

I'm ill. I need my daddy to help me back to my room and give me Calpol. Signe pushes out of the swing door. She is white with what I assume is rage. My father stands between us, unaware of the threat. He winds up his conversation and puts his phone away .

Signe and I both say 'Dad, I..! Then we pause. Then we both say 'I just wanted to...'

My fingers tense. Are we destined to die grasping each other's throats? No. My stomach makes an executive decision and turns me into an arch of puke.

The next thing I remember is being outside the ladies toilets.

Lizzie says...

'Ok, forget 'seven'. How do you spell 'You'?'

In the bathroom, she gently cleans my face. We both stare at my reflection.

'Oh.My.Shitting.God.' Says Lizzie.

My lips have inflated to one third the size of my face. At the front desk, Lizzie asks the staff if they have a doctor on call?

'Yes. But there's a £200 call-out charge.'

Lizzie asks 'Is there a nearby medical center?'

I am hurried down the late-night street, suddenly aware of nothing and everything. People's stares. Cigarette smoke. Beer. My mum on the phone to Lizzie. I am a gasping Spitting Image version of Mick Jagger.

We pass the medical centre three times before we find it. It's a discreet shop front that deals with the undocumented needy with no access to health care and middle-class sick-stained drunks who look like they ate a botox hamper.

Can she fill in this form?

No I shitting can't.

'Can she wait for a doctor?'

I almost tear the veneer off the receptionist's desk and suddenly, I'm on my back.

23. The Afterlife

I'm in a white box, with gossamer walls. There's an unearthly hum. Far, far away I think I catch the voices of my loved-ones, not words as such but hushed whispers, almost like a shadow of life. I am floating, I can't feel my body below my neck.

The only thing that is wrong is that I have the family-tree of all headaches.

Suddenly a metallic scrape and the walls of the room open. Curtains! A nurse comes in and notes I'm awake. She's pushing a box on wheels.

'Any pain relief?'

'Head.' I say.

She picks up a clipboard at the end of my bed. Purses her lips, locks the box and goes away with my clipboard.

Right. I can tell I've pissed the nurse off already and I've only been awake for a minute.

Then there are footsteps and back comes the nurse, with a doctor and my sister Lizzie.

'Hello!' he says far too loudly 'You've got a sore head.'

'Yes,' I don't nod. That would be sore.

'I'm not surprised!' he yells. To the nurse he says. 'Just push fluids, we'll review at lunch.'

They take the box of pain relief away!

Lizzie stays. I note that she has a large bottle in her hand and a 3″ paint brush. Then she pulls back my sheet!

Oh Jesus! Not only do I have nothing at all on, but my skin from the neck down has gone crusty and white!

'Lizzie! I've got gangrene!'

She twirls her brush. 'You're getting calomine by the jar-full.'

She pours it onto my tummy and starts to emulsion. Soon I am covered in a mauve of humiliation.

'Why do the doctor and nurse hate me?'

'Do you not remember anything of last night?' She does a second coat on my shoulder. 'You had an anaphylactic reaction to bed-bugs. You lost consciousness in the medical center and they called an ambulance. But it turns out that it wasn't really the bites that were your main problem, it was the amount of vodka in your blood.'

'I didn't drink that much!' (Maybe I did. I can't remember.)

'They were worried about your breathing and they were worried about your alcohol levels. Anaphylaxis and alcohol don't mix.'

'Throat is sore.'

'They stomach pumped you.'

'Oh.'

The undercoat is finished.

'Dad's here. Your mum's here too.'

Oh God.'

'And Aunty Leah and Uncle Owen.'

'Oh shit.'

Mum and George sit by my bed. Aunty Leah paces up and down the ward, checking for dust. Uncle Owen is lying on the bed next door, waiting for a nurse to come and manhandle him.

Mum kicks off.

'You gave us an awful scare, Miriam. We didn't know what the problem was, and neither did the doctor for a while. Then he came out and said "I've recognised the vomit. It's vodka and coke. Two litres of it..."'

Mum leans in and lowers her voice to a hiss.

'...When they brought you out, what you said!'

George takes her hand. 'Miriam doesn't need to know, Dear.'

'You said some nasty things, Miriam. George does not subscribe to any of the TV channels that you implied he does and *Aunty Leah has never abused that substance or any other.*'

She leans back and folds her hands. 'That's all I have to say.'

There's a clinical silence.

She starts again.

'The horrible, dirty things you said about Uncle Owen....*you're lucky he's a medic.*'

'*Why am I lucky he's a medic?*'

'*Because he think's you were insane and didn't mean what you said. Anyway, I don't want to talk about it any more.....Leah says this wedding has revolved completely around you and your rash. For once I tend to agree!*'

At long last it's just me and Lizzie. I'm being discharged later with a goodie-bag full of cortisone and antihistamines. Lizzie has to break the glaze of calomine on my body to fold me into my clothes.

'I've got your stuff together from the Omi. Dad's paid the bill.'

I never even slept there.'

'You definitely used the room. I packed your make-up bag but your lipstick got all over the insides.'

'Don't worry.' I smile.

Lizzie clears her throat.

'It's what happens with stolen tester lipsticks – they have no tops you see. And I see you didn't return the Celine Dion perfume either.'

Lizzie helps me downstairs. I feel like I'm wearing a crisp packet for a shirt.

'By the way, some guy called your mobile. We told him how ill you were. He was really concerned, apparently.'

Chap 1?' (I've often dreamed of Chap 1 calling me, just as I succumb to a terminal disease)

'George took the phone call. It was a man from Norfolk; could've been that Kit guy I suppose. George says he called back again twice.'

Oh crinkly, grinning, blue-eyed Kit. I want to be back home in Norfolk.

I am met at the door by George. He is going to drive me to the train station and then he is going to extend his own insurance and drive Clio back to Norfolk.

During the journey to the station, he gives me a short lecture.

In this speech, the words 'Mother, worried, income, unsettled, self-centered and childish' loop past me, rotisserie-style. When George does a lecture I can't help myself. I have to look out of the passenger window and hum to myself. Not loud enough to actually be heard, just a puny rebellious hum that only I can hear. The end of the final sentence goes like this...

'.....your own income. You're lucky to have so many people who love and support you and want to help you. Including, it seems your friends in Norfolk. That nice young man I spoke to yesterday was incredibly thoughtful.'

'Oh Kit!'

'He had a funny name. Win, I think it was.'

'Wym? Wym?'

Ugh. Wym! How did he get my number? Can't he keep his anal organising confined to Toft Monks? Talk about invasive.

24. The Big Stink

Norfolk. The county where farmers laugh at hosepipe bans.

I splurge the last of my money on a taxi from the station. The first thing I discover is that my dream of Kit being there to welcome me is just a dream. He must not have got my texts. Once in the door, I whip my clothes off. This rash of mine keeps moving, it's like continental drift. The second thing I find is a leaking bath tap. The third (final?) discovery is that one of the good cats have knocked a pile of Marjory's Victorian chinaware off the dresser. They look like they've gone berserk. I left them a whole bunch of food. When I get to the kitchen I meet a swarm of flies orbiting between the cat bowls and decomposing fruit.

Kit has still not answered my texts.

My dad used to call my mother 'Balebosta', a Yiddish nickname. It means 'A woman who is obsessively domestic.' I did not inherit her skills. Post-apocalyptic house is ignored while I go outside. The softest dress I own is a cute silk number, only useful for seducing a boss. I have a medical condition. It's this or a sheet.

Kit's phone is going straight onto answer machine.

The path to the house is as dry as it ever was. The wellie prints I made a week ago after that storm are still visible but now ossified. Maybe my steps will be a historical find in the far-future; archeolo-bots will be able to recreate me from the shape of my instep. I stumble along the rutted track, everything looks calm and empty but I can hear the comforting roar of a chainsaw in the woods and further away, some distant dogs protesting against incarceration.

But soft, there's another sound; children's laughter.

It takes a clear five minutes to walk to the tennis courts. In that time I have ascertained that Kit is playing tennis with his children. He is generally being ludicrous and causing them to have hysterics. And I can see he's not doing it for their benefit but for the benefit of another person; a blond, lithe cucumber in pink Abercrombie shorts. Anna Smirkwright-Shebitch.

During the rest of the walk across the lawn I groom my mode of re-entry into Kit's consciousness. Off come my flip-flops and I walk barefoot (on tippie-toes to maintain shin length). Add to this a sway and by the time I reach the tennis courts, I am breathless and foot-stabbed on a twig. It's worth it for the double-take from Kit.

Anna turns to collect balls. Min throws herself against the wire. 'Milliam!'

'Look-at-me-serve-look-at-me-serve!' greets Tibby.

Kit's Sellotape smile is plastered on. Damn him and his allure!

'You're back. Did you have a good time?'

(Good time? Did he not read a single text?)

'I was ill.'

Min is trying to crawl up the tennis court wire.

'I was ill, Milliam. I ate too much water melons and I was sick on Plop's knee.'

'So you're doing your own child care today?' I mutter.

'Oh no, Anna did it. She had a day off. She's great, nothing is too much bother.'

Anna addresses me from a distance.

'I heard you'd taken time off before you'd even started.'

'Aren't they paying you enough at the estate office, Anna?'

She gives a little titter. 'I don't get paid to adore The Littles.' (The Littles?)

I find that my jaw is making the equivalent of a fist.

'Well maybe you can tell the office that your stinking rental accommodation has sprung a leak.'

'It would be quicker if you went yourself.' she smiles. 'I'm not in the office today.'

I am off, walking as fast as my foot will limp me. Kit bleats 'Miriam.. Miriam..Miriam' until the chainsaw drowns him out. Back at home, who should be waiting but George. He doesn't handle the sun well, having the duel disadvantage of no hair on top and skin that flushes lobster at the drop of a hat. He's sitting inside Clio with the Bad Cat on the bonnet staring at him, looking like a lion who's killed a wildebeest.

Now I enter the house I am suddenly aware of a cacophony of odour. George has a keen nose and my self-conscience is channeling my sense of smell through him.

'Cup of tea, George?' I say loudly, hoping this will him distract him. He nods, but I see his nostrils going. He's in the sitting-room so I have time to scrape the cat-food off the floor into the bowl, and phlumph! the bowl contents into the bin, then take the bin outside.

'Miriam?'

'Ye-es?'

'You've got a leaking tap. Shall I fix it?'

He can't help himself and why should I stop him? I lead him to the tool shed (past the kitchen bins! Damn!) While he's humming and hawing and admiring the tools in the shed and then tutting over the knackered washer in my bathroom, I do a rapid omni-clean.

Although I try to anchor him to the kitchen, George is an awful wanderer. He likes to pick things up and theorise about their age and quality. Over his cup of tea, he raptures about the rattly leaded windows and the Victorian plumbing. 'But you know, Miriam love...'

'What's that, George?'

'I don't know if this house is sanitary. There's a certain smell.'

I explain about Marjory and her canine offspring but he shakes his head. He starts to inhale his way around the walls. Then he stops. 'Ah. Found it.' He lifts the humane mousetrap. Against the light, I can see the dehydrated and contorted body of a tiny mouse, nose to the air-hole as if calling for its mother.

I offer to show him around Toft Hall but George wants to be home before sunset. I drive him to the station to catch the 17.24. I really should thank him for his kindness. I know I should. I find it very hard.

I say. 'Well George...It's really been, you've been... y'know...you really are the best and everything.'

He says 'I know, love. Goes without saying.' He gives me a sweaty little kiss on the head and is gone.

25. Child Soldiers

The children arrive armed with their favourite things; Tibby and Robsie have pump-action nerf guns, Min a bag full of thread and pre-cut glove puppets. So. A fairly strong hint that I should make gloves, not war.

Glove-making is an intense process. Min is a stickler for craftsmanship and has pulled the thread from her glove four times before she decides she's more the creative and I'm the technician. It is not made easier by Good Cat One jumping on the table and headbutting me.

Bad Cat has not returned since last night. He was so pissed-off about the weekend imprisonment he staged a dirty protest. While I was chipping rock-hard cat poo off the washing machine, he left home and the good cats are desperate. Good Cat Two wee'd on the blue sheepskin rug about an hour ago and has skulked off to a cupboard. Good Cat One is made of sterner stuff. He walks over Min's sewing again and Min gives a shriek.

'Get away cat youw making me luin my sewin!'

Since the Good Cats' rampage, I've stuck all breakables down with blu-tack but how long can it hold against the forces of Robsie and Tibby? The thwack of nerf off china, Min heavy breathing as she spikes her finger for the fiftieth time and the Good Cat drilling its purr into my skull make me flip. Right! I grab the cat and chuck it over my shoulder. He doesn't care, he just goes to the front door to start whining.

'That is The Dangerous Door of Front where Front is.' I warn him.

He repeats his demand.

'Ok, on your head be it' I say, opening the door. 'You'll either be killed by Front or killed by the Bad Cat.'

He's out of the door with the speed of dart.

Like Frankenstein's monster, the work of two combined people comes to life. Our glove creation looks like a muppet fetus. Min is over the moon. 'I learly yuv it.'

Suddenly, drama! Good Cat One being chased by the Bad Cat across the back lawn.

Now the boys want to hunt the Bad Cat outside. I decide I should take the bullet. I've quietly checked. Each gun holds only six darts. I theorise that if I take them to a wide open, thick-floored forest and bring Min's unused weapon, the more spaced out they become, the quicker they lose their darts.

The bullets make a kind of sucking, popping noise, like the sound of fun being drained out of me. After twelve minutes, my barrels are empty but the boys are still fully-loaded. 'Robsie can you – thwack – ow! stop for a – thwack – second and – thwack – ow! I just want – thwack – do you know the idea-of – thwack ow! time out? – thwack.'

The Little Shits have bullet belts! Arghhh, Hamleys have gone too far! First they inflict needle-rage by forcing me to create happy puppet-memories for a child whose mother hasn't identified the letter R for it. And now they've sold two under-tens unlimited amounts of ammo.

I go in and the souped-up grunts follow me, firing all the while. I've created two nuclear meltdowns of excitement. In the kitchen, I discover Min sitting on the knee of an old man.

'Plop!' says Min.

He gives me an empty smile.

'Hi Prop.'

'Who are you?'

'It's me, Miriam.'

Prop's eyes turn inside themselves for a second.

'Where's Marjory?'

'She's gone painting in Poole.'

(I've no idea where she is.)

Prop sighs and holds Little Min close.

'Would you like a cup of tea, Prop?'

Prop says, by way of answer, 'Please don't tell anyone I'm here?'

Min is watching him with the intensity of a stage mind-reader. I boil the kettle.

The Glove Puppet on the end of Min's hand places itself in front of Prop's face.

'Why is awr you sad?' It says.

Prop focuses on the fist of green felt.

'I've four little girls in Kiamutura. Victoria, Dalila, Amelia and little...'

Prop puts his gnarly hand to his cheek, lost.

'A baby.'

I'm not sure if I'm supposed to know already. I concentrate on making the kettle boil with my thought alone. Little Min and the puppet lean on his chest, which rises and falls in heaves like a piece of 19th century steam engineering.

'Lovelace is the most beautiful woman in Kiamutura and my girls are jewels.'

Prop's in the heart of the Dark Continent, some time around 1959. He is lost in the Long Tall Grasses.

I place his tea in front of him and his gaze returns. He tastes the tea and puts it down.

'I can't drink this.' he says in such a sweet way that I remove the cup in shame.

Prop pops Min on the ground and raises himself up. He touches his nose and says 'I've gone doggo.' Then he creaks out of the back door.

At twenty past the allotted time, Kit comes to collect the children.

'Plop was here!' grasses Min.

The spawnless house is a vacuum of peace and quiet. At 7:30pm the Bad Cat comes in with a glint in his amber eye.

At midnight there is no sign of Good Cat One. I go out and make feeble lip-sucky noises and shake a bowl of dry food.

I wake up at 2am with a horrible feeling in my tummy. I rationalise, it's not like leaving through the back door ever made Out Front inaccessible to the cats. And even if he was Out Front, if more than two cars passed a day it would count as a rush hour. This settles my brain. I sleep the sleep of the just.

26. Just Like Sunday

Six-Forty am. The sunshine alarm wakes me again. Hear a Good Cat miaowing and think for a second it's One, but it's Two. One has been gone for fourteen hours.

Kit arrives at 8:45 to drop off the kids and spends forty minutes leaning against my AGA making eyes at me. At last he presses a cashy envelope into my hand. We have slept together and now he's paying me £10 per hour. It begs the question; 'Childcare; the second oldest profession in the world?'

At ten, I shoehorn the kids and their car seats into the back of Clio. They are used to much wider seating arrangements The three 'Littles' have a horror of their elbows touching.

To the south of Lowestoft is Kessingland, not a small independent state run by East-Anglian separatists but a town devoted to sand, all the fun of. It's the sort of place that Morrissey used to complain about. There, surely, even a Hamley's bullet belt cannot last. The kids whip off their Bonpoint shirts to reveal Bonpoint swimming outfits and head for water.

I glance down and up again in time to see Little Min do the most magnificent faceplant into the sand, it's like watching a locomotive train crash into a snowdrift. She is not stoic. Between screams, she says her 'eye-baws aw breeding.' Robsie fires nerf-darts at her at a distance of two feet. Next the kids are in the water and heading for Holland. Min will be the first to drown. They've fired most of their nerf-gun bullets into the sea. I am forced to reveal my rash to the light and go up to my shoulders to retrieve the things I most want to lose. It is horrific. It is like swimming through cement, so cold is it on my abused skin.

Min faceplants again. I make a big show of what pity I have left. She demands that I wash her sandy hands with my carbonated spring water. Who raised this child? The Queen of Sheba?

Using the skills I learnt when training as an imaginary nanny in Switzerland, I tell them all about King Canute who successfully kept the sea at bay with nothing more that a well-build wall of sand and mind-power. Min is philosophical in the face of having orders barked at her in this Little Rascals' remake of Tenko. This keeps them going for fifty minutes and ends in Ibsen-esque disappointment. Hurrah!

I'm home-and-dry until they spot the rollerink.

Being a renaissance chick, I dream of being a fabulous skating, pearl-wearing granny. Twenty-eight pounds later we are booted and suited. Wheeled-fun is not how I remember it. In my earliest childhood, you got skanky red things that strapped to your shoes. These wheels roll like tiny foot ferraris. The boys take off, both looking like Douglas Bader tap dancing. Little Min is hugging the wall of the concrete roller-rink and whining slightly. Getting up speed is fine, it's the slowing that's tricky – the boys do it by crashing into me.

Little Min has let go of the wall. I whizz past her with a buoyant 'wheeeee'. I don't notice Tibby on the ground until too late. My feet do the Russian dance of trying to stay up while the bum slowly predicts the future. Thoughts that flow between up and down are; 'Oh dear, this is going to hurt! Oh dear, now I know why you don't get roller-skating, pearl-wearing grannies. This really is going to hurt!'

It so happens that part of the rink is overhung with gorse bushes. My bottom smashes onto the concrete while my legs are driven deep into the gorse.

The pain radiates from my coccyx up my spine, taking in my right buttock. Tibby misreads my shoulder-jigging as laughter and tries to quip me better.

Robsie says, 'Miriam is crying.'

I lie face down on the ground for ten minutes.

The drive home is a delicate lean, my nose touching the steering wheel like a myopic pensioner. Robsie and Tibby stamp fight each other all the way home while neutral Min cowers in the middle. This means they miss the bloody cloak of gore strewn across the middle of the road outside my house.

I hassle the kids inside to find Kit's in my kitchen, cooking on my bloody AGA! This right-to-roam thing is going a bit far.

'I have a key' he says.

(Of course he has.)

I airfix the kids' eyeballs to BBC 1, then invite Kit outside. I use him as a horror shield because I don't want to face my guilt that is pasted all over the B1136.

It can be smelt without being seen.

'Ugh.' says Kit. 'Was that yours?'

I nod against his back. 'It's very dead isn't it?'

'It's alive with maggots, if that's any help?'

I have to peep around. With a paw at each corner, Good Cat One lies like a big-game hunter's hearth rug. It's so incredibly flat, how many cars does it take to squash a cat utterly? Or does someone own a road-roller?

The only part that still has some shape is Good Cat One's head – its little tongue is peeping out from its mouth, like the most upbeat road kill in Norfolk.

Kit tries to lift it in one piece with a spade but the body starts breaking up.

'You're not removing it, you're slicing it!'

'Dicing. I'm actually dicing with death.'

We decide to leave it until after supper. Kit consoles me with a glass of red wine. 'It's not like you did anything wrong, all you did was let the cat out like normal.'

'Out of the Front Door' snipes my conscience. I grab the bottle and get to work on a dreg.

Kit knows how to wrangle the heated ton of metal, the machine that gives me complexes. I don't do cooking, I have AGAments. He is a man who can whip his meat and veg in and out with great ease. He eats, play footsie and give the kids just enough attention to get them worked up but not enough to keep them under control. During pudding I lose every profiterole I have as child arms sneak around me. Finally they topple asleep on Marjory's disgusting sofa, the remote control in Robsie's hand. Kit and I watch them and his arm sneaks around my shoulder, using the profiterole technique. We stand like this, trying to work out how to get them home to bed. Each sleeping tot in placed on a quilt in Marjory's outsized green wheelbarrow (previously used for clearing dog guano?) Robsie will not unclasp the remote so he goes off with it in his tiny claw. The vehicle is heavy. Kit and I take a handle each and snigger them back up the bumpy track to Toft Hall.

All three children share one giant bedroom in the house. I help them into crisp cotton pyjamas and brush sleeping teeth. I pretend in my head I'm a mother with three happy children and a man who is both my lover and my friend and who will be with me forever. Then I snap out of it because I know that's a disgusting, corporate lie invented by Disney.

In his room, Kit's very politely does not mention my legs that have not been shaved since the wedding. That night we are almost as staid as two nuns (two pervy nuns). I'm a glutton for every stupid word he says. He may as well be singing the hits of Kagagoogoo because no matter how New Romantic his lines, they seem profound and intense to my ears. I am wearing love-speakers.

Morning. I awake with six blue eyes staring at me. I try to sit up but my arse tells me to stay horizontal.

Tibby says 'She's still here.'

I am sensing a general somber mood in the room.

Little Min says 'This is like when Clara was here.'

Robsie's mouth goes anvil-shaped. He shoves his sister hard.

'DON'T mention Clara!'

Tibby says 'We'd better go.'

I feel awful; they seem so disappointed, in either me or Kit or both. I turn and look at his freckled back. He's still asleep. Who is Clara?

27. Bad Things

I did a bad thing.

Kit gets up and goes off to make me breakfast and tells me stay in bed. So I do. He leaves his mobile. To make it worse I don't really feel guilty. I don't even feel guilty for not feeling guilty. I go through his phone address book. There are many many girl's names but no Clara.

So I scroll through his text messages. It's a journey of discovery. I find some from Anna. He and she are flirting. Maybe not obviously, but it feels like it to me. She's asking him for end-of-year receipts and he asks her to come over and get them herself. I know exactly what that means.

There's a woman called Zabina who tells him he's left a bag of washing at her place. Well, that can only mean one thing. I think.

Back through time. Now Jonty's asking him to take his things away. She's as cold and clinical in the text as she is in the flesh. Backwards, backwards. He's forgotten Min's birthday and that Robsie's come home with nits. Before that, there's a long list of things Kit has to take away from The House and things she wants back. What the Hell is a Trivit?

Now Cassie, Vince and Martina. 'Please, Cass, can you go to my office and remove the box of photos in my drawer? Please don't look at them.' 'Vince, could you do something about the cash out of the business account?' 'Martina, I want you to know that any rumours you hear are untrue, and spread by my wife.'

I'm getting close. I can almost smell the rotting little tiny skeletons in the sim card.

'YOU BASTARD! I HATE YOU! JUST SO YOU KNOW, I NEVER LOVED YOU!'

Just then, I hear a tinkling tray with something crystally on it. I fumble and drop his phone just as he kicks the door open.

He's made me the breakfast I asked for; 'Anything but egg!' So, a reliable short-order cook but a dishonest and immoral partner. He's also placed a carnation in a very nickable fine stemmed vase. I eat the toast with a horrible feeling in the pit of my stomach. In this case, knowledge isn't power, it's just indigestion and heartache. He tells me Jonty is coming from London for one night only.

'She does spot checks. She's going to enumerate the bruises on legs and blackened finger-nails. Could you perhaps keep them from messy injuries for today?' (Which would be easier if the money spent on Taekwondo class had been used on sibling inter-relationship counseling.)

'Sooo.' I feel my own transparency. 'You and Jonty. Was it an amicable split, would you say?'

Kit does this thing that Wym also does. A muscle in his cheek starts to grind.

'Fine. Jonty and I just grew apart, it was very organic. So that's a good thing for Jonty, obviously.'

'Obviously?'

'My little joke.'

'Oh.'

'She runs an organic baby meals-on-wheels service. Didn't you know?'

'No.'

'Caters for babies, aged new-born to one year.'

'Well, due to limited mobility, I guess that's the best time to have food delivered.'

'Zactly. So, anyway, Jonty is delivering herself here at six and we're going to have a family barbecue on the terrace, to which you're cordially invited.' (His Lordship honours me.)

I start to dress. Kit's 'gentleman' persona works hard to maintain its composure.

'When d'you think your rash-coccyx will improve?'

The UK is suffering from URP/NR (Unexpected repetitive sunshine/ no rain). The three children chew on their Golden Grahams with the bovine stare of a trio of veal calves.

'It's too hot to go outside.'

I would tend to agree but Puritan Mother wants three hours of 'outdoor free-play' per day. Kit sends me off with a kiss on one cheek and a pat on its opposite, anterior counterpart.

Mindful of the rules about cuts and bruises, we go to feed pigeons in the park. My God, the two boys are like a satanic work of art. It's clear they hate each other, and yet Robsie chases Tibby everywhere. When Tibby stops running, Robsie starts thumping him until he's forced to run again. They orbit around me like a scrapping planet of fists and feet while Little Min tries forlornly to tempt the pigeons, who are wisely staying the flock away.

Back at the ranch, the kids are hot and weary. We've been given some pressed white shirts to dress them in but first I have another fiendish-but-fun plan. We all clocked the giant farming sprinkler in the field near the house and now, ten minutes later we are down to our underwear, standing on the edge of the parched field tip-toeing in between broken stalks of ripened corn. The water jets are quite powerful up-close and the smell of steaming earth is exfoliating my brain with oxygen.

We have not yet dared enter the stream but, this time, we are all going to do it, holding hands. The kids give little squeaks of anticipation as the water threatens with a 'psh psh PSH PSH PSH!' Suddenly THWUMP! I'm almost knocked out – it's a suckerpunch of ice to the chest. I gasp a lungful and check that my skin hasn't been torn off.

Then I notice that I'm not holding any kids anymore.

They are lying some way off, very muddy. Oh and bleeding. Oh. And crying. Oh shit.

28. Social Services

Tibby will just not stop bleeding. The other two are changed but this last one was somehow stabbed in the mouth by a corn-stalk.

Luckily, I have the phone number of a person who has cured every idiot-brain injury I have ever had.

'What do you mean, you've injured a child?'

'I just have, Mum. He's bleeding from somewhere inside his mouth.'

'Ice-cube.'

Ah-ha. Excellent. I have that very medication, I saw one under a loose fishfinger. I find Tibby and pop it in his mouth,

'Well Dear, are you better?' asks my mother.

'Depends what you mean by better. If you're asking if I'm making a steady income, or have a man who loves me for who I am, then still no. The last steady income I had was my pocket money and the last man who loved me for me I dumped when I was thirteen.'

'I meant your rash.'

'It's improving. And I've found another inappropriate man, so here's hoping.'

'You hope for too much, Miriam. You're looking for a lightening bolt. Really you should be looking for someone who can wash dishes and doesn't carp on too much.'

'Like George?'

'Like George. Look for another George.'

Tibby comes through. His mouth seems better. 'It tasted fishy' he whispers.

'Remember!' says Mum. 'Dishes, look out for whoever washes the dishes.'

Mum wants me to marry a kitchen porter.

I come back through with Tibby in his nice white shirt, but now Robsie and Min are on their knees on the kitchen table and have poured three bottles of Black Dog Real Ale and a bag of brown sugar into a large mixing bowl. Min has pink and brown cheeks.

'Millium we made smoovie.'

Robsie has found a bendy straw and is draining the black tar in the bottom. I don't even know how they managed to get the tops off the bottles. The beer is on their hands, cheeks and hair but some miracle delivered the shirts, which are still pearly-white. I know for a fact that all the straws in Marjory's cat-hair encrusted cutlery drawer are re-used. So now the kids have needle-stick injuries, beer-breath and possible cholera. I brush the sticky glub off their hair and face but I can't wash away the widely scattered cuts and bruises. I can only use a little Clinique foundation.

As we leave, I try to pop Good Cat Only into the garden but he darts straight back inside. He's now using the sheepskin rug as a long-term waste solution.

The terrace is already smoking. Kit's square frame shadows the gas barbecue range. He is wearing an apron. I can't tell if what I know about Kit makes me hate him or want him more or both or neither. He turns and lets Anna kiss him on the cheek. And at that very second a face looms in front of me, it's Wym. He leans in for a polite kiss and despite trying to avoid it, I meet him on the lips. Ugh ugh ugh. I have to stop myself from wiping it off with my hand. He doesn't seem to have noticed but there is an embarrassed pause. I grab a glass of wine and place it between us.

'Wine?'

The fun doesn't end, for now Jonty is fluttering her eye-lashes at me. She grabs my hand and purses her eyes.

'Where are the children?'

'Your children?'

They are out on the dry rolling lawn, rolling. In fact, they are all playing with a kind of relaxed giddiness I've never seen in them before.

'Ahhh.' She says. 'They always look so sweet when you see them from far far away.'

There are many things I want to say to this. I bite both sides of my cheeks and pick up a glass.

'Wine?' I offer.

Now entertaining both Wym and Jonty, I want to be with Kit who is entertaining Anna. He is letting her turn his sausages.

'So, Jonty. I hear you cook food for babies?'

She gives a snort that sounds like party popper going off.

'You could say that. Although I'm breaking into the toddler market.'

This must be the only context where you can say that without being in danger off receiving calls from Social Services.

'And I don't do the cooking, Miriam. More than half of my business is concerned with providing breast milk.'

Wow. I can't help it and neither, I notice, can Wym. We both stare at her chest and then guiltily snap a glance at each other. Is Jonty a one-woman commodities market?

'We run a milk-bank, serviced by a number of organically-living providers. My clients get the best milk their child demands. Here!'

Jonty hands me a card. It's called 'La Laiterie' and shows a happy baby getting its milk straight from source (not Parcel-Forced).

Before my stomach curdles, I take myself away to a quiet corner. I sit between Mr Perry and Prop on an outrageously uncomfortable deckchair.

Tibby tiptoes up and sticks a geranium in his grandfather's hat.

Meanwhile, there is a flurry in the middle of the terrace. Anna says 'I thought they smelt beer-ry.'

Kit's voice rises. 'The little shits must have sneaked it from the table'.

I can now see both Min and Robsie. Min has a huge sopping stain behind her behind. Robsie has a brown sick stain on his immaculate shirt front.

'They're pissed!' screams Jonty.

'Bravo!' shouts Prop.

29. Vowels and Consonants

I have had a number of ill-considered careers. After school, a summer of waitressing ended in me being fired after howling my eyes out on the restaurant pay-phone as George read me my A-Level result.

Then I got a job as a satellite dish pusher, trawling housing estates in Basingstoke, signing up impressionable single-mothers to inappropriate tariffs when all they needed was a little grown-up conversation.

After that I made willow-basket coffins in a warehouse in Windsor. I was 'let-go' to make way for three eastern Europeans who split my pay and sent it home to Split.

So I'm either extraordinarily multi-skilled or a failure. I'm the first person in three generations not to go to university. I see it as taking my family back to its working-class roots. They say I'm lazy.

I also worked in a shuffle of geriatric care homes. We used to have chairs for 'problem clients'. The seats tipped back and once you were in, there was no escaping until Charge Nurse felt she had exerted enough control to bring you back into line.

That's why Prop and Mr Perry have been placed in deck chairs. I've stupidly fallen into the trap on my own accord. Now I'm a stuck fly on the wall of an octogenarian bitching-session.

'Bor, hoi 'member the fah-mly gittin' all drehzzedup afor suooper. Hint niver no puurls ur dinner jahkets eesdays. Zall a poile o squit ter me.'

'An hour to dress, an hour to eat, an hour to digest.' Prop aims his leathery finger at the terrace. 'This anaemic shit is what passes for a family occasion. This herd of runts is what passes for family! I'm going to cross each of them off the will, one by one'

'Yew do thaaht, roite.' nods Mr Perry

'You watch me!' says Prop.

'Bout toime too. Lend'em jip'...

'First that one. Then that. And then, definitely that one!'

Three Hebbindons have just exited the French Windows, pretending hard that they've not just had a furious set-to. First the Marchese, then Jonty and finally Kit; he storms back to the barbecue to turn the sausages with such a force, he looks like he would rather drive them into the wall with his forehead.

Jonty and the Marchese spot me. Oh shit. I try to get up. Mr Perry notices my floundering.

'Whars wrong with'ew, gal?'

'My coccyx!'

He pops his eyes 'Yar whaaat?!'

'I was skating. I fell on my bum.'

'Ohh. Yew broke a tile.'

'Tile? No, not tiles.'

'Oi mean yur tile on yer hind, ye daft lummux!'

'Help!'

It's too late.

Suddenly, two 3D views of chest. One is a fantastic landscape of furrows upon lines upon a mountainous tundra of scarrified brown skin. The other chest is a wide bony valley that one could play chop-sticks on. They make it hard for me to collect my thoughts, which are all about the legalities of supplying small children with alcohol.

'Miriam' Jonty breathes 'Minnie tells me the last thing she had at your house.'

'Yes?'

(They're little kids, and drunk ones at that. Surely their evidence can't hold in court?)

'Was a lovely smoothie.'

'Uh...yes, yes. I made...Blueberry and...prune. Organic.'

The ladies lean even closer. I get a waft of the Marchese's warm perfume. She says 'Kit is a good father isn't he, Miriam?'

Jonty blinks at me. 'Or isn't he? You can tell the truth...' Oh God. I wonder if just sitting still might work, in the way you're meant to do with a Tyrannosaurus Rex. Suddenly, a third shadow.

'Kit is an over-sexed pea-brain!' Prop has escaped his deck-chair. 'And the only aspect of child rearing he enjoys is screwing the Nanny! There was no change out of one hundred thousand pounds school fees and what did I get at the other end? Two ungrateful, spoilt, useless, vapid, neutered, sponging cronies who are only going to inherit the estate if I want to see it ground into the dust and then shat upon.'

Really, the upper class do project their vowels and consonants so well. As the final words bounce off the stonework of the silent terrace, both Kit and Wym turn and walk mechanically inside. Prop is pushed into a corner by the Marchese and takes sub-audible threats as gracefully as any man can when he has seven or eight geraniums sticking out of his hat.

I sit forward and edge myself onto my knees and then stagger onto my feet. When a party has been rendered into a lardy mess, it doesn't matter how sore one's bum looks whilst getting out of a deck-chair.

But it would be better if some little shit hadn't filled my curls with used corks.

I listen in the hall. Beyond the ticking of a thousand clocks, I hear someone washing dishes in a sink. It must be Kit, the poor guy. He's trying to purge the stain of embarrassment from his life, Freud would say.

But it's not Kit doing the purging. It's Wym. He's up to his armpits in a sink the size of a Fiat Panda. He looks grim. He doesn't say anything. I don't want him to say anything. I take a towel and start drying. I keep glancing across. Wym seems grateful that I'm here, I think. It's hard to tell. I'm just realising how dark it's getting when the lights go on. Kit has a bottle in his hand.

'Miriam! Come!'

He's making bedroom thighs at me. I see Wym flinch. I think.

It's hard to tell.

30. Territory

Seems that all the prim nights are having a revving-engine effect on Kit. A can lead very quickly to B, even after agreeing that B is a bad idea. We got to A and B and then C. But D was still just a bit painful – so far away from my fantasy scenario that I ask him to stop and wait a few more days. He lies me in his arms instead. He is utterly so gorgeous. He says:

'I never knew I could feel this way about anyone.'

Oh wow. No-one has ever said that to me.

Once a guy starts advancing on me, unless he's ugly or smelly, I just go along with it. Why? Because I'm middle-class, polite, immature, scared of confrontation and pathetically grateful that anyone likes me. This is how all my previous long-term relationships started, which I then continued in terror of being dumped, and so it goes until I'm dumped. After my devotion to 'Chap First,' I reversed years of feminism by playing Cher to a selection of tramps and thieves. Chap Muso played guitar. He also played the field and all I got was a lousy STD. Chap Psychiatric Nurse was a gorgeous jibbering loon. Chap Boss almost killed me in his BMW by chasing a motorbike that had overtaken him on a country lane. He was married. Chap Previous never let me see my friends or even take evening classes. Chap 1 was the most handsome man I ever met and he turned me into a paranoid, needy, stalking quagmire of insecurities.

So I usually roll over under pressure, but not tonight, on account of my butt. To avoid non-coital angst, I go to the loo, and who shouldn't be lurking in the hall outside but Jonty, apparently absorbed with a framed map on the wall. Surely she's too perfect to snoop? The moment the door is closed, she puts her arm through mine and guides me to the bathroom.

'I just want to let you know, from one girl to another, that if you think you're special to Kit, you're not.'

I blink at her. I'm wearing love-bites like tattoos and a T-Shirt that only just covers my bottom.

She leans in.

'Has he told you that he's never felt this way about anyone before?'

She MUST have been listening.

'I'm going to the toilet, Jonty, that's one thing I can do alone.' She does that eye-pursing thing.

'Kit collects girls like a Scout collects badges. Picture him as a horny Baden-Powell.'

I hop back to bed insecure and anxious.

'Miriam!' he sighs in the darkness. 'You have nothing to worry about in Jonty.'

'I can't help it.' I bleat. 'I have issues with beauty and confidence and success and she has all of them and I don't.'

Kit lifts himself up on his arm. 'I'll tell you a secret, Kinky-Locks, but you mustn't repeat it. Jonty has not one gram of confidence and it doesn't make her a nicer person, it only makes her vicious. She's also got some rather disgusting...quirks. Those eye-lashes, you like so much?'

'She has so many of them!'

'When she was plucking her eyebrows hard, she started sticking the hairs back on her eyelids with eyelash glue.'

'Oh WOW!'

'It didn't stop there. One night I caught her – she had run out of eyebrow hair – she had moved on.'

'Where?!'

'Nose hair. She has very hairy nostrils.'

My mind is spinning – where was she going to stop? Did she ever look at her pubic hair and wonder if it was just too long and crinkly?!

'Those eye-lashes are very thick and natural-looking, because they are! Just remember that when you're face-to-face with her.'

Early morning I pad back across the lawn, feeling light with love. There are lots of things Kit has not told me about himself. He is insincere, indiscrete and immoral. But I can feel the craziness coming to get me, and if ever a girl likes to hide in Crazy, it's me.

I get home and, with a cup of tea in hand, the phone rings. I answer with all the innuendo I can muster but it's a loud woman at the other end.

'Miriam?'

'Marjory?'

'Miriam!'

'Marjory?!'

'Bugger me! It's the dogs. They've eaten something – I'm coming home to let Morrison the Vet see to them.'

'You're coming home? When?'

'Thursday night. One day only, I hope, if the dogs play ball.'

I have no idea what the day is.

'Everything OK, Miriam?'

'Fine! Fine! On top of everything...'

'See you Thursday, can't wait to get home!'

What do I do? Do I drag all Marjory's tat back out from the cupboard? I can't even remember where it all belongs. I should have been more forensic about it and drawn white lines around the ornaments before I moved them. Talking about that, what do I do about the largest missing ornament, the twin cat?

On the face of it, I've mown Marjory's lawn, cleared two tons of animal hair from her soft furnishings and brought new life to her bed-springs. But I have a feeling that's not what she cares about. I suspect she will count the cats.

With a glass of white wine, I go out to the road, just in case I have it wrong and it's not the cat after all.

No, that's definitely the cat. I try to grab it by its fur and lift, to see if it will release from the tarmac. The hair comes off in two brown clumps.

I go back inside. The final Good Cat sits in the middle of the kitchen trying, I think, to make a profound statement. It glowers at me without actually making eye-contact. I reply, saying it's no good, it can be as profound as it likes – I don't actually speak cat.

I am now talking to a cat.

Then I have an idea and take out a handful of dry cat food to sprinkle on the dead cat. This should make the cat a more tasty hors d'oeuvre. I'm hoping it will be nibbled away by tomorrow.

While out there, I see Prop appearing on the road. He's been shopping – a bag churns in each hand. He stops and looks at me, looking at the cat food on the cat.

'Hello Prop.'

'Nice day.'

'Have you been shopping?'

Prop is taken aback by my ability to read a situation.

'I have, but let's not tell, eh? Long tall grasses.'

He tips his head to look at my little bit of road that will be forever feline.

'Vermin!' he says.

'Oh, no – that was Marjory's cat.'

'Exactly. He was always giving my birds the eye.'

'Dead now.' I point out.

He appears shocked. He widens his eyes at me and sucks in his cheeks.

'Marjory's coming back for the night.' I say.

'Marjory, eh? An incredible bore to listen to, raving mad to boot.'

'Really?'

'Should've had a hysterectomy, would've sorted her. Stops a lady's mind from wondering orf.'

'You know,' I attempt. 'I quite like your boys. Wym is nice and hard-working and Kit has a lot of....spunk.'

Ugh. I said that because I couldn't think of an alternative word.

'I've made up my mind. Wym can have the estate as I proposed the first time around. She can skewer me like a pig for all I care but that's my view.'

He doesn't say goodbye, Prop just veers away down the path towards the only square meterage in Toft where what his word is law. I am superfluous, so I go home.

Marjory and I favour different kinds of non-hygiene. She likes dirt and I prefer mess. I will need to clean, tidy and then unclean and untidy to bring her house back to its original state. I block out a plan of an hour per room and then I call Lizzie.

'So,' she says. 'What do you think of the news?'

'News? What news?'

'About your dad.'

There is only one piece of news I ever get about my dad.

'Oh no. He's doing it again. He's done it three times already.'

'I know.'

'Is he in some Faustian pact to marry every woman in North London?'

'I don't know.'

'Why he isn't learning from the past?'

'I don't know.'

'I wish Dad was like George.'

'No you don't.'

No, she's right, I don't. George is normal. My dad is a mystery. He's an absentee fantasy; in my mind a secret agent, a horse whisperer, a Wall Street tycoon and, during my ballet phase, Anthony Dowell. Because I never knew what he really did, I was able tell my school friends whatever fell into my head. Truthfully, what he'd never been was there for me. He was so very cool – as smooth as Roger Moore, as cutting as Clint Eastwood. Which is why it's completely out of character that he fights his way to the altar like a crazy pot-hunter at a bric-a-brac stall every time a new admirer blows into town.

It takes two hours to unpack tat. Marjory's taste veers towards brittle china ladies with wigs and wide dresses, leaning on china stumps of trees, waiting for a handsome prince to come riding by. I empathise with them; all my life, I have been a brittle, slightly chipped and dusty maiden; waiting, waiting, waiting for a prince.

31. Power and Satisfaction

Inside, Marjory's place has been restored to its obscene original condition. So, if Marjory is here, am I relegated to guest? I picture a clammy night on the toxic sofa. Then I scan through other beds I'd prefer to sleep in. I text Kit.

I was expecting the kids at ten but they don't appear. Kit is still not replying to my texts. What does this mean? I wonder around outside, listening for the tell-tale sounds of approaching menace.

Nothing.

Then I go hunting. I pass White Rabbit Garden where Prop is apparently polishing individual rose bush leaves with a linen handkerchief. From the look in his eyes I can tell that he has not seen Kit either physically or metaphysically. I press on.

Although the french windows are open, Toft Hall is abandoned. There are no kids, no cleaners, no adults, only the tutting clocks. Tip-toeing to the bedroom, it's empty of Kit. Even his bed feels cold. Where was he last night?

I wonder back outside. There is a cool woodland path and a stinky stream with dried white slime instead of water that swing together around the back of White Rabbit Garden. The woods are ever so still and silent. Apart from a distant whining dentistry noise.

Because I don't allow horror films to dictate my outlook on the world, I follow the noise towards the iridescent heart of the forest. The grinding dentistry now sounds like a heavy creature being hacked apart. Finally, I catch sight of a desolate green-tinged wooden shed. It's large, rotten and crowded by invasive young trees. The grinding is shrill. Even if there were banjos dueling, I would never hear them.

I approach and peer around the opening. Feeding wood into a lethal belt-driven circular saw is a guy in a sweaty olive, open shirt. Instead of retreatwardy thanking my lucky stars I'm not already boxed and coxed, I get closer. The guy is heaving massive sides of wood from a stack. He turns to brush sawdust out of his face and – Wow, it's heir to the estate and hillbilly hick, Wym. He spots me. Damn! My reactions are really very slow. He's turned the machine off and removed his ear-defenders already. My head is crying 'FLEE! FLEE!' but my feet just shift aimlessly.

'Hi.'

'Hi.'

It's a good start.

'What is this?'

'It's a saw-mill.'

'Is this what you do all day?'

'No, it's more my hobby.'

'Hobby?' Oh please. Someone find this man a stubby pencil and a log-book and direct him to the nearest aerodrome.

'I've been getting it to work. The machinery hadn't been used for over twenty years and the building was just abandoned.'

'So ... almost a was-mill.' I quip.

He blinks at me.

'Instead of a saw-mill?'

He moves on. 'I've fixed the generator. Look!'

Now I am taken on a tour of things that I don't really understand but Wym thinks are breathtakingly interesting. I see rubber belts, tight screws, oily nuts and all sorts of other things that I would normally misconstrue for fun if Wym wasn't such a gimlet-eyed man-child.

'I'm just happy,' he gleams 'to have somewhere I've saved that's all mine.'

'Actually, isn't all of this all yours? Isn't that the issue?'

Song birds tweet. Tree tops roar.

Oh dear. I've dropped a metaphorical anvil on the tiny pixie of eagerness. I can't predict when and how my foot is going to slam into my mouth, but often it's there choking me for whole minutes before I notice.

I blurt 'I was actually looking for Kit.'

'Oh.... Kit's with Anna.'

(Why is Kit within half a mile of Anna?)

'She's moving into the West Lodge and I think he went to look over the interiors with her.'

(Oh no, not her interiors.)

I shout goodbye over my shoulder and fight my way out of the woods. By process of elimination I work out where the West Lodge is. Worryingly close to the main house is where it is.

A cute gingerbread-style red-brick thing on the outside, sat in tiny pink roses/lavender walled garden. The interior paint has been chosen by someone with scrunched toilet-roll for eye-balls. It's all curdled lime, peach and turquoise. Combined, they make the colour psych-quoise. From the workmany noises spilling out, I deduce that men are inside working.

'Hey!' I shout in. 'These colours are disgusting!'

The head joiner looks pleased to see me. 'Oi know, it hint my hoydea. You friend o' fAnna?'

'Yup, we're best bestest friends, me and Anna.'

'Cos we're knaakin aff jis now. Jis' give yew her kaeys. Boodiful' (He actually said 'Boodiful.')

Roge gives me a quick tour of the lodge, explains why the shower will only work on cold for now and then hands over the eight keys to all Anna's internal doors. Once Roge has cleared off, I lock all of Anna's doors and then drop the keys down her drain. One by one. Plip. Plip. Plip. I feel a surge of power and satisfaction.

By the door is a newly planted rose bush. I don't read the label but it's barbie pink so I grab it by the neck and yank it from the soil. Plants always used to make me happy. Once I nicked an ornamental cherry tree from outside Basingstoke Water and Sewage Pumping Station. George planted it and asked no questions.

However, after five minutes walking, the rose bush feels heavy and conspicuous in my hands. There's a trail of mud marking my route. I decide to hide the evidence by creeping into White Rabbit Garden and hacking a hole in the mud with my heel. Now Anna will think Wym has stolen the rose. That will spice things up a little.

I spot movement. Shit! I don't want to meet any Hebbindons, not like this. I plant faster, stamping on the rose and leaping backwards as Wym appears at the end of the path.

'Miriam!'

Shit! I pounce wildly at conversation. 'I didn't find Kit.'

He looks at my fingers. They're covered with panic mud.

'No.'

'It's just.' I say 'Marjory is coming back and sharing her bed is very tricky, I keep falling out. She snores and farts. Ahh-hahaha!' The red curtain of shame climbs my jawline. 'I need somewhere to sleep.'

'So that's what you wanted to see Kit about?'

'Maybe, but it's none of your business where I sleep, William.'

'I wasn't suggesting you'd share with him.'

'Oh, I see.'

'How long is this for?'

'I don't know. I need somewhere until one of us flits.'

'You mustn't flit.'

Wym does a long, thinking frown and shuffles a slug off the path. The frown goes on for an extended time and I start to lose track on the topic and concentrate on his expression. He's staring so hard beyond his feet that if he were a baby, you might think his nappy would soon need changing.

Finally he gives a pained twist of the neck. 'I do have a spare room but. It's full of...belongings.'

He shuffles. I've never known anyone talk about something so bland with so much plain agony on their face.

'It's fine, Wym, really. I'm sure Marjory and I can agree a duvet sharing routine. We women are good with compromise.'

Instantly his shoulders relax. 'Good good. Well, the invitation is there if you need it.'

Yes, an invitation surrounded by flood lights, man traps and barbed wire.

Back towards the house that was my house and is now not. By the time I see three gigantic red dogs circling the garden, my sense of power has slumped to a record low. Marjory is standing on the back doorstep grinning, resting her hands on her hip zone.

'Ahoy-Hoy! The place is still a bloody tip! I thought you'd at least want to put your mark on it, and hide all my bloody Doulton.'

32. Kit's Game

Still nothing from Kit. Does this mean he doesn't like me anymore? Is he testing me? Am I paranoid? Has he just lost his phone? Am I actually an existential figment of my own imagination? In the silence, who can tell?

Marjory invites me to sit down and she makes me a cup of tea. Then I remember I've moved the cups from where she had them. There's a bit of running around and us awkwardly crashing into each other. I decide to mark my position as house incumbent by making a scone mix. I should never bake in public. Performance anxiety makes me sieve flour like I'm shaking a maraca.

'So how are the cats?'

'They're fine!' I truthfully say (because Marjory still has two cats which makes them plural and they are both still fine.)

I'm creating a flour dust storm.

She points at the dappled brown fur duster asleep on the sofa. 'Which one's that?'

'Which one? That's Cat Two. Can't you tell them apart?'

'Yes of course but...the light's a bit dim.'

Ah-hah! If I keep the lights off, my luck may be in. Just then I'm saved by the Shrill. Little Min comes in.

'Milliam, we've been to town wiv Anna an Daddy and we...'

'Anna and your dad?'

'Yes and we bought things – we got cussions an cuwtains anacksaysorrys.'

'Were the accessories bright green and bright pink?'

'Yes and blue! It's all weelly pwetty.'

So. Anna's taste in decor is aligned to that of a five-year old. I knew it. Tibby slopes in followed by Robsie. Their father has gone to the cottage to help Anna with her 'soft furnishings.'

Adult, child and animal eat my scones. No wonder the dogs fart like volcanos on the pacific rim. Then we clear the money and play cards: Black Jack. Once Min has tired of her brothers screaming at her for not being able to count effectively to twenty-one, we play Old Maid and then Beggar My Neighbour. It goes without saying that I've never played these games before. I'm from a Ker-plunk and Buckaroo family. The rules Marjory taught us fall out of my brain the moment they go in.

But with dogs farting and scones buttered and cards and kids it all feels comforting and healthy.

But Marjory and mutts have a date with Morrison the Vet at six. Without a 'can I take Clio?' she is gone in a barking yellow flash.

Now we play half a game of snakes and ladders. None of these kids are graceful losers and are not really being refereed because my mind keeps referring to what Kit may be up too. Finally we end with a game that Min says her father invented.

'The run around?' I ask.

'No, Kit's game.'

This is the 'hide everything under a tea towel' test for pre-senile dementia which I believe was actually patented by someone called Kim.

The light fades and as the chess pieces hit the ceiling, I advance to bedtime. This is the perfect opportunity for me to take a toothbrush with me and accompany the kids up the wood-lined lane to Bedfordshire. The avenues are alive with the sound of whinging but by the time we've reached the Hall, they've been muzzled by exhaustion.

I quietly tap on Kit's door. Like my texts, no reply. I open the door.

Lights! Camera! Action!

It's like walking into a movie. The two people in bed are playing what appears to be a mixture of 'Kim's Game' and 'Snakes and Ladders' under the duvet!

The kids are agog. Half of me is paralysed. The other half wants to smash the tag team's heads in. Kit's idiot hand weights are handily close. I take a second to wonder if such a death would be given the OK in court. It takes two seconds for Kit and Anna to notice us. It's caught-us interruptus. I hurry the children out.

Min says 'It's like with Clara again.'

Robsie shoves her onto her bed. 'Shut up!'

I try to comfort the kids but who's going to comfort me? I've seen Kit with his kit off for someone else. My toothbrush waves from my pocket and I feel like a retard.

It takes Kit and Anna a minute to come out. I am an angry horrified coward, staring at Kit's stupid undone shoes below his hastily put-on jeans. He doesn't say anything. Anna busily coos to the children. My feet make an executive decision and exit.

33. Go Faster Stripes

In a crisis I often find myself singing inane songs. I don't know why: I think it's kind of like a frozen screen on a computer. It needs to happen before I can press restart. Being the sister of someone who makes commercials, product placement has taken up a large proportion of my brain capacity. So on the walk home, I sing the 'Canon can' advert, which goes like this....

'You get all kinds of Canon sizes for all kinds of enterprises, Canon big and Canon little, Canon somewhere in the middle...'

I take my toothbrush and lob it into a nearby grassy knoll. I never want to clean with it again.

'...take a gander at this figure makes your copies four times bigger...'

I stamp and sing and cry internally. I am stupid. Why am I so stupid? Why do I let a stupid guy drill a hole into my heart and then pour lead in it?

'...you'll have all their eyelids batting when they see you photostatting.'

I have fallen in love because I am blind and weak and in need of something: security, closeness, friendship. That's not so disgraceful, but surely I knew he wasn't going to deliver?

'...the widest range you've ever seen, copy-copy-copy goes your Canon machine...'

Kit's not the problem, he's just an asshole who didn't know when to stop playing. Why did I let it happen to me?

'...if your company's only teething, all you need's this tiny wee thing....'

I already had the crazy love, next will come the crazy breakdown. An escape is called for. If anyone can, I can. I come home to find Marjory massaging Dog One on the couch. Good Cat Survivor is still there, curled up beside her.

'It's bad news, Miriam. I assumed Blossom had simply sniffed something dangerous on the beach...'

(Sniffed something dangerous? Where is this dog being walked? Sizewell B?)

'He's eaten something rotten – a dead seagull perhaps.'

(Ugh. Man's best friend, Man's worst dining companion.)

'But there was wire attached according to the X-Ray. Blossom's going to be bloody-well operated on. Next Monday.'

Monday? Today is Thursday. I am not going to stay on this sofa, I'm not going to stay in this entire county. I spot the time; it's ten past nine. I tell Marjory to race me to Beccles train station.

'I would have to leave Blossom,' she notes. I agree with condensed sympathy. 'But the other boys will guard him.'

I am already emptying the dirty clothes' basket into a bin-liner.

Marjory makes plans for her twenty minute absence from her animals. 'And you know' says she, 'that cat has not budged all afternoon.'

Now is my chance. 'Oh no, Marjory. That's Good Cat One, now. Good Cat Two must be out.'

She blinks at me and the cat. Maybe I've taken it bit too far?

'Oh!' she looks at the cat again. 'Oh yes, you're right.'

I win!

We dash out of the front door.

She really has taken to this Go Faster thing to heart: she does most of the journey on the right-hand side of the road. The train's already in the station saying 'Beepbeepbeep!' I make it through the door by first allowing it to ram itself shut on my hands. When it re-opens, I leap to my freedom – my confined capsule of escape. Suddenly I'm watching Beccles pull away. Marjory waves from the other side of the window. A wave of nausea rises through me. What am I doing?

The journey into the sunset of London is spent in self-recrimination and all the while my subconscious sings the 'Shake and Vac' advert. It's no good, I can't get any positive metaphors out of having my carpet smell fresh. My life is skankier, stickier and more stained than it ever has.

It's a long walk from Liverpool Street to Bloomsbury. Thursday night crowds bray and shove. Luckily no-one feels like mugging a girl with a black bin liner clasped to her chest. Huntley Street is sepulchral. Starlings squabble in the tall trees, the homeless people have put their cardboard curtains up in their car. This is an oasis of post-war newsreel in a twenty-first century mosh-pit.

Nothing has changed about Tom's flat either. Apart from the huge bunch of rotting flowers awaiting me outside the front door. A mag-alanche of glossies lie sloppily on the rug under the letterbox, their news quietly bio-degrading. There's also a gold-edged envelope. I sit with it in my hand. I try to distance myself while I read the words:

PHILIP SHORT AND
(Wife-to-be-for-the-Minimum-Term-of-Five-Years)
VIVIEN CARMICHAEL
REQUEST THE PLEASURE OF YOUR COMPANY
(Oh please, if my company was such at hit you would have made
more out of my existence)
AT THEIR MARRIAGE.
(You've invited me not to a wedding but to a marriage, something
that can last as long as twelve years in some cases?)
R.S.V.P.

At the bottom, an address in Fulham. My father lives within five miles of me and I had no idea. My brain rolls at another assault to its self-esteem. Before I let myself think again, a safety campaign for 1983 takes over my mouth.

'Get a routine show your intention, fire prevention fire prevention. Check and make sure you shut every door, I mean your life could depend on your bedtime rou...'

SHIT! I knew something was missing.

Bike.

I moved Tom's fixed-wheel racer before I left last month. It was stowed securely under the living room window. But some idiot has left the living room window open by six inches. But no-one could slip a bike out of a six inch gap.

I go search. It takes thirty seconds to frisk the flat. Then I look outside. I peer and crane and despair. Then I return to the flat. I inspect the paintwork of the sill. There are two deep scratches with yellow streaks. Go faster stripes.

How could someone get a racing bike out of a window with a gap of only six inches?...They'd have to... with the... I mean, it's not possible...

34. Gift Horse

I watch eggs boil on the hob. Staring at a pan is a very safe activity, the perimeters are clear.

The giant, fetid, mushy bouquet festers on the table. The note from my mother reads 'Flowers as beautiful as my daughter.' I know it's not her fault but I'm a sucker for metaphor. The whole flower thing seems calculated insult. I put them in a vase anyway just so I can tell her I did and as a reminder that my life on earth is finite. If I'm not careful I'm going to end up like a stinking bunch of flowers and I must pull my finger out, find the man who loves me and a career that fulfills me.

I eat my eggs. They remind me of Norfolk. My thighs are touching. My hair is frizzy. I'm rubbish. When I've eaten my eggs, I still feel empty. I can't even eat myself happy.

A text pings in from Kit. He feels 'just horrible' which is good but despite that, he reminds me we were never really an official couple. Oh weren't we? I text back that he's right that we weren't an official couple. I would never become attached to a man whose children are so inured to finding a fresh lady in his bed, that they treat it like Daddy's embarrassing fungal infection. Stupidly I didn't insist on my pay from Kit before I left. So I only have £19.55 in the bank. I walk to Tottenham Court Road to withdraw it, passing shops where the staff would actually push me down and stamp on me if they knew the true state of my financial affairs.

The cheapest way of traveling on the tube is to find an old ticket and then lie in wait for children going through the wide gated barrier. You step up behind them and give the ticket-lady a significant look and point at children. It works every time.

I'm on my way to Fulham to see my father. People go and visit their fathers, don't they? Do they usually have thudding hearts, dry mouths and a sense of doom?

Coming out of the tube, the heat hits me in the face like a frying pan. There's a shaggy old loon at the entrance in nothing but cycling shorts dancing to some very heavy ska from an 80s ghetto blaster. He has that ten-mile stare. He looks like Prop.

Fulham is a deadzone for tube stations. It's a two km walk from Hammersmith to Meadowbank Close. There would have been meadows here once I guess, on the banks of the river and there's nothing a London developer loves more than a friendless meadow. The road itself is a modern Basingstoke-style cul-de-sac. The difference is, this terrace looks directly onto the Thames. 39b Meadowbank Close is hard on the riverside, up a few steps. It has pots of geraniums in front of the windows and on the paving. I stand outside it for a while, wandering up and down and generally loitering. It's the same terror that I used to get when aged four, standing outside my parents' bedroom in the icy dark of night, too scared to knock on their door.

Then I clamber over the geraniums and peer through the window into a dark sitting-room. Yes, this is definitely my dad's place, I can see his guitars on stands. I get the sense no-one's there. Now I feel brave enough to knock on the door. No answer. So he's not there. I want to stay, in case I see him. I also want to run in case he sees me. Just then, my phone rings. I jump, I knock a pot of geraniums over. There's now high grade compost all over the steps.

It's my darling wee unofficial sister, Lizzie.

'Hey-de ho! Tell me what's new.'

I tell her. I hear her groan and repeat my lines. 'So, you hadn't seen him all day and you were deeply suspicious so you walked into his bedroom. Right. What next?'

I tell her.

'Right. I'm ahead of you now. You packed up your bags and ran?'

'Yes! But how...?'

'You always do! You are the headless chicken of emotional turmoil.' She's never gentle, just fair.

'And now I'm standing outside my father's house.'

'What, you're in Fulham?'

'Heeeey! How d'you know he's in Fulham?'

'Er, because I take an interest in family affairs?'

'I do too!'

'Miriam, you're only interested in your navel. You're only interested in your family if they're gazing at your navel too.'

That seems a bit harsh from my best-beloved.

'Have you been talking to Tom? What does the bike-humping Smurf want?'

'Oh, can your bile. He rang to tell me his company have been offered free weekend tickets to V festival.'

'Let me guess, Tom did the Virgin advert and Branson's paying in goods and services?'

'Something like that, but don't look a horse-faced entrepreneur in the mouth...'

'Huh?'

'What I mean is, stop stalking your D.N.A. source, come home to Basingstoke and collect your ticket.'

35. The vips

I hate reality; it's grey and grim and bitchy. A festival will make me forget that I only have nineteen pounds and fifty-five pence to my name. I have every right to text Kit and ask him for my outstanding pay but that would follow hard on the heels of my previous text which said I wouldn't take anything from him even if he was shitting gold bullion.

I don't need money anyway; all I need is the air that I breathe. But the air in London is made of granules of dog-poo and my hair acts like a natural filter system. Without one sachet of Deep-Conditioning Hair Mask a day I end up with coir. I may as well write 'Welcome' on my head and lie by a door. Next in the queue is the leg-hair, made of space-age nano-wire care of maternal hirsute Welsh D.N.A. I knew I was in trouble when, aged eight, my mother told me that 'A man likes a mustache on a girl.'

George and my mother live in a house that is not unlike George. It's square, post-war, red, lacking in topiary and trying hard to fit in. We moved here when I was eight. Until then, home had been a huge ex-rectory gone to seed. I loved it because it was a world of exploration and endless imagination. My mother hated it because of the drains and the rats. Basingstoke is tidy, neat and contained by a road network. My mum loves it, I hate it. It's a town that is proud to know its limits.

I can see Mum's little runaround packed and ready to go in the driveway. Who should be sitting on the doorstep but Lizzie's best friend, Consumpta. Consumpta is Irish, jolly, out-spoken and independently-minded. I don't like her. She asks questions, and when she isn't doing that, she contradicts nearly everything people say to her. She also stands way too close with a kind of Irish intimacy that makes me want to shove her.

'Hiya! So you're coming too?'

'Well. Lizzie IS my sister and Tom IS my brother.' I direct an eye-dagger that she deflects with bloody-minded self-assurance.

'Right so. I've brought my three-girl tent, it's gonna be grand craic.'

I step over her and go in. Lizzie's on her knees in the hall, forcing a sleeping bag into a tiny container.

'Why's Consumpta here?'

'Because Tom said as many people who wanted to come, could come. Miriam, if you're going to spend this weekend complaining, you might as well stay here.'

Lizzie is pink and narky-looking. I tiptoe away.

Isn't Consumpta latin for tuberculosis? She is no way consumptive unless she's medicating herself with dumpling stew. She talks all the way to around the M25, it's like being under fire. I lie in the backseat, menacing the view with my eyeballs.

At last, we reach Essex to discover we are going to be staying in a festival VIP area. Not THE V.I.P. area, just a 'vip' area. The vip camping ground is for people like us who have got their passes through work or a competition. Isn't there a band called the Freeloaders? Still, having my name ticked off on a clip-board and then having a 'vip' access band for free makes my shallow heart beat warmly.

Consumpta's tent is a flowery thing that she bought in a factory outlet near Dublin. I remember one horrible disorientated night at Womad, being as I was very drunk and eighteen, when the night was spent staggering through a sea of green dome tents, crying and asking everyone if they'd seen my tent. Shape? Dome. Colour? Green. That won't happen here. This tent is a giant sanitary towel wrapper.

vip has a number of fringe-benefits; a private area next door to the real V.I.P. area, a big eastern-themed marquee with plastic chandeliers, drapes and cushions to lie on and real toilets with water. The down-side is that other vips are rude, grasping and thick. In the distance, the thup-thup-thup-cheer-cheer-cheer has started. Someone's having fun. I persuade Lizzie and Consumpta we should slum it in the main arena.

POP! *peoplepeoplepeopleSmell of Burgers!*

Now this is a festival! Crowds move in aimless pathways of intent, between gig and food, tent and stage, drink and loo. Drunks, narcissists, kids with tended afros, students with idiot-dreads. There is way too much humanity out here. I can't turn off my natural tendency to judge every person I pass, creating a rolling background commentary that goes; 'orange-peel-thighs cankles goose-neck michelin-tummy dreadful tattoo short-shorts, samey-samey-same...'

Just then, I spot a girl with a really nice red rockabilly dress. We approach and I see she also has a jewfro, poor girl. From the back, she could be me. I decide to give her a thrill and tap her on the shoulder as I pass; we will have a sisterly exchange about the vagaries of frizz. She turns.

'Aw jeez-in-a-jeep!' gawps Consumpta 'Will you look at that, Miriam, she's your feckin twin!'

I am thunderstruck. Lizzie fills the gap.

'Hi there Signe. I guess Tom got you a ticket too?'

36. Token Drunk

This festival would be bearable if I had Lizzie's attention but I'm fighting for it with the Irish foghorn and whoever Lizzie's incessantly texting on her phone. She leads us blindly around the site, texting all the while.

Now she's careered into the area that is devoted to Healing. Stepping inside the enclosure is like taking a walk through a mental-health respite day centre. It's important to keep moving and to avoid eye contact. Smirking, laughing and pointing would be frowned upon, if frowning were allowed. Everyone smiles as if they've had happiness-thumb tacks driven deep into their skulls. It's a chakravalanche. Lizzie enthuses about activities that could be eased out of existence by carefully balanced medication and counseling. Before you can say namaste, Lizzie's signed herself up for 'Laughter Yoga' or public humiliation, masking as soul-enrichment. Lizzie's self-harm takes a while. At its zenith, she's dancing in a circle, artificially laughing while wagging her finger at some hairy guy with no shirt on. (In this area, it's a No to shirts and a No to suntans but a Yes Please to wispy body-hair and stringy beards.)

That's when I split and find the drinking zone. At this festival, getting drunk is an art form c/o Franz Kafka. You go to a kiosk and buy a token with money for a specific drink. You stumble to the bar and take your drink. To save time you could drink it while walking back towards the token kiosk again to buy another.

Soon I'm tipsy and alone. Perfect! That's never a recipe for enriched soul-searching. Using my elbows as weapons, I anchor myself in the middle of a tightly-packed crowd in a marquee, warm mud/beer/grass steaming up my skirt. The girl singer is being surprisingly Freudian with her Stratocaster and driving the guys crazy. Her songs are beautiful and I'm a morbid music-listener, always reading just a little bit more into a lyric than is strictly healthy. I lean over the railing at the front, all aching, heart-break and longing driving over me like a truck. Luckily no-one can see me bawling, apart from a perplexed rock-goddess. There is reflected light on the cheeks of the person next door. She's also crying. Poor thick her, poor thick me. My brain re-assembles the features; it's Signe, again! I put my arm around her. Soon we have each others' tears and snot on our vintage shoulder pads. When we make it outside, she coughs up that she's having Samson issues. It turns out that he unpredictably loses his temper, suffers from some male form of PMT and is a self-adoring bully.

She's put her foot down and gone to this festival alone but is anxious about the crowds. To make it worse, she thinks she may be pregnant. I help by taking her to the token queue and with the ten pound fifty-five pence I have left, join her in a stiff drink.

Lizzie and Consumpta eventually sniff us out.

'Is Signe drunk?' points Lizzie.

'I'm not!' slurs Signe.

'Oh leave her alone,' says I. 'She's got man problems.'

'Och, like every other woman.' Consumpta moos.

Lizzie stretches smugly, showing off her xylophone rib-cage figure. 'I don't have man problems.'

'You don't have a man.' I counter. I see the glint in her steel-tipped eyes. I smell trouble.

'Actually, Miriam. You know your brother...'

'Oh nonononono.'

'Well, we are. As soon as Tom's back. We're in love.' She juts her neat little chin defiantly.

'But what it'll do to the family?' says Signe.

Lizzie's mouth drops open; 'Will it ruin the harmony of the Short family? Y'know, Tom stays out of the country because he can't stand listening to you all complaining about how each of you had the bad manners to develop into babies. His happiness and mine has nothing to do with bloody atoning for something your father did thirty years ago.'

(I hear Tom in that speech. He's been priming her, which means the feelings really are mutual. Worse luck.)

A square shadow passes over our table.

'Ahh. This is nice, my three favorite girls together.'

'Oo, apart from me!' That comes from a shiny American in a brand new Pacamac.

Dad stands before us, his gleaming charm oiling the grass around him. He gives a stomach-churning smile.

'So, we're all on the guest list. Tom is a generous boy, isn't he?'

Dad and Vivien pull chairs up and completely misread the leaden silence as a respectful invitation to start conversation.

'Did you get the wedding invites?'

We all nod. Never has there been such a muted response to a wedding since Adolf and Eva. Dad ploughs on. 'While you're here, Miriam and Signe, could you be bridesmaids?'

Vivien adds 'Well, Miriam should be Bridesmaid. Signe is a Matron of Honour. Soon I'll be a happily-married woman too.' Vivien is sliding with roller-skates into a nest of vipers.

'You know, I've moved country and now we've just moved house and that's very be stressful. Now we're getting married. I'm not sure why we're doing all those at once but of course, your father's been married three times before so he's had the practice a-hahaha!'

I look at my dad. His face appears to have had all the expression rubbed off it with a duster.

'Sure this one's a keeper.' says Consumpta.

'Oh, you Catholics like sticking with marriage, come hell or high-water,' says Dad.

(When was marriage to my mum, or to Inga or to Sheila ever Hell? And what high-waters exactly? He bailed out before it became humid.)

'So Signe, you're a good Catholic girl. When's the baby coming along?'

Everyone looks at Signe. Signe looks at me. I look at my feet. She lets her rum-and-coke do the talking.

'There's nothing wrong with our relationship! Samson has very strong views and he's a very moral man. I wish everyone would stop putting him down!'

That pretty much smashes all conversation with a tent-peg mallet.

'Well. Red Hot Chilli Peppers are starting on in ten minutes.' Dad says. 'We'd better go.'

I get up and give him and Vivien the obligatory hug.

'I'd love to be your bridesmaid. Thanks.'

Then I feel my toes being squashed into the turf. Signe dives onto Dad. 'I'm really flattered too, Daddy. I'm so pleased for you.'

Many things annoy me about this 'wild' living. People singing at 2am. People tripping over our tent cords. Consumpta snorning like a banshee. Birdsong at 4am. Then the sun at 5:30. Bloody relentless nature!

Festival mornings are fun and games. The light-on-work actors who populate the arena are dressed as aliens, so as to better interact with children. Poppy, Gypsy, Archie et al are being shepherded from face-painting to Indian drumming to paper-hat decorating to raffia-skirt making. I slip through a railing to a marquee at the end of the site. Last night this tent had two DJs rotating two different kinds of music. The people who dance in the tent are given headsets and can chose Channel A or Channel B as their sound tracks to dance to. When you pop your head in, it's a little like 'Laughter Yoga'. Everyone is dancing in silence.

The tent is currently empty apart from a few black T-shirted technicians walking around with armfuls of headsets, rolls of gaffer-tape and stubble. There's also an unattended box of vinyl. I start to flick through it. I can't help it. I have no record player but do have kleptomania. Just then, a pair of sensible safety-toed boots appears in shot. I stop fingering the records and stand up, red-faced and blinking. There's a ruddy-looking guy gawping at me.

'Ha... I collect Vinyl, just seeing what you've got?' I lie.

'Miriam?'

Uh-oh. I have no idea who he is.

'It is Miriam?'

It clearly is.

'You probably don't remember who I am.'

Clearly not.

'It's been about twenty years.

Oh. Ahhh, It's Chap First.

The last time I saw him he was 5 ft 8" and wore braces. He is now significantly taller. The braces have gone.

He asks 'Would you like a drink?'

I nod dumbly. My heart is battering its way through my ribcage. First love meets first heart attack.

He turns and looks back. 'I'm going to get two drinks. Miriam, don't go anywhere.'

37. The End of First

I haven't seen Chap First since I was thirteen and a half.

I stand at the door of the marquee, feeling queasy memories wash over me. He was the perfect example of the Boy-Next-Door.

Our red-bricked semi in Basingstoke shared a second-floor balcony. On weekends, before breakfast, and while still in our pyjamas (his Luke Skywalker, mine Holly Hobby) we would tip-toe between open-plan sitting rooms long before the adults were awake.

We did everything together. Or, at least, he allowed me to do anything I liked to him. Dressing up as action film characters gently evolved into clothes swopping became double-dare strip shows became secret kissing became kinky body examinations. Our pre-pubescent romance was full of paranoia. Our parents, we thought, had the investigatory powers of the Stasi. There was never a cupboard dark enough or a corner hidden enough to stop me feeling I was being watched. By the age of thirteen, we twigged that our parents were as keen to avoid our affair as we were in being discovered. Our main dating issue was keeping our dental braces from snaring.

Then I left for boarding school.

I didn't even dump him. I just didn't get back in touch even though he wrote his phone number over every available object I owned at the time. When I came back for half-term break, I blanked him. Completely. He followed me around, bemused and then incredulous. I didn't have the words or the emotional depth to let him know that my new career as 'desperate school loser' was making my head implode. His questioning frown as he passed me in the street made my stomach double up Rubik-style with dull embarrassment.

Real estate came to my aid. His parents moved away when I entered Second Form. Being my first-ever boyfriend, I expected all other men to be as biddable and patient but time and time and stultifying time again I made a beeline for the noisy, popular motormouth who caused the world to rotate around his ego. I should have noticed the quiet ones in the corner, the ones being inconspicuous and invisible. Like him.

I did ring Chap 1's dad when I left school, and got his new address. I don't know why I didn't write to him. I wish I could send a letter from now to then.

Chap First comes back with my drink; a Southern Comfort and

Lemonade, the bottled dental decay that I secretly tippled when my parents were out. I salute his recall.

'I can't believe it's you!' he says. 'I saw someone yesterday who looked exactly like you. I ran after her but she looked like she was going to hit me.'

That is usually Signe's reaction when someone calls her Miriam. 'And then today, you're here.'

We start off by making polite small talk. I find out he's happily engaged and has a baby. He finds out that I'm a successful ghostwriter and triathlon competitor. He has a great job, recording live performance to be streamed on the internet. He gets technical and I remember what a sexy brain he had. Once the drink has settled, polite becomes intimate. He recalls the first time we attempted very heavy petting. The pets were the puppies that he invited me to see in his bedroom. But there were no puppies to be seen, not that kind, anyway. He talks about our distant relationship in detail, I can only recall snatches. Other guys I've dated had wind-up egg-timers ticking away in their brains until it was their turn to hog the conversation again. Chap First listens carefully, only querying the places where I've made up bollocks.

We wander the festival alleys aimlessly. The second wave of humanity is starting to replace the 4ft arena-rats who are now kicking or hanging off the backs of hapless character-suited actors. One thesp who has spent the morning enacting 'alien' in a delicate papier-mâché spaceship is trying to stay in character while piping desperately through a voice-changer:

'Pleeeese leave my spaceship alone. I do not need the help of earthlings. Do these children have parents? These earth-beings are becoming irritating.'

Then the evening makes the fairy lights come on in the trees. We are still walking. My history is wooshing past me like an express train. I am thirteen again; I am full of hope and optimism. The world is my oyster-bar. I have a boyfriend back home who loves me for who I am, but he's a bit stringy and gangly, and basically, a wimp. Because I am thirteen I know I can find better. I will date a musician who will become a rock-god. The nerd will be ditched while I use my feminine wiles to inch my way up the cesspit of life. Idiot! My leg mentally kicks myself in the thigh. Then I do it again. By the time we have walked around the site once more, my brain is limping at the needless loss of a very good man.

We go into a marquee to watch a singer, a skinny public-school boy wearing cherokee headgear. I can't remember if the songs are any good. I'm too busy trying to work out how to extricate Chap First from his fiancé situation. Not-married is better than married; there still is time isn't there? He's remaining on the correct side of the fence. I have leapt right over the fence. I am in the next-door garden, stomping over rose-bushes and flower-beds.

After that, we visit his green tent in the Production Camping Area (like vips but muskier). Anticipation rocks me to my core but all Chap First does is collect a four-pack of beer and hands me one.

'I'm creating a boozy barrier between us.' he says.

Ah. I've been rumbled. Romance has knocked me sideways like a bowling pin but all he's rolling with these days is a platonic beer and clean wholesome friendship.

On the way back, he holds my hand to lead me through a tidal wave of people going to watch Coldplay. I can't work out if it's him I want, or myself magically restored to being a teenager.

My phone buzzes. I notice and ignore a worried text from Lizzie. There's one from Kit, asking when I'm coming back. I momentarily remove my hand from Chap First, but follow his feet like a willing child as I construct a witty/scathing reply to Kit. By following Chap First's boots I can text and walk and once I'm done, I grab his hand again and give it a squeeze. His hand feels different, flabbier. Then I gently realise that these legs have different shoes on. And he has a different, mildly surprised face on him. Fuck! I have been following the wrong man.

I shake my hand free and turn around, trying to see where Chap First has gone but the swell of the crowd is too much, I'm pushed backwards to the main arena. At last, I fight my way to the silent disco, but it's silent and empty.

He's gone completely.

I head for the Production Camping area and in the colour-sapping darkness, look for his green dome tent in a sea of green dome tents. He isn't there.

I have his mobile phone number – I'll text him. I hide in Production Camping toilets to escape Chris Martin's gloomy piano thrashing. As I remove my phone from my pocket, I also realise I need a pee. Undoing my buttons while texting is a mistake. My phone releases itself from my grip, does a slow turn and lands in the water with the grace of a dolphin.

'This would not happen into a bog-ordinary portaloo' is the first thing I think.

'Oh shit!' is the second as all my pixels fade and drop off the screen. My phone is dead.

Now outside, shivering and tearful, I'm drunk and it's dark and I'm on my own again.

I cry myself back to vips, home of the panty-liner. Meanwhile Chris Martin smugly reminds me about the chasm between life and how easy it's meant to be.

38. The Lego Box

The first feeling when I wake up is that something really brilliant has just happened. That feeling is slowly overlaid by a tide of shit as I realise that a number of very stupid and bad things happened just afterwards.

I open my eyes. There is a yellow post-it note stuck to my make-up bag which has been placed in front of my eyes – and vertical too, so I can read it lying down. It is a hand-written rant by Lizzie who is now peacefully asleep to my right.

The note says 'We were all worried sick about you yesterday! I texted you hundreds of times – don't you have any credit?!! Stay in touch today if you want a lift home. Leaving about 10. PS. We had to push you out of the way last night, you were sleeping in the middle of the tent. How come you're even self-centered in your sleep?!'

I check my phone. It's still dead. I check Consumpta's wrist, with its mammoth idiot Swatch on it. It's 8:10 already. I leap out of bed. Someone smells like a baboon's cage. Me. A neighbour's solar shower is hanging on a tree so I nick it but it's not warm, it's bloody freezing.

At 8:30, the outer fence is still closed. I have a primal urge – Chap First is still within a mile of me – it is essential that I find him. Trying to climb over a wire fence is harder in real life that in either films or my dreams. It hurts and my arms refuse to lift the rest of my body up. In the end, I walk to the end corner of the site and crawl underneath, scratching my back and covering my chest in crud. It's now 8:55.

My legs run/walk/flip flop at speed straight to the silent disco tent. My stomach churns. I'm prepared to do something dramatic, perhaps hit him over the head with a large club and drag him away. Or beg, or threaten to become a nun or something.

The crew are there – all black T-shirts, beards, sun-shirked skin and five-month beer pregnancies. They shout single words at each other and tie up their arms with cables. No Chap First. I ask for him. He's gone to the entrance to let his fiancé in. She's come to pick him up.

I'm made irrationally angry by the obvious error – Chap First is my property. Just because I was too lazy to post a letter to him twenty years ago didn't give him the right to form relationships with other people. He wasn't given permission to move on.

'You can wait. Or leave a message for him in his flight case' says Grizzly Crew Man. He points at a box that looks like an extra-sturdy giant egg carton.

I open it. The box has all kinds of Chap First's personal things – maglites, leathermans, gaffer-tape. It smells of coffee, incense, aftershave, roll-ups. It sends me back to his teenaged L-shaped bedroom. The posters on the wall, the CDs in the shelves, the sink on the wall. But in the box, on the inside lid – a photo of a woman. She's very beautiful and has ringletty hair, like mine only nicer. She has clear skin and dimples. Like me but prettier. The main flaw in the photo is that I can also see Chap First, looking smitten, pressing his cheek to hers. And there's another issue. This photo has a baby – peachy, button-eyed with a mop of soft curls. I feel something crack in my throat.

Thoughts trickle through a part of my mind that I've spent years trying not to access.

Could it be that Chap First has a life outside my own? Could it possibly be that this is simply my reward for life-long thoughtlessness? I hear a loud voice in my ear and realise it's coming from inside me. 'Keep your cock-ups to yourself. There is no need to share them with anyone else, especially innocent bystanders. Stop, look and listen. Then move on, idiot-hole.'

I close the box and step back. Then I run away, feeling like my intestines are attached to that box and are being pulled out like an unravelling jumper.

I arrive back at vips just in time to see Lizzie and Consumpta starting to pack the tent.

'The skinny boy from next door? You spent the whole day with him? Didn't you use to call him The Whinge?'

I did. I hate me. I want to give my thirteen-year-old self a slap.

My sister and her friend bustle and pack without reference to me as my ego slowly disintegrates into the mud. I wander away from the morning full of evacuating tents lying ribbed and baggy like trampled giant used condoms.

What am I doing? When did it start? If I spin around and face my problems will they mow me down? And when did I start running? I can't remember a time when I wasn't being pursued by black, shredded fears; half-lit banshees just behind my shoulder. If you split the white noise that they're making you can hear my teachers voices telling me how stupid I am, my mother and father fretting over me, my siblings hissing at me; everyone everyone in a trail, tied on to me like cans behind someone's wedding car.

My brain is a vast bucket of lego. I pull the blocks out and examine them, but there are more blocks below. Soon I am surrounded by Lego blocks of anxiety, confusion and self-doubt. There are layers under layers. A stupidly emotional dead zone girlfriend, a dumpily naive teenager, a confused child, a frightened toddler, an annoying baby.

I am stumbling over cracked beer glasses but to me it's a sea of lego blocks. A square shape shadow on the horizon, carrying a large water container. It's my father.

I call after him.

39. It's Complicated

I think he can tell I've been crying, but the festival haze of carbon escape and mud might be shielding me.

'Give your Tateh a kiss.' He croons in a cranky embrace. I test him for any emotional sympathy. All I feel is his muscly back and well-covered ribs. 'Great to see you here,' he lies. We pause and I glance over my shoulder. There's a breakfast van still on site, serving the last of the roadies. I haven't eaten for almost two days.

Dad sighs, pats his pocket and nods. 'So let's get a coffee.'

Ever since I was young, if I've heard some good music, I'd fantasize a scene where Dad might enjoy it too. His blessing is an instinctive need. It's like ducks/water, dogs/bones, me/paternal approval. It has never ever worked; the little primate in me is stymied by his complete inability to engage with my brain. It's not that he doesn't like me, he just doesn't want to be anywhere near my thought processes.

Dad talks to the staff of the van. He talks to a roadie. He may even try to talk overflowing wheelie bin to avoid speaking to me. At last he has to sit down.

I open my mouth and out comes the lego for a full ten minutes without pausing. I say a lot of words and it goes well. I use another word which is wrong. I meant 'opaque'. What I said was 'tights'.

'I mean to say, my childhood wasn't translucent. Other people have memories. I don't.'

Dad leans back in his chair as if he's willing it to carry him over the hills and far away.

'The thing is, I'd like to get to know you. Before the wedding.' I suddenly feel guilty about this. It sounds a bit selfish. I pause and watch pallid festival wraiths stumble past, then a trailer of rocking portaloos.

'But you know me. sweetheart.' He says. 'Remember all the things we used to do? I took you on holiday.'

(When we went to Rome? I got lost in St Peters. Instead of running to save me, he took 'funny photos' of my expression as I panicked. Or the time he and Sheila invited me to the Caribbean? I was cared-for by a Bolivian au-pair who was a trained doctor but now made her money as hired baby-wiper. She was bitter and angry. Tom was tiny and screamy. I ate too much ice-cream and got a vomiting bug.)

'We went to the theatre.'

(Shudder. Aged fourteen, I was induced to watch Kiss of the Spiderwoman in a tiny fringe venue with a floor-level performing area. We got front seats. He thought it would be an education. It was.)

'Ten-Pin bowling.'

(Broken thumb incident.)

'Sunday museum trips.

(Dad's single-mother hunting ground.)

'The holiday in Rome.'

'Really Dad, this is not what it's about.'

Dad eventually tilts his coffee at me.

'When are you going to get hitched, Miriam? Someone must want a girl like you?'

Note the 'someone.' Also 'A girl like you.'

I don't really have the time and he doesn't have the inclination to examine the many complexities of my love-life. So I lie.

'I'm in a relationship.'

Dad nods. He's trying to placate me. 'We might even get engaged.'

'Tell me when it happens. If it happens.'

Bloody Dad.

This has been my best shot to clear my head.

The pretty coffee girl comes and offers free cups and biscuits to finish off their last batch. She winks at Dad. Everyone loves Dad – he's perfect. Maybe I'm going mad.

I am dunking each corner of flapjack into my coffee, making increasingly poly-sided shapes out of the square when Dad grabs my hand.

'Look, sweetheart. It's not that I don't think what you're saying matters, it's just that people of my age don't think about this stuff. It's not me; it's my generation.'

I'm not sure how to take this. All his relationships were 'Complicated.' It sounds like he's passing the blame for his marrying, begetting and scarpering onto the 1970s.

Suddenly Dad is smiling and it feet like being caught in a beam of warm evening sunshine.

'What are you smiling at, Dad?'

'I was just remembering the look on Keith Moon's face when he blew his drum up live on American TV.'

Right, that's it. I give up. I've had enough of my family, they shield themselves from me with invisible full body prophylactics. The spectres at my back are closer then ever, I want to run away again. But I'm too broken to know which way to run. Everywhere I go there are land-mines.

I ask Lizzie to drop me at Chelmsford station. I have absolutely no money so sit hidden in the stinking train toilet. During the two hour I stare out of the window in a self-hate session. At least I think it is; I can't tell anymore whether the hate I feel for myself is real, or made-up drama queen nonsense.

40. Badger Ugg Boot

'You're back!' barks Marjory

She is right. I am. It felt like a lifetime but having unsuccessfully hitched the eight miles back to here. No, sorry, I did get a lift for one mile, from a digger driver. I had to lean over him in the cab as he drove a little slower than my normal walking speed. So I asked to get out again.

At the very long straight between the roundabout and Toft Monks, my black bin bag, which has been my suitcase for the last four days, made like the value product it is, and split. There is no pavement or path, so I have to make do with the lumpy verge that causes me to stumble often enough to look like a grass-chewing nut job. How easy it is to make the transition from cute, rambling gypsy-chick to dusty middle-aged care-in-the-community client.

Marjory's dogs bound at me, glossy, ginger and stinking of rancid barbecue. Blossom has recuperated.

I spend an hour in the bath, allowing the water to wrinkle my skin. I would stay there indefinitely but Marjory has a life to get on with.

'Bad news, Miriam.' Marjory sits me down heavily at the table. 'When I took you to the station last week, I forgot to close the front door. It was open when I came back. I think one of the cats is missing.'

'Oh. Oh dear.'

If I didn't feel so bad, I would be rejoicing and feeling bad about rejoicing and play-acting that I'm very sad. Even Robert De Niro would find it hard to display that expression. I want to make her feel better, so promise to find the lost cat. Marjory seems to happier after that. She goes off to her room and reappears ten minutes later with her bags packed again and the dog leads in hand.

'Right, Miriam. I'm going before Prop gets here.'

'Prop?'

'The crazy cove's asked me to bloody-well witness yet another version of his will. If a girl has her head screwed on right, she'll keep it well out of Hebbindon family business.'

'Yes, there are lots of skeletons in Hebbindon wardrobes.'

'Skeletons? That family's a bloody ossuary!'

I climb into the car and Marjory drives me back to the station, a journey of two stumbling hours reduced to fifteen minutes. Marjory seems to not notice either my croaking throat or red, puffy eyes. She has the stamina of a barrel-organ and talks the entire time.

'No one Hebbindon likes anyone else in that family. They nurse as much hate as the Mafia but none of the loyalty. If one of them can bloody-well stick a knife in another's ribs, they will. Wym hasn't spoken to Kit since his wedding day. I'll tell you about it. Hold on, just got to overtake this bloody truck.'

The unbridled Marjory screeches into the face of on-coming traffic. Once we've recovered the left side of the road she says, 'So, after THAT happened, Wym moved out. And of course, then Kit ran off with the Nanny.'

'The nanny?'

'He'd only been married for five years when Jonty wanted to work. They brought in a nanny. He tupped her within two months.'

'Tupped?'

'And ran orf. Disappeared with the nanny, then ditched her and re-appeared, six months later.'

I leave Marjory in the unpredictable care of East Anglian Rail. On the way home I try not to picture Kit and the nanny or think about him with anyone else. A sort of girl totem pole is forming in my head. I'm sure he's trying to spread the love but really I know the only thing he's spreading is herpes.

When I've parked in the drive, I go back out onto the road to look at what remains of the cat formerly known as Good. The badger looks like a single grey Ugg boot. I go home to review my impact on the world. I kill cats. I kill mice. The last three people who I thought loved me didn't. One person I wish I had loved cruelly went off and fell in love with someone else. I disturb my father and worry my mother. My sister is dating my brother.

This is a time for The Smiths. I pack up Royal Doultan figures, singing 'Last Night I Dreamt Somebody Loved Me' whilst wrapping Marie-Antoinette in headlines from the Eastern Daily Press. I'm interrupted by Prop and a skinny young man with sweat-pits under the arms of his shirt.

'Where's Marjory?'

'Hi Prop! She's off with the dogs.'

'For a walk?'

'No, for good.'

'This is Marjory's niece. She'll do won't she?' Prop says to the limp rag of a man. Prop pulls a brown manilla file and a pen from the carer. 'Miriam. It is Miriam, isn't it? You'd like to help me wouldn't you?'

'Urh...'

'Great. Good. Sign here.'

41. Signed and Dined

By the thickness of the file, it seems to me that Prop is a will-changing recidivist.

The guy is a solicitor. His forehead glistens. He and the situation are smelling increasingly fishy. The document has bits of coloured tape that say 'Sign Here!' It may as well add 'And make it snappy, we're desperate!'

I'm guessing Kit's going to come out badly from my signature. I make-pretend I'm reading the document. That's what they do in films.

Just then, the front door knocker goes. Lawyer hands me a warm biro.

'Would you like to sign now?'

'Hullo?' says the door.

Prop grips Sweaty Lawyer.

'Dammit! It's one of them.'

The lawyer says 'It's fine if she just signs now.'

Knock-knock-knock.

'Hullo. It's Wym.'

Do I hate Kit enough to cut him out of his inheritance? No. He's a lonely kid who spent too long in a single-sex boarding school. He's trying to escape demons and the only winner is Durex. Would a whopping pile of money and responsibility make him feel better about himself?

The sitting-room door opens.

I follow Sweaty Lawyer's finger. It is pressed so hard, he's melting the paper. I sign.

'HAH!' Prop snatches the will and holds it in the air. The lawyer grabs his pen and weaves straight out in a cloud of stress and body-odour.

'It's all done!' whoops Prop. 'I have it, signed by a witness. Miriam....' He squints at my signature. 'Miriam Sport. Well she is a good sport!'

'Oh no!' Wym turns ash-grey, static and horrified. Yes I've idiotically stumbled into a localised war, blindly ignoring warnings, huge road signs that read 'Family In-Fighting Ahead.'

'Prop. Please don't do this. Think about Mother.'

'Mother? What about Mother?'

'She'll be dreadfully hurt.'

'Hurt? The woman's never been touched in her life. The Marchese's jolly-well been backing me into a corner like a beastly attack dog. Has nobody noticed? Has no-one remarked at the sound of shattering glass? I'm a target for vases.' The old guy's shouting technique uses only the upper-part of his head, while keeping his jaw completely still.

I try to send Wym a message saying 'I'm sorry, it wasn't my idea'. He returns a look that says 'This office is now closed. Try later.'

He puts his face in his hands. 'I'm just asking you to see reason, Prop. It really doesn't matter who comes into what part of your estate. It's how we cope while you're alive that bothers me. Anyway...' Wym waves his hand in my general direction.

'I don't know if this is legal.'

'Legal? What about legal. Your mother's a bully. Having her haranguing me in my own apartment, that's not legal.'

Wym turns. 'I only came to say 'Supper's ready.''

Prop claps his massive hands. 'Yummy-yummy. Miriam, come to supper.'

'Ah, no I don't think so.'

'You're my guest.'

Wym sighs. 'You may as well. You're part of the drama now.'

One hour later. The room we're eating in is smaller than I expected. It's not much bigger than the table. There's a ridiculously huge fireplace at one end. The ancient candy-stripe wallpaper is singed and smokey. Some time in the 1970s, they knocked a hatch through the wall. The oblong light from the kitchen reveals The Young Miss Perry marching backwards and forwards accompanied by steam, pans, tea-towels and muttering.

I sit between Wym and Prop. Although I was eager for a square meal, the tension has cauterised my hunger. Young Miss Perry starts lining covered serving-dishes up at the hatch-shelf. A Ride of the Valkyries-type click-click-click approaches, and in marches the Marchese.

She gives me a beady look and continues to her seat. 'What's the City Girl doing here?'

'I invited her.' says Wym.

Young Miss Perry comes in to carry the dishes from the hatch to the dining table. I can't help but question the operation. Wasn't the hatch put in to shorten journeys from the kitchen? Is none of the family capable of lifting dishes from the hatch-shelf?

The Hebbindons sit benignly while Young Miss Perry swarms about in her navy jogging- bottoms. She plonks two stem glasses in front of me, huffing under her breath.

'Oi wahren expectin' yew.'

She work-ethics out of the room and we sit listening to a nagging clock.

I'm not good with silence; it's as bad as holding your breath underwater. The pressure builds until I can't help blurting.

'My family only eat in the dining room at Christmas (shut up) The rest of the year it's covered in piano music and washing and George's Hornby (really, shut it) It's a shame really, more people should dine like this (STOOOOOP!). Erm....'

The Marchese sniffs.

'This is not the dining room.'

The door swings opens. In rolls Kit. He surveys the room and lands on the nearest innocent dining chair.

'Miriam! You said you weren't coming back, ever.'

'And yet,' says the Marchese 'Here she is.'

'I'm not sitting opposite him,' pipes Prop. 'He's bloody pissed!'

'Say Grace.' shoots the Marchese.

'No.' replies Prop.

The Marchese doesn't flinch.

'William. Say Grace.'

Wym tensely mutters a rope of Latin words.

The Marchese is the only one with eyes closed. Kit picks up a knife and looks at his teeth in its reflection. Prop frisbees his deerstalker hat across the room. He reveals a leaking fountain-pen stuck behind his bacon-rind ear and one blue-ink sideburn.

Young Miss Perry returns and opens the covered dishes for us, before eventually leaving. Really, were this family's ancestors quadriplegics or something?

Now we have the massively uncomfortable charade of each person holding the dishes and politely inviting their neighbours to serve themselves. I am more likely to eat the inside of my stomach before this meal.

'Well, William. What did you do today?'

'I was up at the timber-yard.'

Kit snorts.

The Marchese treats this as a opener. 'And Christopher, you were...?'

'Dealing with the import licenses for the asparagus. I think it's going to be a good investment.'

The lamb casserole can't hide the stink of bullshit.

'That's good,' says Prop. 'Because today, Miriam and I wrote you out of my will.'

42. The Half-Wit

Everything in Toft Hall goes quiet. I'm not sure what to do. I'm quaking at the Marchese's approaching reaction. Meanwhile, I feel I've committed harikari in terms of Wym and don't want to do anything that would further embarrass him. I'm certain he sees me as dangerously unbalanced. Whenever I'm in contact with him, unsavory things happen. If only I could explain that it isn't me, it's just the things that happen around me.

The clock's toc-toc-toc hammers in the vacuum. Never has the urge to jump up and run around gibbering grabbed me more (outside a church service).

Just then, I feel a hand on my leg. It's not from Prop but Wym. Luckily he does not squeeze my leg. If he heard the scream that I've honed, Pavlovian-style, from my groping Uncle Owen, he would give my thigh a wide berth. But he keeps it open, palm down. It's a kind of calming, protective, warning gesture.

I now feel brave enough to gaze upon the Marchese. Her EE cup rises above the table top like a hot air balloon pumped with fury.

'You. Despicable. Ugly. Little. Tramp.'

She means me.

Wym squeezes slightly. I lurch.

'Who are you? Where do you come from? Who invited you into our family circle?' She hisses and stands, her chair jumping obediently back. She has a weighty-looking napkin-ring her hand. Another crash. Prop is also up, knocking his chair flat.

'I invited her and Miriam graciously obliged,' he pipes. 'To what? Where is this famed family circle? Last circle of Hell, more like!'

'How DARE you dismiss fifty years! How DARE you dismiss the sacrifices I made, the exhaustion, simply, exclusively to serve you and the children. It's due to my effort that we have a stable home!'

Prop lifts his upper jaw. 'I HAVE SUBLIMATED MY ENTIRE EXISTENCE!'

Kit leans back on his chair and brings out a bottle of beer from a sideboard. He opens it ostentatiously and so draws Prop's tirade.

'Him! He's no more entitled to my money than is the fishmonger who calls on Fridays. Laziness? Kit has the patent! Woodbridge? Useless. Harrow? Useless. If he did win his colours, it must've been for lying, cheating, stealing, sleeping, eating and tossing-orf. How has he improved the human race? You can't find it, cos he hasn't done it.'

I retrieve Prop's chair and he sits, angrily stabbing his tepid plate of stew.

Kit lifts his bottle.

'I'm not letting you write my biography.'

The Marchese turns and closes the hatch doors in a way that can only be described as ominous.

In a voice of brushed metal she says 'I am going to reverse this latest signature. That woman is an ignorant half-wit and you are a senile incompetent. I'm going to warn the solicitors never to deal with you again because you're mad, as was so clearly proven today.'

The Marchese narrows her mascara and then clicks out of the door, Queen Victoria on stilettos. There is an audible exhalation of breath. Young Miss Perry pops through the hatch doors.

'Durrs enywanwan their food moicrowoived?'

We begin the silent silver-on-china grind and cut. Eyes settle on plates, jaws chew gristle that is not entirely food-based.

'Salt please, Kit.' says Prop.

In the middle of the table is a wide wooden circular dish. It's raised, with a wide canopy and piled with condiments of every kind. Kit turns the wooden platform, which spins until the salt and pepper arrive opposite Prop. A strangely eccentric affair, it reminds me of the toy train gravy-boat developed (misguidedly) by my step-father one Christmas. Prop snatches the salt off the carousel and then I notice that the salt is pink and hump-like. A breast. So is the pepper. Prop offers them to me. I thank him for the mammaries.

They appear to be an antique...um...pair.

Wym has long removed his hand but I can still feel its warmth. He gives a tiny throat clear that I realise is the signal that he's about to try and speak.

'You know, Prop, if you're worried about money, I met with the new farm manager and the accountants, and we all agree that, what with subsidy initiatives we should make an annual growth in the...'

'Bollocks to growth!' spits Prop lambily. 'I'm not worried about the estate going broke, it's Kit's bally character.'

Kit sets down his beer bottle. 'And I'm not saying I should have any share of the farm either, I just need enough to fund the asparagus project.'

Prop glowers. 'If I give any portion and then lie down in the drawing-room and die, it'll all end up bloody Jonty's pockets. Why you couldn't keep your cock dry, God only knows!'

Now there's a lot of blushing, glowering and measured chomping. I really don't feel hungry even though I've not eaten sensibly for about two weeks. In the long and weighty silence, I steal diagonal glances at Wym and Kit, for the first time together side by side in my view.

They share the same bolt of chestnut red hair, stubbled freckled skin and high-boned facial structure. But it's funny how Kit and Wym cling to their duplicate mould in different ways. A smile on Kit's face is devilish, glinting, inviting. On Wym, it's momentary, a fleeting tic. The downward sloping eyebrows on Wym are heavily weighted by gloom. On Kit, they have the worst kind of phoney puppy-dog appeal. These two men are the perfect subjects for a nature versus nurture study, not that any visible nurturing was involved as far as I can tell.

At last Wym and I are excused. We escape out of the french doors and down the terrace steps. There's a freshness in the air; summer is running out of battery-life.

Wym tries to clear the gristley indigestion with uncontentious chat.

'On Thursday evening, we have some old friends coming over. We're probably going to make up some croquet teams if you're interested?'

'Of course – I love croquet!'

Yes. It's right up there with my love of quoits and french boules.

Wym does quite a lot of Price Charles-type anxious fiddling with things and feigning interest in far away things. Now I see what his mealtimes are like, I muse on the chances of him having chronic stomach issues. I also sense a desire to sit him down and feed him beans on eggy bread. He looks like he's trying to tie granny knots in his lips with his own teeth.

'You know, most of our suppers have been like that, in the last five years. Forever, to a degree. That's essentially why I moved out.'

'Would you like some eggy bread and beans?' I ask.

He smiles – at least, I think it's a smile. 'Thanks. But I've just eaten.'

43. Pumpernickel

I do a stocktake in the fridge. One pint of green-top milk. Two rashers of value bacon, an open tin of tuna. An open tin of cat-food. A bag of mixed, ready-chopped salad and some pumpernickel bread.

The hummus at the back I bought when Lizzie was here. Some eclectic jars (rolled mop, tahini, dried yeast and marmite) are left from my shop harrying. The rest Marjory has imported. So it's a cup of tea and with pumpernickel dunked into it. My stomach gurgles. Having always tried basically to be a good girl, I've always hoped that God would step in. What I need now is a miracle. Or failing that, some work.

I am still wading through my own shallow mental mire, and with no phone for two days and a cavernous stomach, it feels as if fate is thrusting a detox on me. A meowing from the laundry room reminds me it's time for the cat exchange. If self-pity starts to take me, I like to remind myself of all those who have it worse. The Bad Cat for example is the hapless victim of captivity, exclusion and prejudice due to colour or preconceived notions of 'beauty'.

But he is a truly ugly cat.

I feed the Last Good Cat while my tummy growls. The smell of Whiskers is making me salivate. That's never a good sign.

Suddenly a knock at the door. If it's Kit, I'm going to tell him to keep his erotomania away from me. If it's Wym, I'll invite him in for bacon rind, pumpernickel and a hug. I stride to the hall with my top shirt-button slightly undone. I throw the door open and squeak 'Seee-nah?!'

'Didn't you get my text?'

'No? How did you find me?'

'Lizzie gave me directions.'

I'm completely lost for words/reaction. Signe has never phoned me, written or visited in my entire life. I can't see why this should change now. She's not smiling or frowning or even pouring a bucket of water on my head. Apart from the Norfolk mosquitoes rustling through her curls, in the overhead light she looks like a marble statue in a Gap trenchcoat. Her lips part.

'Can I come in?'

We noiselessly walk through to the kitchen.

'It smells of dog.' She says.

'This house?' I do 'surprise' as a look. It's funny, I'm sure the house must smell of poo but it's become part of my nasal norm. I can't smell it, on the house or on me.

'Tea?' I say.

She nods.

Then I say 'I take it with milk and half a sugar? You?'

'Same.' She says.

We sit across from each other. In the bald, overhead light Signe looks worn. She looks at her tea. 'I tried to stay somewhere else. I went to Dad's but he wasn't in. I couldn't go to my mum's, she wouldn't understand.'

'Understand what?'

'She'd make me go back with Samson. She likes him.'

'Ahh. Oh.'

'And he knows all of my friends. He doesn't know you. This is the last place he'd expect me to come.'

Good ruse.

'How long are you staying?'

'I don't know. Not long, hopefully. And I'm not a charity case. I can pay my way.'

'Oh no need for that' I say, making my eyes large. 'Are you hungry? Would you like some bacon and pumpernickel, or perhaps tuna and pumpernickel?'

'I brought a few snacks for the journey, they'll go off if they're not eaten.'

My stomach fidgets. Her bag zips open and starts making like a magic caesarean; it's bearing fruit. Bruised apples, speckled bananas, flapjacks, rice-cakes, a half-full bag of hand-fried crisps and curling coronation-chicken sandwiches. Suddenly the world feels right. Everything will work out just fine. God loves me because here's my miracle. We have a picnic. I donate two bottles of black-dog ale. We talk, laugh even as we try to work out how crisps can be hand-fried. At midnight, Signe suddenly changes tack and pertly announces she's tired. I don't know if she understands the concept of one-bedroomed living but I'm not about to land it on her tonight. I tuck her into my bed.

With the last of my drink, I step outside and sniff the air. Night stocks, honeysuckle, degrading cat. A nightingale is singing I think – or maybe it's a distant car alarm. The sun sets, blue and grey streaked with red, like a badly shaved Italian chin.

Inside the dog-hair sleeping-bag, I sack race to the sofa. Not my choice, but alternatives are limited, seeing as my bed-surfing days in Toft Hall are over.

44. Freud Central

I am poor. I have always been poor. My pocket money used to come through George who held the purse-strings with the grip of the Boston strangler; £1/month, which was non-negotiable until I reached 16. From ages 16 to 21 my mum wangled an extraordinary £40/month. First I saved for a pony, then for a piano, then a motorbike. At 19, I left home and the pony fund bought me a second-hand oven, a washing machine and a *Good Housekeeping* diary. Good-bye childhood dreams, hello prematurely-grey reality.

At last I pupate from the sleeping-bag. Signe's already up, complaining about my bed being too narrow and squeaky, (what with its sprung frame, mattress, clean sheets and all). Meanwhile, I'm covered in a fine layer of dog fur. I'll have to shave to get rid of it.

Signe runs to the loo and throws up. I make a list.

1. Get up.
2. Put a stop to this sofa surfing.
3. Phone up Inland Revenue and tell them to stop doubling my fine. I'm never going to submit my tax return now. Why can't they get over it?
4a. Clean Clio.
4b. Clean my clothes. I can't survive by reversing my knickers.
4c. Clean the burnt scone out of the top oven.
5. Fix my phone/call Tom

I do the last thing on my list first. Call Tom. I don't think he actually likes me contacting him.

'So Tom. If I dropped the phone in the toilet, how would I fix it?'

'How the ...? Never mind. First. Is it still wet?'

'It happened a week ago.'

There's a gap of about ten seconds. I guess it's because New Zealand's so far away.

'OK. Put the phone in a bowl of rice for two weeks. Dry rice.'

'Rice. Are you joking me?'

'No.'

No. Tom doesn't joke.

'Lizzie says you're coming home soon.'

'Yes, in a week so you'll have to move out of Huntley Street, *if you're ever there*. I'm coming back via the US, I'm DJ-ing in Santa Monica. Hand the key to the caretaker if necessary.'

I plunge the phone into a bowl of rice and my head in the oven. My younger brother's jetting around the world, DJ-ing and brain-storming new campaigns. I am chipping carbonised lumps off a furnace-hot oven. This is not how I saw life panning out.

Where is Kit? Dare I ask anyone? Is he immured in the terrace? But what about Wym? I feel affection for him. Could he be my last choking gasp at fantasy? I just need something, even a crush on a pop star to get me through. I really can't bear the idea of sitting alone with nothing but my own wrinkly, ugly soul to stare at. It scares me.

Luckily I still have Signe. She demands a drive to Beccles. I demand a full tank of petrol. She stares at Clio with distaste. The car is still shamefully filthy, I now recognise. The rear window is one vast petri dish.

Cute, time-locked Beccles now feels like an embarrassing parochial armpit. Signe complains about the tight parking spaces, the badly cared-for municipal planting, the Moebius strip traffic system. She shows only minimal interest in the Teddy Bear Shop (run by a nice bachelor who may or may not be a serial killer) There's a Lyons-style tea and cake corner shop, all maple wood, aspidistras and girls in pinafores. My last few pounds are spent on her and all the tea and cakes in china.

I scan Signe for a reaction but there's barely one crumb of interest on her marble face. My efforts are so many fat turkeys of hope trying to jump the Bernard Matthews fence of emotion. I ponder on Signe, who if anything, is even more messed up than myself. My father has performed a remarkable sleight of hand by creating the internal angst in his daughters but letting them blame each other. If Signe and I could just find our common ground...

'I tried to talk to Dad at the festival.'

'Why, do you have problems talking to Dad?'

'Don't you have problems talking to Dad?'

'Not as such.'

Right. Silence resumes. The waitress takes our order and adds 'Wow, I can tell you two are sisters.'

Signe blinks slightly.

We shunt our cakes around. At £2 a slice, 40p is left on the plate in the form of crumbs and butter- cream. Signe goes so far as to cover her mouth while she chews.

This is ridiculous.

I go to the loo to allow her to consume her cake in private. In the mirror, I see I've gnawed my inner lip, causing a stress ulcer the size of Corsica.

Right-lobe repeats the mantra 'You have no need to impress anyone but yourself.'

Left-lobe rocks backwards and forewords gibbering 'Why does no one love me?'

I go back out to tinkle of china, pouring of tea and posh screeching.

'Insinuating little hussy! If I ever find you inside my home again, I'll have you arrested.' Signe's being given an exercise in public humiliation by The Marchese.

I peer through the greenery. Signe actually looks shocked!

'Hey!' I handle the Marchese by the shoulder pad and wheel her around. The look is priceless. Six seconds of consternation.

'So, belittling your own family isn't good enough. Now you pick on strangers?'

The Marchese's neck flushes around the pearl region 'I thought...Well you're clearly sisters!'

'Half-sisters' Signe and I correct in harmony.

'If she's like you...'

'SHE'S NOT! She happens to be a good Catholic girl. Leave her alone and SCHLEP YOUR BILE BACK TO THE HALL!' In Beccles, all teaspoon tinkling has stopped.

The rope of pearls undulates slightly. The Marchese backs up and tries to leave smartly. Hard to do when you're forced through a revolving door.

We drive back home and nothing is mentioned. Not by me or Signe or the elephant in the back seat.

I change into safe, comfortable ready-to-work leggings. The phone rings. Signe's unwilling to answer it so I have to dash and hop out of the bedroom.

'I've been ringing all day! Is your phone broken still?' It's Lizzie. 'Have you seen...er... Signe?'

I repeat that because phonetically it sounds quite good. 'Have I seenuh Seenuh?'

Signe does a dance on the spot, which I interpret.

'That's a negative. I have not seen Signe.'

'Hmm. Why did that sound like a lie?'

Uncomfortable. Lizzie's possibly the only person I never lie to but Signe's monitoring my outgoing messages.

'Is she there? 'Cos she did ask for your address last week.'

'Odd.'

'That's what I thought. Could you tell her Inga's panicking? Make her call her mum, before the police get involved.'

'Right. If she WAS here, I'd certainly pass that message on.'

'And by the way, ask her how she's feeling of a morning.'

Pregnant Pause.

'Ah.'

'Ok. Toodle-bye. Have fun... *On your own!*'

Any work I might theoretically have to do is made impossible by Signe sitting at the table and psyching me out. What's wrong with her? It's like she expects the world to perform and she's on the judging panel.

'Look, just how long are you planning to stay, Signe?

'Why, do you want me to go?'

'No, I just don't want to sleep on the sofa anymore.'

'I'll sleep on the sofa.'

'You can't sleep on the sofa, you're pregnant.'

Signe's mouth opens ever so slightly. 'How do you know?'

'You told me.'

'No I didn't! I just said I might be.'

'Well your whole family's freaking out. Your mum wants to call the police.'

'Why didn't you tell me?'

'I didn't want to, what with your condition.'

'My pregnancy isn't going to suddenly go away because of my mum. She's only doing what Samson's telling her – she think's he's the flippin bees' nob.'

I don't want to correct Signe's badly mixed metaphor. I must create a diversion. I weakly suggest we take a look around Toft Estate.

By the time we reach White Rabbit Garden, my myopic sense of self-worth has flatlined. On the path a sprinkler creates ozone and rainbows. I guess it's trying to cheer me up. Six foot flowers mosh gently in the breeze. I take her down an avenue of foxgloves when the gate is opened by Wym. He's still some way off so I pull Signe's arm and we edge back along the wall, ducking peach and pear stems.

'Miriam?'

Shit! If we can make it to the gap in the wall, I might be able to get Signe back to the house without being met. But Wym has predicted my move and pops out at the gap, panting and baffled. Bafflement is a bit of a go-to expression for Wym. I grudgingly point and mutter 'Hi Wym. My sister Signe. Signe, my...Wym.'

45. Baby Lamb

We all move backwards down the very tight path, clashing and apologising.

'The Marchese was just here. She.' Wym grinds his jaw a little. 'Well, I can see where she made her mistake. She's, shall we say, embarrassed?'

'Shall we call it incandescent?'

'OK.'

'I guess she wants to shred my tenancy?'

'No! How could she? I'm in charge of leases.'

Ah-ha!

'Wym, Signe needs a house for a few weeks. You haven't got anything, perhaps a bit run down or sub-standard you could let her have?'

'I can find out. If you just step inside?'

We step.

The kitchen is large, brick floored with an oven like mine but in red. I refuse to be impressed. I have fAGAtigue.

Behind a pod mountain, sits Anna. She's shelling peas at Wym's bloody kitchen table. The last time I saw her, she was being topped-and-tailed by Kit.

'Anna! You do like to root around in the veg box, don't you!'

Anna gives me an icy smirk. Luckily, I'm hiding behind Signe who repels all frost with her own arctic front.

'Anna's been doing the accounts with me,' burbles Wym. 'We're just about to have lunch. You'll stay?'

Wym never smiles much. He stretches closed lips at varying degrees. Certain inclines tell the observer he is worried or embarrassed. A minute raise of one side proclaims to the world he is as happy as a cat on Mouse Island. Like he is now.

'Do you know I've been raising lambs over the summer? I've got one here.'

'Aww. Really?'

I look around the undulating brick floor, listening for tiny hooves and warbling bleats. 'Where is it?'

Anna leans back and opens the heavy bottom AGA oven door. There is the lamb. On a bed of mint. 'I slaughtered it here on the farm.' beams Wym.

Ugh.

'Is she a vegetarian?' sings Anna.

Wym breezes on, regardless of female static in the air. 'Anna, do we have anywhere we could do a month's let for Miriam's sister?'

Anna gives a precious sigh. 'Oh Wym, not a thing. And we have such a waiting list too.'

Signe and I exchange an unspoken thought. Sisterhood so long coming, here at last!

Wym goes out to quickly deal with someone who has something that needs something. For the ten minutes of Wymlessness, Anna says not a single word except a stabbing 'Scuse me' as she washes some rocket in a sieve. I simply can't help myself; the thought starts seeping out of my brain.

'Sievewright. I guess your ancestors must have been sieve makers?'

She didn't like that.

'And what about you? Miriam Short? I guess your ancestors were midgets. Am I right?'

I would like to say that I've got a perfect return for that, but actually, I'm speechless. A glance at Signe. Still no crack in the enamel.

Wym returns with a bottle of red wine and places it on the AGA to warm. His kitchen's a mix of chocolate-box cottage and bachelor cave, kitted out when British companies ruled the gadget world, fifty years ago. I'm very suspicious of the intimate relationship between Anna and this kitchen. She knows where the cutlery drawer is. She and Wym flow around each other. I don't know why that should be a bother but part of me likes all men to remain single for my convenience. I know there are arguments against this, like the populating of the planet, but that's how I tick.

As one of two girls who don't enjoy eating in public, supper is a bit of a trial. Wym asks about Signe's social work job which makes conversation as animated as can be expected. Anna just sort of rests her eyes on me. I have nothing startling to say because although I know quite a lot, it's spread over a wide area at a depth of one inch. I don't like revealing my matt gloss of knowledge in such dangerous surroundings. So I fall back on my old trick of flustering. When lifting the water to my lips, I clutch and jerk it, overshoot and allow it to flow around my lips and down my front. My dad's nickname for me is Shlemiel, which is Yiddish for 'The girl who always spills her drink down her shirt in times of stress.'

The food is amazing and I can see Wym would like me to eat. I'm pussy-footing around an aubergine but it's fighting back. It's Anna's fault I'm poleaxed by a vegetable. Her smirk is so barefaced – what has she got to be so smug about?

Oh of course. The realisation coincides with the end of the first course. As plates are recalled by Anna, I politely invite Wym outside for a second.

'Did you enjoy the lamb?' He asks

'No.'

'Oh.'

'I would've enjoyed it if Anna hadn't been using a mental laser-pen to excavate my brain.'

Wym opens and closes his mouth.

'She was here when the Marchese came, wasn't she?'

'Yes. I couldn't really stop her.'

'And she heard everything?'

'Yes.'

'Then why? WHY did you invite me for a meal with Anna? Didn't you feel it would be inappropriate after that?'

'I didn't think of it. I thought, well, you're both nice people!'

'Nice?! Wym, I feel like thwacking you with a frying pan! How on earth can Anna and I possibly like each other?'

'I don't know! Why not?! You tell me?'

Wym looks...well, I'm not sure. His lips are very tight. He appears distressed. It dawns on me that he has probably had very few dealings with groups of girls. How would he know that to invite three ladies to lunch was to beckon the wolf-pack?

'I'm sorry I'm narky.' I say 'My sister is staying with me for an undefined period. She won't budge from my bed and I'm sleeping on a couch that has a tog-rating of 500 mites per inch. I'm just irrational and tired.' Wym does a thinking frown.

'I did offer you my spare bedroom once.'

'Of course but that offer has legitimately expired now.'

'How long is this for?'

'Somewhere between finite and indefinitely.'

Wym looks suddenly grim. 'Can you wait until six? Then I'll have time to – clear up.'

'Hey. I don't want to impose!' (Liar. When have I not wanted to impose?)

We stand by the doorway as the hedges soak up shadow. The dusk is fetid with roses and a hint of smoke. All of a sudden, Wym lurches, grabs me in his manly arms and says

'CRUMBLE!'

He dashes inside.

My heart is kissing my lungs. I take a deep breath and inhale burnt apple and adrenaline. I return to Wym's kitchen in time to catch the tail end of something. Everyone's staring at each other like before a 3-way shoot-out. Signe's jaw juts towards Anna. I'm too late to hide behind the door and too nervous to stride in so I trip over the edge of the brick floor and make the entrance of a drunken octopus. But I'm ready to back Signe; an almost exclusively egg-based diet means my nails are super-strong.

Instead, Signe says 'I'm tired' and bluntly walks out. I gave a startled 'Oh' and follow. She won't tell me what happened, she only says 'Wym's dim. His girlfriend's a bitch.'

46. Hoopla

My case trundles up the drive, leaving a trail of dust like the last stage coach quitting town.

When I told Signe I was going away, there was an assumption on my part that she might ask me where. All she did was ask for a door key. The key facts are, that I will be back morning, night and most of the day for Cat Exchange and computer internet trawling. But leaving the frizzy rhinemaiden to stew I hope will resonate with her on some very basic level.

Wym is waiting at the door – with a glass of port for me and a peck on the cheek! The peck transfers directly to an odd ache in my stomach that I suspect will not be sorted by Alka-Seltzer. The thought of 'But what if Anna really is his girlfriend?' flits across my brain. I catch the thought in a mental paper bag and squish it to mush.

The upstairs of his house is nice, it has white wallpaper with tiny blue flowers and book shelves in a library area. He points out his room and then takes me next door. It's tidy and large with a double bed and a dressing table, sitting empty of anything to dress with. There's a window seat with views over W-R hedges towards Toft Hall and beyond that, the flat infinity that is Norfolk. A fire has been lit in the hearth.

'What a lovely room.'

'Yeah.' He sighs. 'It's bigger than mine.'

He points at a door in one corner. 'And you have an ensuite, a very cold ensuite, I'm sorry. I've not used this room for a number of years.'

There is another door.

'What's that?' I ask

'That's my room. Or at least, it's an interconnecting dressing room. I've put all the...belongings in there.'

I nod with feigned indifference.

'Look, I've got to go up to the farm. Make yourself at home. There's milk in the fridge in a jug. Do you mind unpasturised? And we'll see you and your sister on the croquet lawn at six?'

I curtsy my reply. Then it's just me, the house and whatever is behind that door.

I fiddle with things in the room, put my nose in the cold bathroom, then sit in the window seat. I lie on the bed. Anna could be Wym's girlfriend, or she could be Kit's girlfriend. Who knows how things work behind closed doors? Letting slip about the jiggery-pokery to Wym could set a cat-rescue league jail break amongst the pigeon fanciers' convention, and even I recognise that less drama will be good for my wellbeing right now as opposed to more.

It doesn't stop me from being curious though.

The dressing-room is locked, of course. I bob down but can't see anything through the keyhole. There is a key in the lock! Yesss. I scan around for something to slip under the door. If you ever want to keep me out of a locked room, don't leave the key on the far side of the door. This bedroom is nearly bare, eventually I make do with a towel, threaded under the door gap with a coat-hanger. Then I gently, gently push the key out of the lock. It falls with a muted clank onto the towel.

I pull the towel back. The key does not come.

Urgh! I hook it with the coat hanger but the key is too large-arsed Victorian to slip through the crack.

Bugger.

There must be another way.

Wym's bedroom opens. It's neat but full of guy things. Neat CD stack, neat stereo, a neat TV screen. It smells of man perfume, coffee and candles. On the left, beyond his fireplace is his dressing-room door. I try its handle (my pulse-rate tells me that my anaemically faint- hearted blood-stream has already pulled out of this venture).

The door is locked.

After this skull-duggery I exit the room in a crisis of conscience. In general I am a well-meaning person and I'm not often bothered by guilt. Back out in the hallway I think about my karma. So this is how I treat someone who has been nothing but a gentleman to me? Have I forgotten already how low I've slunk in my treatment of others? Suddenly there's a shout in the hallway.

'Miriam – I need a dress!'

Good. I think about Signe and sense good old fashioned Freudian bile surging. Then I feel balanced again.

When there's nothing left in my wardrobe but a ball gown and corset, it's time to wash my clothes. Tonight's like that. Signe squeezes into my rockabilly outfit and I'm in Seduce-the-Boss Kimono. The evening's still warm. The scent of home-killed button-sized lambchops and tiny-lamb burgers lays us a trail towards the Big House.

In position already are some couples I don't know. Wym and his busy side-kick Anna remove grey, wood-lousy, electrical-taped mallets from something that looks like a disinterred child's coffin. According to Google, croquet is simple; there are about three rules. But as none of the Hebbindons are actually talking to each other, diplomacy's another issue. Eventually we are broken into four teams of people who do not want to scratch each other's eyes out. The Marchese and Prop sit pitch-side, separated only by a drinks trolley.

The hoops are embedded in a kind of H-Block formation. It's a knock-out competition so most of the players hurl abuse from the sidelines until their turn. Wym and I are opposing a beefy man called Chalmers and his wife, a narrow blond named 'Dessie-Darling'.

When asked what colour I'll play, I blurt 'I like my balls the way I like my men, black and...uh...rolling. In it.' The wrongness of this goes off the meter.

It's such a civilised game. The sound of mallet-on-ball is just the sort of 'plink' intended when the word 'plink' was invented. The only positions in the Kroquet-sutra are 'the-slight-lean', the 'ponder', the 'dramatic-plotting-grin' and the swipe, front-facing or sideways. Add to this the 'dance-of-dismay' when the ball bounces off the hoop instead of through.

Free-flowing bile and distrust seeps into the game. When an opponents' ball is shunted out of the way, they are practically sent into the next county. At last I make the first hoop and clink Chalmer's ball. I line up the twinned balls, put my foot on mine and rocket his ball into a flower-bed. Suddenly a chorus from the sidelines – the Marchese's waving her arms.

'American rules! The City Girl's playing American rules!'

What?! It seems I've undermined the foundations of an important class edifice. Wym shows me the less-satisfying British method. He puts his arms around me, I should be fine with that but actually I'm painfully uncomfortable.

Once the shot is played, me and my ego retreat to the edge. Having excellent hearing (to my occasional advantage and regular downfall), I hear and translate the hard syllables the Marchese mutters to Anna.

'And you have to feel sorry for her. How on earth could she possibly ever fit in? Simply horrid. It's kindness in the long run.'

'Oh don't worry' replies Anna. 'I'll knock her back to where she comes from!'

47. The Theory

In deciding to play well at croquet a girl must turn off the brain of Haribo. When I don't make the hoop the natural instinct is to wallow coquettishly. But I'm keen to improve, to become the Navratilova of croquet. But it's hard to concentrate when I see Signe and Anna having a long, friendly, close conversation.

Signe was always bound to fit in. She has icy poise and an odd first name. While I'm thrashing bits of turf and causing Wym to flap around me, I note that Signe, Anna and the Marchese are taking a 'turn around the lawn.' What that means is a kind of slow, mobile bitch huddle. Signe's frosty armour has intrigued Anna. Whatever slim alliance I had with my sister is rolling out of the playing area like tumbleweed. I watch them circle when I should be playing. The other competitors are becoming impatient and as my abilities are hopeless, this situation does not improve.

'Dessie-Darling' has the opportunity to tap her ball the single foot to the finishing pin or turn back and thwack my ass to the next post-code. It would be meaningless and cruel to do that, so she does it. My ball is made of some outdated solid plastic; the bastard child of resin and bakelite. 'Dessie-Darling' gives a golf-pro swing and launches it across the lawn, off the edge of a path, past the perambulating ladies and into the longer grass. It is a metaphor for what the upper class like to do with interlopers. With as much ill-grace as I can restrain, I give the match up. There is leaden clapping from the side.

Out at prole-meadow, I hack about in the grass looking for my ball, blubbing slightly. Wym trots over. I wish he wasn't wearing idiot chinos – why can't he be louche like his brother?

We now swish with our mallets, looking like the special-needs reapers who were given the plastic scythes to play with.

After a while, Wym says 'You're crying.'

I shake my head and rub the cocktail of tear'n'dribble up my wrist. Wym makes his arm raise, moves as if he built it with Meccano and places it on my shoulder. I turn and hide my damp, red, blotchy face on his chest. He is exactly the right height for me. Not too tall (the agony of back pain means I will never accommodate a tall man again) or too small (the flat shoes, the apologies, the male insecurity.)

'You'll get better at croquet. Or if you don't, we'll not play it again!'

(A stupidly gallant statement, to pretend he would ban croquet from Toft Hall on my account).

'It's not that!' I inaudible into his chest 'I just don't belong anywhere.'

'You do! I think you do.'

'No! I never have. I've never found a place where I feel at home. I'm homeless, I may even be on the wrong planet!'

'No-one belongs anywhere. If it makes you feel better, I don't belong either and my family have been here since 1818.'

There's yelling from the sidelines. We break and search more. It's useless, the ball has dematerialised. The croquet majority shout that they have a spare (inferior) wooden ball and can get on with that, while we continue tramping the grass down, re-searching the same spots.

Then we give up.

The lawn extends to a large, disused fountain. After this point, the mowers halt and the grass grows gradually wilder. Far-flung flowerbeds are tangles of ancient, knotty lavender and scabby, spotted geriatric roses. For every ten meters further distance from the house, there is a halving in the amount of attention the grounds receive. The cracked fountain has a scum of waterlilies on the evaporated waterline. White doilies of lichen cover the parapet. We turn and watch as players hit, appear to freeze and then the 'tink' reaches us half a second later. I'm outside this scene – it's like watching a film. Why do I always feel so alone?

'I think.' says Wym 'You should try staying. Settle here and see if it grows on you.' He points at a doily. 'Like the lichen. Takes a while but it does grow. In the end.'

I stare at the water. He stares at me staring. Then he says 'Oh!' There is my croquet ball, floating in the water.

'She didn't hit it that hard!' He says. 'Neither she did.' says I.

I note that both Anna and Signe are still huddled.

It goes without saying that Team Wym/Miriam take an early shower (as it were). He goes to the house and I go to the drinks table. Prop snores in his deck chair. It's chilly now but no one has thought to cover him. Eventually I go in search of insulating material. Rug-hunting takes me on an interesting tour of the square footage that some people think they can get away with financial free rein. I find the actual dining-room and, yes, it is very, very large. The table is longer in feet than I can estimate. There are sideboards and silver and the smell of soap and soup and smoke and (the non-alliterative) Antiquax. Toft Hall is redolent with it. (And I thought it was a spray to deter ducks.)

Finally I stumble into a small room that I can make out nothing of except a bright computer screen and Wym's silhouette. He jumps up before I can retreat.

'Sorry.'

'No, I'm sorry.'

'Sorry!'

'No, really!'

This could go on for a while.

'I'm looking for a blanket. For Prop. I think he's cold.' Wym leads me to the dark kitchen. Of course, there is the tartan mountain on a sofa. He shakes and folds one and hands it over and then leans in and kisses me. The random-generator that uses my entire body as a control bot leaps into a reaction. I fall back, flap my arms as if trying to stun a wasp and make blurbing noises.

Wym's bottom lip drops slightly.

'I'm sorry.'

'No, really.'

'I just...when earlier you were crying, I thought that you, that it...'

'No, really, I was just crying.'

'Sorry.'

'It's fine.'

'Sorry.'

This is entrapment entropy, neither of us can escape our apologies. My cheeks seem not only to radiate but cause a disembodied feeling of being my own audience as if I'm rising on stilts. Just then, the kitchen door opens and Signe and Anna walk in on us, carrying trays of quivering glasses. Four people hover in tension, before Wym leaps back, strides past the looming ladies and out into the shadowy corridor.

48. The Hockey Match

Signe and I have our first proper argument on the way back to White Rabbit Garden. 'Seducing men is not a sport, Miriam, it doesn't make you a better or bigger or even sexier person, it makes you a predatory bitch!'

'I wasn't seducing anyone!'

'Samson was fine before he danced with you at that wedding!'

'You are not going to stand there and blame me for all THIS, on me!' I wave my finger all around her, mainly aiming for her head and her womb.

'You know, you're not the be-all-and-end-all of perfection!'

'I didn't say I was.'

'You seem to think you are. You seem to take it as an insult that any man has a girlfriend who isn't you! Have you ever noticed exactly how ignorant, manipulative and completely self-serving you are? You and I have have nothing in common.'

Stomp...stumble...drag... and stop. I stall at the wall of White Rabbit Garden. Signe marches on, curls huffing until they fade in the gloom.

I don't turn the lights on. I sit in Wym's kitchen in the blue/grey dusk. Outside the trees rush wind and birds whoop into the distance.

I don't understand. I don't understand anything. I don't understand anything from the deepest speck that fires from inside my brain to the world reeling around me. I'm dizzy, I need to be sick. I sit on my hands to stop them from slapping me and telling me I'm stupid.

Just then, the shape of Wym passes the kitchen window. I tear out of the kitchen and double jump the stairs, arriving at my bedroom just as the front door clicks gently open.

Creakcreakcreak.

Pause outside my room.

Finally a whispered 'Miriam? Could we talk about what happened just there?'

'Could we not?'

'If you prefer.'

I'm tense and shivering, even my kneecaps are juddering. I daren't move, I hold my breath. He must be able to tell. All men eventually recognise I am a skin-flaying frantic; the world is full of men tip-toeing away from me.

At last I lie in bed and stare at the ceiling. Not eight feet away, I am sure Wym is also lying in his bed staring at the ceiling.

A night of wakeful sleep and sleepful wake. I feel an ache in my thigh. Then I think I feel the same ache in my hip. It's moving, I'm having an aneurysm. I try to track the aches and they seem to move all over the place. My heart occasionally chunters and bumps. If I die now, I won't have done anything with my life. At all.

Morning hits me. I am still alive, but somehow that rush of thankfulness and new-found verve doesn't overtake me.

The kitchen is empty but there's hot coffee on the AGA and poached eggs inoffensively lounging in a pan. Wym's leather boots on the floor are pregnant with the shape of his foot. His coats hang on hooks wrinkled at the elbows. He's everywhere and nowhere. I'm torn between needing to escape and wanting to hide in my own wardrobe. As if hailed by my thoughts, Wym bounds in. Oh God.

'Good morning.'

'Yup. Hi!' I wave. Ugh! Stupid stupid.

'I left you some eggs.'

He shunts them around the pan.

'I've got to go over to the farm this morning.' says his back. 'I'm meeting the dairyman; I've got mastitis.'

'Really!?'

'In the herd.'

'Oh, of course!'

'I thought you might like to come see the cows?'

Come see the cows. I chew the cud for a second. 'I was going to have a bath....'

'I'll wait.'

'No no! Don't let me keep you.'

I lock myself in my ensuite. I'm panting and holding my chest, I look like Joan Crawford.

The bathroom is neat and barren. On closer inspection, the bath has a layer of dust that gives it a seventies porn-star kind of look. I clean the bath, I run the bath. I take a long long time. Wym kissed me before I even tried to seduce him. I've very rarely been chased. When I have been, there's usually something wrong with the chaser. As the water goes cold, I go through every possible scenario, in which I turn him off with my hysteria.

An hour later, I descend safe in the knowledge that Wym must've gone. But he's not! He's still bloody waiting!

*

So then I'm mincing (if mincing were not an unpleasant term to use, when visiting cows) along the drive. Wym's wearing thick boots. I'm in flip-flops, which I point out are often used by Sherpas to climb Everest.

We make dusty conversation. There seems to be a strange set of magnets in our clothing. One minute we bump together, the next we're repelled. Soon the air is full of static.

The talk shudders back our distant pasts. I tell him my theory that the childhood song 'Wind the Bobbin up' was actually written by an agoraphobic weaver. Who else would desperately point to the window, ceiling, floor and door? It's a cry for help.

He doesn't seem to have a view on this. But he does tell me that he was sent to Woodbridge Prep School aged seven. I express dismay and mutter things about child abuse.

'Oh no, no it was good. No arguing, no crockery being thrown. It made a change. I liked it – to start with.'

'Then what?'

'Well, Kit was often in trouble. Rustications, near-expulsions. After a while he started persuading me own up to his trouble to stop him being thrown out.'

We walk on. I picture a mute, knocked-kneed Wym standing in front of the headmaster's door. I stare at his worn, safety-toed boots. He's staring at my dusty flip-flops and my mud-lined toes. I feel sympathy for him. Sympathy is not love.

At last we turn onto the West Road. I must have driven past this building many times. It's a huge rural statement, complete with clock tower and archway; built to convey prestige and to hide the slurry lagoon.

Inside the arch is a courtyard with strange concrete footpints to buildings long gone. Sheds stand shoulder to arse and there's a smell, reminding me of a varnished wardrobe I used to like chewing as a kid. It also musters up the stink of a three-week old hamster cage.

Wym leads through a chipped-paint blue door to a high-ceilinged office. This room is populated by rural ruddy faces in blue overalls. Wym perches me on a huge pre-war desk and disappears for a moment. A number of blue, watery eyes blink at me. I finger the cracked wood and try not to look at them. Chicken-wire in window, maps on wall, red field outlines on map, feathers stuck in cobwebs, dog paw prints on filthy linoleum.

Then Wym comes back through with papers and a box under his arm. He smiles at me, I smile at him. We leave together, him and me while the watchers blink.

49. Moo Stained

I thank my lucky stars I've learnt so much about agribusiness from my Ladybird Book of Farming. Milking has already started. Cows wait outside at the shed, kicking it occasionally. They're hunched and each delicately moving a pulsating milk float beneath them.

The close association of shit with sterile milk somehow goes against all I expect in a nice pint. Mud-stained doors open onto a room that looks and smells like the swimming pool I shivered beside at school. A guy in blue overalls is sweeping water with a broom into a hole in the floor. I note why the flip-flop is not the chosen footwear of dairymen. Wym lifts up the lid of the huge tank-sized metal tank and there it is – the milk lake I heard so much about as a child.

Wyn tells me, coquettishly, that nearly everything he does is 'cowcentric'. He monitors me for tell-tale signs of interest. I give it to him in shed-loads and sparkle when he offers me tough wellies, a pinafore and slightly stained rubber gloves. Soon I'm wearing more dried effluent than at any time since the age of three.

On a scale of one to ten, my interest in the milking process falls at around two point five. But Trevor, now my mentor, is almost rupturing with keenness; he is lactose super-tolerant. He has been 'in dairy' since he was a boy. So were his father and grandfather. That's a sign it can't be so bad – gradually I'm eaten away by an urge to play momentary milkmaid.

Through a door, we're in a large concrete and steel zone. At worst it looks the kind of place Hannibal Lecter entertains his guests. At best it could be the most down-at-heel mechanic's garage, complete with inspection pit and unidentifiable machinery. There are already six cows attached to pipes and twenty more waiting. They stare down into the pit, listening as Trevor feeds me bovinformation, slice by slice. I lose track almost immediately.

Trevor's cows are 'units'. These Moo Units are Friesian. This is good – they don't break down as often as the more commonly produced unit, the Friesian Hybrid. Each unit has two months 'off' per 'rotation'. What's more, Trevor's units do more 'rotations' in a cycle than most. He's on a roll and I'm unable to butt in. What kind of rotations can a cow do apart from on a rotisserie?

Trevor's conversation travels laterally along cattle planes. He tells me about the many funny milk accidents he's had. Then he tells me about giant diary farms in America. I hear about his dreams and hopes for the future. They have computers and self-milking cows in America. I suggest that the cows need bras because their posture is dreadful. He says there ARE cow bras, in America.

Meanwhile the UK cows are impatient and seem to be blaming me.

There's a long list of things to be done if you want to get milk from a cow and once you're on the bovine bike, you have to keep peddling.

Things that surprised me about milking.

As the barrier is lifted, the first half-dozen cows fight and jostle into one of the six milking stations. The seventh hangs back with resigned patience. Cows can count up to six.

- Cows are huge. Bigger than I ever imagined. Their back legs are all muscle. Trevor has to warn which cows are likely to kick me. Cows have personalities.

- Udders aren't uniform, every single one is different. Sometimes they're close together, sometimes on opposite sides, sometimes they're ostentatiously long, sometimes tiny. Some have freckles, some are peachy pink. Cows are individuals.

For an hour at least the cows keep coming. It's an endless stream of black and white, mud and milk. I look for someone to save me, but Wym is nowhere.

I'm given one large-eyed unit as a special treat. She has mastitis and is uncomfortable. Her udders are boiling hot and veined. Her milk must be kept separate as she's on antibiotics; milk and medicine doesn't mix. She's very ticklish but docile and gives my shoulder a sniff, then gamely cleans out her own nostril with her tongue. I dignify her with a name. Alison.

Trevor points at her. 'She's done fourteen rotations. She's at the end of her cycle.'

'Will she be retired? Live in the field?'

Trevor gives a plummy grin. 'She'll be sold for burgers.' My face drops. He quickly adds, 'Better quality burgers!'

Alison's milk takes a long time to come and in the end, it will be tipped down the drain. The whole process makes me sickened to my stomach. Alison may well be sickened to her four stomachs.

'Alison,' I sing 'I know this world is killing you!'

Meanwhile, Trevor is as keen as mustard, eyes gleaming, hands a-rubbing, draining his units of milk and rotating them to their deaths. He's an oxy-moron.

The field beside the dairy is a breath of fresh air. It's green on blue with a few sheep and quite a lot of crows, some of them riding the sheep. Before you can sing 'Swing Low, Sweet Cheviot', Alison and her pals join them, udders distended and flapping gently in the breeze.

Wym is standing beside a Land Rover, talking to a guy in overalls. Is that a grin I detect on his face when he sees me? Has he done all this to level me and my work ethic?

'Hey!' I glare 'I've done your dirty business for you.'

'Did you have fun?'

'Fun? Yes, fun. Fun poo and pee under my fingernails. Fun sore arms. Fun never ending cows and fun Trevor. Great date, Wym!'

Wym looks at the guy and the guy looks at Wym. Then Wym looks at my grubby flip-flops.

'Trevor's not be the most metropolitan person in town I grant you, but he's been here for two hours already this morning and he'll be here two hours longer, milking one hundred and thirty cows and then hosing the dairy. And then he'll go home and do all the paper work and then he'll come back and do it all again in roughly eight hours.'

'Sorry!' I stumble, 'It's just that my arms hurt. It just seems like a pint of milk is not worth the effort.'

Wym puts his hands in his hair and the guy beside him clicks his tongue.

'You're right!' says Wym. 'It's not. It would actually be cheaper for me to buy the milk from the supermarket and pour it back in the tank.'

I don't think he's kidding.

'But why do it?' I bleat. 'It doesn't make you any money and your cows, by the way, have a horrible lifestyle!'

'You want happier cows, then pay for it. How much would you pay for a pint of milk?'

I'm too embarrassed to tell him that the milk I like best is from the bottle nicked from a neighbour's doorstep.

Suddenly I've dived into a huge pile of moral silage. Wym crickles his nose as if I actually stink. He turns back, says he has to finish with the vet. He'll see me later.

50. Butterfly Net

My scrubbed feet dry against the AGA. I have never thought of myself as a City Girl until today. Never has the idiocy of my idea of life been more demonstrated. A pile of dung has been dealt by me to the laps of Wym, his farm and everyone who works on it. If there was any time to pack my bag and go back to huddling in Huntley Street, whinging about the £1.89 price of two litres of milk, now is that time.

Somehow in of spite my health, my youth, my good-locks and my stable, middle-class upbringing, the way I take on the world means a bad impression is created in every quarter. It seems I am so much less than the sum of my parts.

Before this thought starts to work on my conscience, my phone rings.

'Signe! What is it? If this is more abuse from you, I'm putting the phone down.'

Whimpering...then.

'I don't know. Oh god!'

Oh shit! Is it labour? What do I do? Think Holby City, what would they do?

'Are you in pain?'

'Yesssss. Noooooo. Where are you?'

'Is the baby OK?'

'I don't know! I think so.'

'So why are you ringing?'

'I'm going mad, Miriam! This house, this bloody blue house. It's going to crush me if I don't get out of it!'

Uh-huh?

I'm slightly chafed of the hands and I've had roughly two hours sleep. My brain is fragile and full of new information that is knitting my synapses into a headscarf. But cold, self-contained and spiritual Signe is having a breakdown and that's something that shouldn't be missed.

After her call, visions of a suicidal Signe showcase in my brain and eventually take me to the cottage. Walking back alone through the oxygen-rich afternoon is like a champagne infusion.

On the morning after my father's 50th birthday, we kids slouched about bleary-eyed while Dad made off-the-cuff predictions to our futures; Tom will end up in Borstal or Goldman Sachs. Miriam will be a long-term unemployed artist. Signe will join a nunnery or some other career where you ostracize people. (Signe became a social worker. It was her disdainy)

Signe willfully makes herself lonely. Of course, she'd already been in a convent; it was a case of nature finding a nurture-hairshirt and liking it.

I get to the cottage to find the Bad Cat loose and a tense Good Cat feigning nonchalance from the highest cupboard. The house smells vile. There are flies buzzing around. I've only been gone a day.

Signe sits at the table, the blue paint perfectly highlighting the bags under her eyes.

An hour later, she's in Clio, traveling in silence. The supposed breakdown has turned into brooding resentment. She wants to go out but doesn't want crowds. She wants to see things but doesn't want to walk. So, the world is our shriveled, midget oyster.

I cruise the lanes looking for a crisis tea-shop. It's a fruitless drive.

The little I know of Signe comes from overheard family gossip. I know she was sent to school at four, becoming the youngest member of a holy ghetto. There were tales of huddling behind bookshelves for hours, of being denied the use of the only toilet. She was caned daily for having her socks rolled down, for talking about menstrual blood, wetting pants.

Signe reefed her emotions and eventually made it to the adjoining Secondary School. There she had a massive breakdown, dropped out and escaped teenage pregnancy; a miracle of non-conception.

She answers my perfectly normal questions with abrupt single word answers. After an hour I have run out of normal, bland topics. I branch out.

'What do you think of Dad marrying again?'

She looks out of the window and shrugs. 'It's not a surprise.'

'I wish he had stayed with Sheila.'

'I wish he'd stayed with my mum. Everything was fine back then.'

'I guess love is complicated?'

Signe turns and stares at me. 'Love is no excuse.'

Signe's motto for our times.

At last we pass an odd, white breeze-block building. It says it's a butterfly farm and café. I don't care what it is, my tongue has gone numb which means I have to get my proboscis in some sugar soon.

Enter and turn left; you're in a nice yellow gingham pale-pine tearoom. Pass through net a curtain on the right, you're in an old guy's impression of Borneo, with naif acrylic painted vines on breezeblock. Tropical plants press against the dirty perspex roof. There are some ecstatically institutionalised starlings and butterflies the size of five pence coins or dinner-plates. They're black, shimmery blue, white or neon, flapping nightmarishly slowly or manically fast like wind-up toys. Signe I notice, is twitching and lurching. As am I. We've both recalled that curly hair is splendidly snaggy and large insects are dangerously snag-prone.

Just then, the flap of StartRites on concrete; two thrashing, swishing boys come in. Tibby and Robsie. Shit! That means...

Kit. He's been avoiding me, to my relief, for weeks now. He looks shocked but can't back out now, not without wrestling retreatwardly through a net curtain.

'Miriam.' He grimaces. 'What a surprise.'

'Hi Kit.'

'Hi there!' I say to the swishing boys and sticks.

'They love it here' says Kit. 'We come every week.' (A week is probably how long it takes for replacement butterflies to pupate and prepare for more swishing.)

Kit turns to Signe. I grudgingly do the formals. 'Oh, yes. This is Signe.' Kit is staring at her.

Signe's blue eyes are glazed and pin-pupiled. She has a plate-sized black butterfly attached to her hair; a fascinator with legs. I'm not touching it. To prove the fact, I leap backwards. Signe's bottom lip quivers. Then Kit gently reaches into her hair and extracts the monster. Hmmmm. Very gallant. I know where this is going.

51. The Tic

I left Signe to manage on her own in the cottage. Our day trip had been hijacked and ransacked by Kit, sitting opposite us in the Butterfly House cafe, batting eye-lashes and brushing Signe's hand, while his sons revolt in the soft play area. Despite her blue eyes staring right through him, he doesn't realise that Signe's heart is kept in a vault in Switzerland.

The only way that this helped me, was to reinstall Signe's usual level of emotional security. I drove Fort Knox home in silence then walked sluggishly back to Wym's. 'Love is no excuse.' I'm aware of my need to furnish my heart with the correct accessories. What exactly is it about Wym, heir presumptive to a massive estate, that attracts me?!

Wym comes home, tosses his creaky coat on a peg and says 'Hello.' He smells of oxygen and tired muscles. He starts supper. I watch him making lamb mince and pine nut sausagey things which he wraps in courgette sleeping bags. I peel sweet potatoes for him. Our elbows keep touching. I realise that my heart, that's usually so concerned with number one, is now traveling abroad, trying to find Wym on his own emotional terrain. I wish he was mine. The fantasy of him is plastered across my brain like badly aligned wall-paper.

I move my food around. It's delicious but my stomach has shriveled to a tiny, confused pickled walnut.

We wash dishes. Again with the elbows. I keep my arms close to me but somehow we still knock together. He does this thing where he lifts a dish to wash, pauses and purses his lips at me. He looks agitated, I think. It's hard to tell.

I say, 'I'm sorry I was so rude about your dairy.'

'I apologise for throwing you in at the deep end, should have realized it's not what you're used to.'

And there it is. The confirmation that I don't belong.

'But you don't love farming.' I attempt. 'I saw love today, it was all over Trevor. He lives for farming.'

Wym's facial tics are always interesting, they're like watching a game of Tetris except it's muscles that he's stacking.

'It's not about love, it's about duty. We're not your average family.'

That statement sends me into a crisis of reaction. I mentally grab my eyes to stop them rolling.

'The Hebbinons have been at Toft for centuries. We're married to the estate.'

'And like good Catholics, you can't divorce? You do lies, cheating, insults, secrets, mental and physical abuse and crockery throwing but not divorce?'

'Not divorce. Kit divorced and look where that left me; taking the consequences again. So I don't recommend you marry any of us.'

A supermassive silence lands in the room. I look at my feet. Wym looks at the ceiling. Then he says in a strained voice.

'I'm sorry if this seems blunt, but. Are you sleeping with Kit?'

My head wobbles like a springy toy.

'No!'

I'm safe enough to hide. The only reason I'm not sleeping with Kit is because Kit's not sleeping with me but Wym did not set the error bars of the question wide enough to take that fact in.

'That an incredible piece of none-of-your-business, William. One trip to your dairy doesn't mean we get to share sex histories. So are you sleeping with anyone? Are you married? Are you gay or bi-sexual?'

'No, no, no and no.'

'What, no sex ever?'

'Yes, of course. I'm not a virgin.'

I regret instantly. He's holding a tea towel the way a hamster holds sunflower seed.

'Sorry.'

'It's me who should be sorry. The whole thing was crass. I'm not very good at this.'

'At what?'

'What I'm trying to say. You're the only woman I've invited to the diary. My mother obviously knows it, and Anna goes there for accounts, but you're the only one who, well, I thought you might.'

'I did I did!' I say, though I'm not quite sure what I'm answering.

He starts to twist the tea towel until it can't be twisted any further.

'I thought I might ask you to think about becoming in a relationship with me.'

The strangled syntax strain out from a swallowing, constricted throat and tight teeth. I look him straight in the eye. His right eye. He's solemn and unblinking, like a teacher waiting for an answer that he thinks is obvious. His nose is a little long, his chin is slightly pink but the sides of his mouth are freckly. He reminds me of Chap First.

'Alright!'

If this was Kit, the table would instantly be swept clean of everything on it for some merry-making. Wym is very different; instead he turns his back and boils the kettle. We are going to have a summit, I can tell. A tea-cup curtain descends between us. We sit down and he leans back. 'Do you have any significant relationships I should be worried about?'

Hmmm. There are seeds of jealousy in the newly-ploughed earth.

I could mention Chap First, but now I've had time to think about it, I can't helping wondering, if he liked me as much as he said he did, why the hell he couldn't stay in touch? I have a feeling that indecision and a thumb-sucking id run the show in his brain.

Then there's Chap 1, a man so utterly poster-boy pretty that when he removed his affection it turned me into a bizarro internet stalker. I will never forgive a man who can (even unwittingly) warp me into someone I don't recognise. Despite the scars and rubble in my heart over these two cases, neither of them would have worked out. And the others in between? So many weird shaped pegs being smashed into square holes.

So I say...

'No, no other significant relationships.'

Wym looks at his cup and says 'Good. I couldn't go through all that again.'

Meanwhile, a tickertape runs between my ears. 'Why is he enquiring about my love life, and yet he's not mentioned a peep about his own?' I muse that I've never really come across male reserve before. Actually, I'm too busy looking at the turn of his neck disappearing inside his shirt, a neck I will soon be able to kiss. I choose a place just below the earlobe. That freckle will be mine.

Wym stands up, massages the back of his chair for a second, then clears his throat. 'I have to go up to the big house right now. I have an appointment with my parents. Please don't wait up.'

Usually when men ask for a date, they tend to want to hang out with me, not with their parents. I am minded to tell him so but have been subdued by his martyrish confession box. And then he's gone. He didn't even smile, I am quite certain of that. To say the least, I'm jangled.

Later, alone in my bedroom, I review the conversation so fresh in my memory. It was brimming with emotion and meaning and slurry and then he gave me a sort of eternity ring made out of cow poo. A wave of brightness courses through me. I'm wanted! Someone wants me! The dammed up reservoir of my heart opens up and the electric water pours in.

But wait, then that he asked me to dissect my love-life. It makes me feel like a fallen women, which I possibly am. Then I remember that this is the twenty-first century and women only fall when pushed or tripped.

The quickest way to level this playing field is to do some practical detective work.

52. The Great Escape

It's cold and scary. The space is about eight foot square with a window and two facing doors. I've closed Wym's connecting door, so the only light is moonlight. I have a visceral need for the loo. The space is stacked to eye-level with cardboard boxes. I've absolutely no business here. It's Wym's fault for being a Man of Mystery.

I didn't turn the lights on for fear of being seen from outside if Wym came home suddenly. I blindly walked my fingers over his fireplace, a topgraphy of tweedy things and sharp things; spilt wax, biros, receipts, a feather and – a bowl of keys! A bunch of bunches. One heavy Victorian key was on the top. I could sense it was the right one.

I start with a shoebox. It opens and gives a whiff of kodachrome. Photos; lots of them, mainly outdoors – under trees, on a lawn. It's a family gathering on an overcast day. Ruddy-faced boys in woolly jumpers and cans of Carlsberg. Ladies with headscarfs and Cross-your-Heart chests. Cords, pearls, up-turned collars, red-eye, red cheeks. It's seeding in the time of Charles and Di. By the light of the moon, I recognise the Marchese – black hair swept back, looking no more endearing then than now. She has a haughty 'Jackie Kennedy' thing going on; a filly who has been consciously well-sired. There's a narrow man with feather-like brown hair, arms to long for his sleeves and a coy smile. He rests his elbows on the heads of two boys – all freckle and full-on teeth.

Prop. And Kit. And Wym.

Here are Wym and Kit together, playing jolly games of lawn badminton and climbing trees. What caused their split? Why is 'Happy Family 1982' now 'Painfully-Divided Family 2003'?

Now I open a zip-up case of toiletries; lavender talc, facial cream, elderflower eye-gel. Uh- huh...really, Wym?

Black bag. Jumpers that smell of scent. Ladies jeans. T-shirts, strappy tops. My stomach starts to ache. There's a rational explanation and I'm not going to like it.

A larger box. Silvery tasteful cards. Oh God, Miriam don't open them. 'Congratulations Wym and Helena.'

Wym and Helena. Wym and Someone Else. I've unlocked Pandora's dressing-room.

Out of the corner of my eye: a white, headless, emaciated figure, floating 3ft from the ground. All body fluids make for emergency exits.

I blink. Blink again, it's moving.

It's not moving.

Edging forward through the moonlight I brush the apparition.

It's a wedding dress.

Just then, Wym's light goes on.

Shit!

Shit!

Shit!

What the Hell am I even doing in here? How would I explain it? I must escape but there's nowhere to hide. Maybe if I crawled behind the boxes and just closed my eyes? His shadow crosses the glowing crack of his door. Maybe now's the time to be brave. I should just step out and confront him. A piece of metal inserts itself in my heel, making me silently hop and curse. It's a huge key! Still lying at the back of my door where it fell. Jam key in the lock, turn – *crash, thrash, thud-thud-thud –* olympic dive into my bed.

The floorboards stop creaking and the house becomes silent apart from my brain conjuring sound-effects. Is that him in the changing room? Looking at boxes? Scratching his head? Creasing his brow? I hear phantom rustles for about an hour.

So Wym is married. He's married to Helena. If he cared about me, he would have told me so. Miriam was an idiot to presume anything. I house the most useless, self-centered, wretched collection of cells ever brought together and labeled brain. Like a grounded fish, I flop my mind on the banks of sleep. 'He will never divorce. Never.' Gasps the fish.

Dreams come wonkily and leave early. I wake in yesterday's dress, sweated damp. What a mess I'm in. What a mess my life's in. Good people die every day and still I hold on, wasting air and health.

I pathetically weep in front of the mirror for a while and further hating myself for being interested in the drama of my outrageously ugly reflection. The itch to flee grabs me like internal eczema. I snatch up my bag and stuff my remaining clothes. Flip-flops flit down the stairs past the dark kitchen.

Out of the front door. I'm free! I've escaped!

Wrong. Bloody Wym is gardening at dawn.

'Where are you going?'

I gauge that walking mutely past serves me best.

'Miriam!... *Miriam!*'

A growl vibrates up, up, up through my throat and become the embarrassing moment when internal thoughts become so loud they drown out local bird noise.

'WHO'S HELENA?!'

Wym pushes his garden fork into the soil.

'Miriam. That is a very long and difficult story.'

'And you won't tell me?'

'I want to tell you but I can't.'

'Fine. I've had it with your family and secrets. My family might not be perfect but at least we have the good grace to divorce before we try to kill each other. Meanwhile your family think genuine warmth is something you buy in the AGA showroom!'

'It's just more than I can deal with right now.'

'Ok. But from here, you're no better than Kit.'

Wym's eyes open and his mouth shuts. If a look was a sound, we'd hear a branch being ripped from a large tree. Now is a good time to flee White Rabbit Garden.

On the stumble home to the cottage, I try to console myself that by hiding my feelings I would be lying to myself and him. Telling lies is something I'm trying to correct in myself.

I gently open the back kitchen door just at the moment that Signe comes rushing outside, shouldering past me with a flaming rag outstretched, Doppler screaming

'Your pants are on fire!'

They are. They were my lucky pants too.

We look at the AGA. I've piled up so much washing on it and pent up so much heat, it's almost glowing. I peel off my clothes. Knickers with elastic melted into bits of rind, dresses with burn holes; nearly all my most-loved and cleanest clothes parched or dead. The clearing of the smoke and the inspection of scorch marks and the discussing of the future of my wardrobe keeps my mind off my own future. With the loss of my lucky pants, it looks bleak. My life has turned into an open municipal dump, complete with the seagulls of outrageous fortune and the JCBs of delusion.

Signe by comparison, is homeless, three months gone, has abandoned her job at no notice, is hiding from her abusive, controlling husband and is avoiding her neurotic mother.

Signe needs a womb with a view.

I need a fresh start.

The cats need someone who can keep them apart.

By 10:15 am, I'm driving what remains of thirty-something earth years' worth of belongings down the blanched concrete A140, along with clothes (unscathed), clothes (varying degrees of scorch but wearable), accessories, make-up, a laptop, 4" of blue panic knitting and a phone in a bowl of rice.

Signe has agreed to be me for Marjory, and possibly Prop. She will not sign any documents. She understands the rules of cat exchange. I imagine her making merry Hell with my persona but I don't care anymore, she can have me as was. I'm going to be completely different. Miles rush past. Dead flat terrain grows nipples, then proper undulations. Every sign for London, I follow singingly. By the time I get to Dagenham, I curse the person whose idea it was to bring their car to London.

One-Thirty pm. Clio rolls into Bloomsbury and the Brigadoon stillness of Huntley Street. Tom's flat is a cocoon. Nothing has changed, not the washing in the sink or the magazines behind the front door. It's just as I left it before I first left it.

53. The Ligger

Oh bollocks. Bollocks to bollocks. Bollocks to the causes of bollocks. I have a car. London has a congestion charge. This conflict means I must crawl out of bed, get roughly dressed and drive out of Westminster before the Magic Eye spots Clio.

The closest free-zone is Dad's place at Fulham. Once I get there I think, Bollocks! I might as well drive somewhere now. I drive to Kew Gardens.

It just so happens that Kew expects money at the gate but there is a fail-safe way of getting into these kinds of places for free. Wait long enough and you always find a crocodile line of children being guided by two or three harassed teaching assistants. You choose a school that looks like it's from south of the river, full of little imps. Then you follow at a slow pace. When you get to the gate, you stand close to them, look harassed and slip in behind.

Kew Gardens has had a tough summer. The grass is bleached with islands of green where sprinklers are trying to save the most expensive specimens. If you listen closely, you can hear the sound of a thousand trees pining.

When I was about twelve and my Dad lived in Barnes, he took me here for a Sunday outing. This was our final trip with me as a child, I guess. Tom was five and utterly obnoxious. What had been adorable cheekiness from a button-nosed, toddling cherub were now red-faced, sweaty haired tantrums. When things didn't go Tom's way, he lay on the floor, pounding his chunky clark's sandals on whatever pissed him off most. Dad never blinked one eyelash.

When at Kew on this occasion, I looked down at Tom writhing on the floor, knowing I could never get away with that kind of thing in front of George, (revenge being a more Hitchcockian affair in Basingstoke; controlled, repressed and subversive). I had a glass full of ice. Dad was at the counter, exchanging the cake that had caused the crisis. I looked down at the grubby little cuckoo and poured the ice down the front of his T-shirt.

The funny thing is, this kicking midget became the ultra-sound, popular, cool-headed twat that he is now. He qualified as a lifeguard aged fourteen. He can fly a glider. He trekked across Iceland. He got four As at A Level and a first from LSE.

My highest achievement was the C in A level Art. But then, I never kicked anyone.

I wander into the cafe, abuzz with people, crummy tables and uncleared trays. When the eventual balloon goes up and we're forced to fend for ourselves I will come in to my own. I am the human cockroach, I will live and live. The corner table has a recently abandoned pot of tea, one sandwich untouched and half a carrot cake. By laying my coat and bag on the table, I mark my territory, then remove the bits of food I don't want (old crusts, the chunk of cake touched by someone else) and gently re-engineer the left-overs to be mine. Then I demand a clean cup and fresh milk from the pink-looking girl at the till.

I don't know anyone else who does this, and I should rightly feel ashamed but here and now the only feeling is the incredible lightness of living invisibly like being a bird in a tree. My pockets are always lined with two gram sachets of sugar. Of course, I could go find a job, make some money and eat legitimately but that would seem like hard work.

After an hour of rotating demands, first for hot water in my tea, and later a fresh tea bag for my water, I wander out and wallow below a tree. Is Wym thinking about me? No, I think not. I feel completely invisible and untouched. Maybe I'm a ghost.

But even ghosts become tired. Clio returns me to Fulham, neurotically lisping 'Panic, you're out of petrol!' through her orange low-fuel light. At Meadowbank Close, I stick Clio in Dad's drive and then push the keys through his letterbox.

Oh shit. But what if I need the car again? Dad's never here. Bugger. I hunt around for tools and find a coat hanger in the bin. I unwind and bend it into the right position, then thread it through his letter box to root around on the doormat.

I'm amazingly sneaky at getting into places, I should work for MI5. As a teen, I was never entrusted with a house key, so secret trips home from St Phil's meant break-in. If I tied a garden rake to the swingball pole and poked it through the dog-flap, I could unhook a tiny window at back of the porch. One time George and Mum went away for a week. They locked the inner glass door and George left a box of chocolates on view to tease me. By unscrewing the carpet edging strip and pulling the carpet away, I was able to slide a record sleeve under the door, push the key from the inside of the lock onto the sleeve and drag it onto my side. Then I unlocked the door, drank all the alcohol, ate all the chocolates and left a note for George thanking him. George was completely perplexed.

And all because the lady loves Milk Tray.

So to find Dad's front door suddenly swing open with my hand attached to a wire, stuck in the letterbox is a surprise. Vivien peeps around, holding a rolling pin.

'Oh! Hello!'

'Hi there!'

'What's with the wire?'

'Er well. I'm trying to retrieve my car keys.'

Vivien bobs down and hands them to me.

'Here you go! Hey Missy, I'm glad you're here. I need a girl's opinion.'

This is the first time I've been inside the Fulham house. It has the feel of the many pads Dad has occupied. The same thick mocca-coloured carpets, the same cream walls, the same easily recalled paintings and ornaments that move with him. We walk through a G-planned lounge with the most amazing view across a slate-grey Thames. Through the bedroom (my Dad's bedroom!) to an anteroom with mirrors and clothes. There are eight wedding dresses hanging in plastic-wrap.

'Listen Honey. I can't get these adjusted until my seamstress gets back from the Philippines. But you're a size twelve aintcha? I really want to see them on, could you try'em for me? Couldja? Honey?'

54. The Car Crash

Vivien is definitely going about her wedding in a way that the British part of me finds cripplingly embarrassing and slightly unnecessary.

Recently I've been vaguely noodling about what would happen if I ever did meet a guy who was dumb enough to marry me. I've always planned a trip to the registrars.

OK, I have added a little more to the scenario.

The registrars would not be one of those horrible, ubiquitous 70s buildings that you see in other people's wedding photos, but a nice London Edwardian affair. I would wear a deep olive green silk dress. We would go to someone's house or garden afterward and be cheered by our best friends and close family. We would dance to 'Grow Old with Me' by Mary Chapin Carpenter. We would eat avocado on ginger oatcakes and mango sorbet for pudding. It wouldn't matter how tiny the wedding was, because it would be clear that we both cared for each other and our love was the most valuable thing in the room. Then we'd honeymoon in a shack of a cottage in Dorset for a long weekend and spend the whole time curled up on an old iron-framed bed.

So, yes, I have given it a little thought. But not as much thought as Vivien. She's a wedding brainiac.

The changing room is a salon of nuptials, a modern Marriage à la Mode. One large photo album is full of cake and another has a forest of bouquets. The last two days have been haunted by wedding dresses, I'm trapped in some kind of ivory silk loop of fate.

Vivien pulls the cover off the first dress. It looks like one of those bleached but very complicated creatures from the deepest parts of the sea. It has a masochistic number of hooks and eyes. It takes nearly twenty minutes to undo them. I point this out to Vivien, making only fleeting reference to the length of the wedding night and the rule that Viagra should be not be on the guest list purely through necessity. So this dress comes off before it really goes on. It is a lovely material though, and as I run my hands over it, I feel my fingertips sending me a coded message.

The second dress has some buttons but the main drag is a good-ol' zip. I breath in and once I'm sealed, I feel I've been poured into a Smarties tube. My stance is poised, up-right and, as far as slug-silk can manage, protected like a knight going into a battle.

'Just like Diana!' gasps Vivien.

She does not mean I am a car crash of the imagination but that I resemble a blushing princess. I peek around the edge of the mirror. It's a pathetic, stupid, sniveling infant in a fairy costume, waiting for Mr. A.H Prince. I imagine Wym. I imagine Wym and me and a big church. I imagine the ghostly Helena jumping up and screaming. I imagine the wedding shuddering to a halt. It can't be helped, it's a game of fantasy downfall.

Another six dresses wait like bottles of gold-top in a queue but the rate of thrill correlates inversely with the number of buttons tied. We don't even do up the corset of number six, we both think it looks like something Madonna would wear, and I step out of it voguing 'Like a Virgin'. Did I mention we've already consumed a bottle and a half of Sauvignon Blanc?

By now it's dark. The Thames' slate conveyor belt churns past the window. We splay ourselves on the G-plan, supposedly to look at bridesmaid dress colours but instead to get the inside track on how Vivien met my father. She's all teeth and batting nylon eyelash and she's far too close and too tactile, but the story's startling.

She and her ex had been renting a house off my father for a month. My father was using the next-door building as a site office. He heard her singing. And then he heard her arguing with her husband. Then the husband walked out. My Dad had to 'help her with the fuse box'. That evening they 'played Scrabble' (which she assures me, just means they played Scrabble). Then they talked for hours. Then the husband came back. My father had to retreat to his own side of the wall. When she came to hand back the keys at the end of the month, he grabbed her and kissed her. It was very romantic.

It is also very unsettling and, as I keep discovering, when I hear about love plus my father, tears seem to come as part of the package. In this case, I'm blubbing distilled white wine. My story of Wym and the floating wedding dress spews out from some spinneret in my front lobe. Vivien tries to drunkenly get her head around my issues but it's so much damp tissue on the Lake Windermere of strife.

At about one am she gets a text. 'Oo, your father's on his way back. He'll be here in half an hour.'

Panic! I've got to escape but I'm in no fit state to walk home. It's about five miles, through a muggy London night, swarming with zombies and vampires. Vivien is very concerned but I am resolutely drunk. I stagger away, like King Lear in plimsolls, scarifying myself and the world around me. Who do I hate more, Dad, Wym or me? Who do I love more, me, Wym or Dad?

It's a journey of about six miles and, as is common with drunken staggering, it's not the length of the journey but the width of the pavement that is the main issue. Like all natural, tear-stained idiots, I am protected by the patron saint of drunks (Saint Monica, so I'm told) all the way back to Bloomsbury, even after walking around the British Museum, I think, three times.

Then I did a bad thing. Worse than normal, anyway.

It's about five in the morning. The sky is already blue. I'm exhausted, semi-sober and bleeding of foot but so nearly home. I see a lorry pull away from the back of Planet Organic. It's left a big, cellophaned pile of something. And a stack of another thing. And a box of something else.

The pile is a shipment of tinned soup.

The stack are boxed pizza bases.

The something else is a heap of bottled echinacea water.

I took a layer of soup, a portion of pizza bases and a glug of water bottles. I don't know how far Saint Monica's coverage goes but I'm hoping I can count on her if this subject comes up later.

55. Little Black Cloud

Some time after eleven, the phone by the bed jabs me in the ear with a stiletto knife. My elbow is hungover but I attain the handset at my first attempt.

'Urr-oh.'

'Is that you?'

'Dad?!'

I sit up. I don't want him to think I'm still in bed. The darn coir organic duvet is noisy. He probably heard it rustle.

'So you made it home safe.' His voice muffles and I hear him call 'She made it home safe.' Then he returns, close up at a full volume whisper.

'Listen, Sweetheart. If you ever make Vivien worry again like she did last night on your behalf, I'm going to get very upset.'

My stomach drops.

I try to interpret this as fatherly concern; folded and inverted concern.

'You could have stayed the night at our place but you insist on walking out into the night, pissed as a bloody fart and talking nonsense. Vivien didn't get to sleep until after six and that nerve massage appointment she's waited five months for, FIVE MONTHS, she missed.'

It's just concern. Vivien is my father's conduit for concern for me. 'Shape up, Miriam! Your mum says the whole family rings her to complain about you.'

'Dad, I...'

'Shape up, Girl!'

'Say sorry to Vivien.'

He shouts into the distance 'She says she's sorry.'

My hearing is very good. I make out Vivien's voice

'If only we could help the poor thing.'

That's it. Interaction over. I pull the covers over my head.

A shower. A black coffee. A toasted pizza base and marmite. A bottle of echinacea water. Another coffee. But I can't shake the feeling there's a black cloud tied to my foot and I'm dragging around behind me. I know in my heart I have to shape up. Everyone's been telling me for years. My beloved Primary One Teacher, Mrs Woods, told me so. Chap First would have told me, if I'd given him the chance. All the staff at St Phil's were adamant that I shape up. The OU agreed. My mum strongly hints that I should. George politely suggests that I should. My brother, sisters, uncles, aunts, grandparents, ex-boyfriends, school-friends nag me about it. Ex-employers, police officers, medical professionals, cold-calling telephone bods, credit-card payment goons, agony aunts and accusing photographic models in lifestyle magazines all agree I should. Even the dying succulents on Tom's windowsill are telling me to shape up. Which is why I don't want to. Not for them, anyway. I'm only going to shape up when I want to. One day I'm going to shape up so much that I'll be a gigantic tetrahedron on the horizon, just when they least expect it and just when they think that my shaping up is a non-starter.

London days cross the cheese-cloth curtains. Some time during the evening, after rush-hour but pre the evening's street cocktail of fun and fighting, I have black tea and pizza base. I knit as well. The adding of a stitch to a stitch feels like it's being woven straight from my head. I could produce a jumper made from the white noise that fuzzes in my ears. Sometimes I think if I stop and look at my life I will just lie on the floor and scream and scream. Then what would I do?

Wandering over to Tom's CD shelves, I see he has neatly cataloged his entire life's hoarding. There are ones that I gave him (passed-on, unwanted presents) and ones that Dad gave him. I know because Dad gave we three fatherless children the same CDs, loaded with bloody Bob Dylan and Fairport Convention. Tom's perfect collection may look as if he cares but I think it's more to do with his grasping nature. I lost every CD I've ever owned. Chap First gave me lots of mix tapes with songs to melt my cold heart. I binned them. It's not that I didn't care, I was just clumsy.

On the bottom shelf is some vinyl, because Tom is the kind of tit who has a record player. I leaf through them. He once played 'Bridge over Troubled Water' so often that I stole the record and cooked it in the oven, turning it into a flowerpot. Then I find something that tears a hole in my time/space continuum. An EP with a bright, hallucinatory cover. 'A Child's Medley of Nursery Songs.' This used to be mine! My first ever record!

The needle goes down gently on the record and the crackling starts. It's Kenneth McKellar and whoever his female equivalent was. And it's 1980 and I like drinking cremola foam and eating Soreen loaf. 'The Frog he would a-Wooing Go'. I might have been a pretty confused ankle-biter but I was quite happy that way.

How could I not be, when I could listen to the feminist hit 'Where Are You Going To, My Pretty Maid?' What's Tom doing with this? I blame him for stealing my childhood memories, my little sunny cot, my wooden highchair, my daddy. I can't reclaim my father it seems but this record belongs to me. It will be mine again, even though I have nothing to play it on.

When I turn the record over, I inspect its grooves, one grainy ring per song like the years of a tree; the DNA of my infancy. I notice someone has scratched something in the middle, beside the hole. The letters were there when I owned it but I couldn't read them then.

It says 'This rekord is S.I.G.N.E.S'.

56. Therapeutics

Sleeping in London is like being in a room with busy wallpaper. All through the night my dreams are decorated with police sirens, someone calling for 'RON!' and someone fighting a wheelie-bin. Finally the dawn-chorus of morning mopeds. The foxes howl and yelp in the war for the control of the bins. I sympathise, I too am starving. I'm becoming my own Big Brother contestant. Soon I'll down to trapping rabbits. In Tom's cupboard is a jar of wasabi paste and a bag of black wild rice. And the stolen soup, which really doesn't aspire to being appetising, it's happy to stop at 'wholesome'.

I'm also running a temperature. Everything from my nails to my eyeballs to the balls of my feet hurt. The day is full of falling asleep and waking up and walking around.

This flat is a pin-drop fish tank. The feet walk over silk rugs, oak floor, smooth concrete, silk rug. A private alcove in the corner of the kitchen is utility booth. There is a window in this booth that opens up widely above a chasm. There's a drying pulley that stretches across to the opposite flat. The space is about six meters wide and an echoey, windless forty foot drop. The window opens wide, and the vanishing point seems alluring.

Tom keeps his wine in here. They're all twentieth century dates and dust. I am already half drunk on self-pity and hunger. The cork opens on my new friend, Bottle One. The kitchen sink is an archeological dig of meals eaten over a period of increasingly constrained budgets. Each plate reminds me of all the things that have happened since they landed in the sink. An impartial witness might see encrusted guacamole. I see months of emotional free-fall, a limitless horizon of self- examination and an empty-gut wish to reverse time by at least three months and best, twenty-two years. I drag a scum-glazed glass out of the sink and let loose a cloud of tiny fruit flies. Two hours later I'm asleep with Bottle Two in my arms.

I sleep like a sunken ocean liner. At some point, I wake to find my teeth as dry as cuttlefish and my nose cemented. Wheeling along with painful footsteps, I go into the sitting room. It seems to have changed. There is a single round footstool in a completely empty space, and infront of that, I could swear there is a small girl. She's not on the stool, she's sitting on the ground, with her hands on her eyes and her head crammed down. Her knees shine in the light, they're muddy.

I realise that I'm still asleep. And this is me.

Little Me is three and a half. She's confused by the events that crush in on her and she doesn't understand, so that's why she's sitting like that. The instinct is to go cuddle her but she doesn't want that, she just needs me to tell her that someone is here. There's a kind of dark spectre floating above her, all judgement and hostility, threats and death and scary possibilties. She's frightened of it. I am still terrified of it. It's an act of bravery just to hold my bladder. I creep towards her and, standing with my back to her, try to create a shield with my hands to surround her. Each swish of my palms paints a shining white stroke. It either took no time, or forever. But the shield was meant to protect her. I hope it does.

Then I get a drink and go back to bed. After such a strange event I'm surprisingly calm, except that I jerk and clutch my water into my face. Fighting ghouls to protect my inner child only goes so far with me, so it seems.

In the morning, I open my eyes to a sun-filled room and discover that the wine bottle has been pulled onto my face and all over Tom's white coir bedding.

The sitting room is normal; no child, no footstool, no spectre, no shield. The flies, thought, have multiplied. They're tiny and fat with maroon bodies and yellow eyes. I get to work with a handy magazine but after another hour, they're no longer landing on flat surfaces. Instead, they queue on wall corners where I can't get them. Are they super-intelligent? Telepathic? In terms of evolution where generations turn over once a day, am I creating a master-race? After twenty days I will have regressed to a twitching magazine-flapping fly swat. The flies'll be ordering organic merlot online. Traffic rumbles, emergency sirens holler, a drill cranks. My tummy groans.

I sniff the wine-stained coir mulch. Would it stew up? I go and get a new duvet and hey! There's a big bowl of white rice in the airing cupboard. It's wrapped around my mobile, still trying to dry it out.

A watched pan of rice never cooks, I remind my salivating eye-balls. But at last, my hand shovels rice topped with brown soup to the back of my throat. I make sea-faring noises. Once the initial eating compulsion has passed, my free hand tries my phone and it switches on, just like that! Like a cresting wave, messages roll in. The first twenty-five are from my mother.

My mother is so conflicted she could set her own perm with purest anxiety. Cursed with 38-22-36 credentials, in 1976 my mother (against her better judgement) was voted Miss Portsmouth and then Miss Hampshire. My father was on the panel. She was unable to advance to Miss England, due to her suddenly contracting a pregnancy. God only knows how that happened. My father has often hinted at the surprise he felt when he realised his pneumatic wife was a prude.

My mum left her pharmacology doctorate and within a month went from counting the enzymes on the coating of tissue cultures to counting paired socks. She really does, especially under pressure, count things. It's marginally better than rocking backwards and forwards, glassily repeating 'Why? Why?'

Her motherly advice to me was often warped by a logic that saw filth in everything. One example: 'When a lady undresses of a night, she must hide her panties and brassiere under her day clothes in case her husband should see them and be shocked.'

Go Mum!

(I do actually hide my underwear, though. To not do so would make me feel grubby.)

So, thoughtless marrying can be a curse, but with my father it's a contagion. Maybe I should call and apologise again. That was the angriest I've heard Dad ever be, since that time during his fiftieth birthday when I got right royally smashed (after witnessing Tom and Lizzie snogging). I stood up to 'dance' to 'I Fought the Law', broke my own table, smashed the crockery on the table, broke someone's glasses and threw myself out. I'm glad I'm not like that anymore.

More messages arrive like eggs from the mobile phone chicken.

Beep... 'Miriam, it's Lizzie. Call me, Slaphead.'

Beep... 'You didn't call. I am affronted.'

Beep... 'Hi Slapper. Still no hear, are you dead? If so, can I have the rocking chair in your bedroom?'

Beep... 'Miriam, it's me again. Have you heard from Signe?'

Beep... 'Look. Signe's gone missing and Inga's gone loopy. That Samson guy's staying with her. It doesn't look good.'

Now an interesting Thames estuary, Spiders From Mars accent. Am I being nagged by David Bowie? No, it's Tom. 'Just reminding you to quit by Sunday. Keys go back to the caretaker.' Apart from being partly hysterical, these messages are all historical. At last, today's messages. Good luck comes in threes.

Beep...Miriam, it's Tateh. I want to let you know how concerned we are about you. You are a very loving girl, but you can also inconsiderate and contrary to those who worry about you the most. I have placed three hundred pounds in your account and I'm about to try your landline.'

If ever a message can turn a person into an electron of reaction by sending me in every direction at the same time it's this one. My father only ever approaches me with grim warnings and a long stick with money attached.

Meanwhile, the messages continue.

Beep... 'Er. Miriam. It's Wym. Can we talk?'

Beep... 'Miriam, it's Wym again. Please, have you seen Prop?' Doesn't he realise I've run away? Does he think I've eloped with his father?

Beep... 'Miriam. It's Wym again. Please call me back. We've lost Prop.'

Is this a clever ruse to make me call him? Using his father as bait would be an unWymly thing to do.

I call and call and call.

57. Heart Disease

Once upon a decade ago, it was easy to get guys to look at me. They did it when I wasn't trying. Then after a while, I did try but only a bit. Now I try like mad and I'm ignored. Right now I'm in a fetish shop in Soho. I notice that I'm surrounded by a lot of embryo girls in skimpy tops and that the only person looking admiringly at me is me, whenever I find a mirror, so as to check I haven't warped into a wizened crumpled hag.

But I'm not really shopping, I'm actually hunting for a crumpled grandfather.

It started like this.

I repeat-dialed Wym most of the evening. The story of my life, a good man forever engaged (if not already married). My mind throws me flashcards of gore. I've already given Prop up for dead, but what about Wym. Why isn't he calling back? Is he OK? Has he any history of heart-disease? I imagine him lying belly-up with his tongue hanging out.

I try Signe. No answer from her either. Is she OK? Has she slipped in the bathroom? Why do I visualise blood-splattered tiles and single-woman-alone-pregnancy-horror headlines?

Now a desperation to know what's going on has me by the neck but it's just ignorance on top of ignorance. Six hours go unslept. I veer from circling agitation to self-obsessed gloom. No-one's returning my calls because I don't count. I don't count because I'm an idiot. Why am I so unlikable? I think I'm one of the nicest people I know! Despite my behaviour, my heart has always been in the right place. But anyone can say that. Even Hitler thought his heart was in the right place.

Wallowing is a comforting way to waste a morning; there's a kind of Calvinist purity about it. I don't need other people, I'm happier when they aren't forcing their stupid expectations on me and making me all tense and sweaty. I won't miss humans one little bit. But I will miss love.

In between times, I call Signe, I know she can hear me as she never goes out. She is properly anti-social, a fine trait for a social-worker. After seven tries, the phone is picked up!

'Hirrow?'

My first thought is that Signe has had a stroke.

'Hello?'

'He-irrow.'

'Who is this?'

There's a bit of breathy huffing.

'Is it Milliam?'

'Min? Is that you?'

'Herrow Milliam. We've been eating basgetti.'

I hear a snatched 'Give me that!'

'Signe? What's going on?!'

'You tell me, Miriam! You never mentioned that every person within five miles is certifiable.'

'Well, they can be a little...'

'At seven-forty this morning, Kit arrived on my doorstep with his kids and ran off without them! You haven't told anyone I'm a social worker, have you?'

'And didn't he say anything?'

'Just some nonsense about a crisis and he'll be back later.'

'Oh dear.'

'And the kids, I hate kids.'

'Well. It's good to practise, what with your condition.'

'I made them spaghetti. I even whizzed up the sauce. They've spent an hour sifting and picking out every strand of vegetable. I cook a proper nutritious meal and they're acting like forensics at a mass grave.'

I can see that between pregnancy and the future, Signe will have to give birth to a nervous breakdown before she can ever be a groovy mum.

So Kit's back in town. I decide to ring his bell.

'Hello Kit!'

'Miriam, sorry about this morning. But you know, with the way things are...'

'Oh, I heard. I'm sorry for your loss.'

(I recall that Prop's will with my added swindling signature will come into effect any time now.)

'Wym and Anna are in town. Everyone else is scattered about in the woods and fields. We called the police.'

'The Police? Good God, how did he die?!'

'Erm. He isn't dead, Miriam. At least, we hope not.'

'Oh.'

'He's just missing.'

'Oooh. Ok, I take back what I said about being sorry. At least, I am sorry, but not for your loss.'

'He is lost.'

(Damn, Miriam, reclaim the higher ground, somehow.)

'How are the kids?' He continues.

'I don't know, I'm in London.' (Yay, crawling upwards!)

'But...'

'But what?'

'I saw you! I spoke to you!'

'No! Do you remember my sister? Well, you flung the children at her and shouted gibberish over your shoulder as you ran away.'

'Oh shit!'

'Which you know, Kit, is a useful metaphor for how you carry on your life.'

Kit clears his throat.

'Signe could be coping.' I say 'Her shrink said she should be able to cope, if she tries to remember that the kitchen knives can't actually talk to her.'

'Are you in London?'

'That's what I said.'

Kit stops talking for a second and I hear Norfolk noises; birds twittering, breezes blowing, police radios crackling. 'Miriam.'

'Ye-es?'

'About a week ago, Prop said he was going to go up to the club in London to meet a friend. Well, all his friends are dead and The Arundel's been seriously re-packaged. It's still a men-only club but not the kind that gives out its number. So, anyway, I just smiled and nodded and forgot about it. But, he's taken his best suit, so there is a chance he could be there.'

'In the club?'

'In Soho. Meard Street. Was called The Arundel. It's now called...well I don't know what it's called and I can't ring. It's private.'

'Can't you get the police to go around?'

'I'd like to keep this low-key if possible.'

'But there's also a good chance he could be in the fields around Toft Hall?'

'Yes. Or in Toft Monks. Or Beccles. Or Norwich.'

'In fact, any of the fields in Norfolk.'

Or, think I, dragged under the chicken house after being eviscerated by inch-long ruby-red fingernails.

'How's your mother taking this?' I ask.

'Not well. I just told her to pray to St Anthony and hope for the best.'

'So, I'm going to a gay bar?'

'Yes.'

'In Soho?'

'It's where all the best clubs are. And Miriam, I owe you one.'

'Oh no! Really, I don't want anything you could possibly owe, Kit. This one's on the house. As it were.'

58. Magnolia

Meard Street is fooling itself into thinking it's more than a back-alley; what the more sophisticated cats call Mews. There are big doors leading to slightly basemented rooms. Most windows are frosted. There are few signs. It's a bit lurky.

Three Meard Street has a black hi-gloss door with a tiny panel that reads 'Members only admitted. All other callers to rear entrance.' There's a big brass knocker so I grasp it and pump at the door. The crashing sound amplifies inside. My chutzpah fails as I wait in front of the eye-hole and the knocker. The knocker is long and chunky, and hits two –

Oh. My. God.

It's a massive willy. Or 'Dong' might be more appropriate (if appropriate is the word). The skin on my hand blushes. Ugh ugh!

Then I take a photo of it. That's going to be my new phone icon! I'm just wondering where to go next when at last, footsteps. Sneakers on wood. The door unbolts and swings.

It's a man. A boy to be truthful, he's very slim and lithe. Maybe he's the son of the owner. Probably not.

'I'm looking for a man.'

He smiles knowingly. 'Uh-huh? Ah-ny man or ay specific man?'

He's an exotic boy.

My explanation is a failure so I'm invited down to the reception.

The first thing is the smell – funk. The lobby is disturbingly dark; lots of wooden paneling. You can almost see the Old Boy's club trapped behind the expensive fushsia flock wallpaper. It's the architectural equivalent to seeing a Tory politician in a PVC gimp suit. There are leather seats and tables with bowls of condoms. The walls have life-sized brass-rubbings of spartan men. Spartan men wrestling, spartan men washing each other, spartan men... Oo-er.

Smiling boy goes into an adjoining room and brings out a nice, clean-looking chubby man in pink cashmere.

'Strangely enough, there was a funny old fellow here yesterday evening.' says Pink Sweater Man.

'Very well-presahved for hes age.' Says Bimbino.

'But not a Lord Anybody, at least he looked a bit like a tramp.'

'So much for his best suit!' I mutter

'He was complah-tely lost. We tried to invite him in.'

'But the old chap seemed a bit put out.'

'We were busy, a lot of clients were signing in.'

'He took off, at speed.'

I know how fast Prop can speed.

'He thought it was the Arundel.'

Pinky is apologetic.

'The Arundel closed some twelve years ago. We are The Magnolia!' I look around. Nothing about this place says Magnolia. Pinky shows me out of the front entrance. He could be a nice accountant or a self-employed architect.

'I did ask him where he was going. He said:

'"Where d'you think? Bally London Zoo". But I don't know, where could he be now?'

Gay-Club Accountant grips my arm and hands me a creamy card; magnolia-coloured. 'There's our number. Call me when you find him. But, please if you could not hand the card to anyone else. Our club is strictly by invitation.'

I wonder back along Wardour Street. I'm a bit out of my depth in this part of town. I've set my gaydar to max but the mix of faceless private clubs and heady dens of intrigue I find a bit perplexing. Or latexing.

First I ask at every shop if they've seen a smelly old Lord in tweeds. All I get are creased brows. This job is hampered by its in-built glitches; no-one believes me or understands me. It takes ages and my search is scattergun and unrefined tactics. I try to think like a detective and become more discerning. From now on, the only shops I enquire in are shops with stock that interests me. This one is called 'Pony Girl' and is a fetish shop. Leather? Tick. Rubber? Tick. Tickling sticks? Tick tick tick.

Once the girl has served the tittering Japanese tourists, I do my rehearsed spiel, which tries to deliver the Prop story in as précis-ed but credible a way as possible.

'Oh right.' (She's from New Zealand). 'So, old bloke? In, like, this hairy suit? He was a lovely guy.'

'He was here?! Really?'

'Yee-ah. Late last night though. He wanted a fetish doll.' The girl points to a display of carved African figures.

'Theyah jis display. I tried to explain. Then he said if he danced for me, could I give him the doll? Then he did this crazy nuts dance.'

'What was the dance like?'

'Just some foot-stamp thing. Nuts.'

'He's just an old guy!'

'I know. Security showed him out.'

'Weren't you concerned?'

'In this shop, if I was concerned for every weirdo, I'd lose my job.'

I keep walking. This is ridiculous. Prop is lost. I don't know where he is. I don't know where he's gone and I don't know where I'm going. I don't know where my life is going. I am lost. I should be looking for me, not him.

London's still far too hot. Four months of top-oven temperatures have singed the streets; the air is exhausted. I wish to be back in Norfolk. From my lips to God's ears, my pocket starts to vibrate. It's Wym, sounding tired.

'So, you've not found him?' I ask

'No.'

'Neither have I.'

'I didn't know you were even looking for him. Where are you?'

'Still in London.'

'Why would Prop be in London?'

'Kit said something.'

'He did? He called you?'

'He needed childcare, and when he heard I was in London. Hasn't he spoken to you?'

I can almost hear Wym's mouth juggling in the distance. 'We haven't really spoken yet.'

'My God, your father's missing and you're still not speaking? You've got Norfolk and Suffolk constabulary on speed dial but you two can't bring yourselves to exchange a bit of information?'

Complete silence.

'Wym are you there?'

'Yes.'

'Just give me a few clues. Where does your father like to go in London?'

'I don't know. It's not the sort of thing he'd tell me.'

'Can't you think of anywhere?'

'The last time he did this...'

'The last time?'

'Yes, a few years ago, he went missing in London, he was found camped underneath the George and the Dragon statue beside Regent's Park. It may be worth looking.'

'Why did he go there?'

'He just said it was safe. I don't know why, I didn't ask any further.'

'Listen, Wym. William. I hardly know you or your family. But you've got to do something about this relationship thing, before before you regret it.'

Static and silence.

'Miriam, thanks for your help. You don't need to really, Anna's running everything to do with the search. She's very, very able.'

59. Crocodile

There's a distasteful sense of point-scoring going on here. I bet Anna's calculating her odds as she organises the hunt. And as for Kit not talking to Wym? Well, Kit's a player. This shameless profiteering could be a new Endemol game show; 'Pensioner on the Run. Find him and live off the gratitude forever!'

However, I know that if I find Prop, it will get me one step closer to the Nobel prize that I once wrote an acceptance speech for when I was twelve.

The London air is thick with carbon. On the march along Marylebone Road, I count three women shopping in bikinis. No wonder Prop is AWOL. Follow the trail of G-strings and I bet I'll find a Lord clog-dancing for all he's worth.

My phone Wyms.

'Hi Miriam, no luck here still. Anna's now on a train to London!'

'But, but I'm searching here! And I'm doing a good job too!'

'But you haven't found him.'

'No'.

'I've given Anna your number.'

'Gr..ate' say my teeth.

The statue of George and the Dragon is on the furthest side of Regent's Park. The bronze raptor/Saint battle scene is cast away on an island of grass in a dual-carrigeway. I can see why Prop felt safe here. I do a wide sweep and see he's not there. I double back. This is impossible, ludicrous, hopeless. A search party may as well just stay in one place and watch the world pass just in case Prop swans by. I walk up the road, following a school party; a wriggling, giggling crocodile of grins. I soon find that I've unconsciously tagged on at the end. My phone shivers but it's a number I don't recognise.

'Hello?'

Lots of crackle and static. And the background sound of a train.

'Miriam?'

It's bloody Anna, microwaving her smirk across the networks.

'I'm coming to London.'

'Sorry, can hardly hear you.'

'Wym doesn't want to bother you any further, he's told me to take over from you.'

'Sorry, I didn't get that. Wym says, "Anna, screw who?"'

'No, Miriam! I said I'm coming into London. Where have you looked, where are you looking?'

'Well, I'm just going to Shepherds Bush Market. Prop likes...bush meat.'
There's a crackle on the line.

'Say that again?'

'Bush meat. Monkey, elephant. He told me he spends whole hours there. Reminds him of Kenya, long-tall-grasses and all.'

The school party cut back into the park, between the high fences of the zoo and the rowdy playing fields, I have football boys braying in one ear and monkeys whooping in the other.

'Rea-lly?'

'Yah! I was just going to look there.'

'Shepherds Bush?'

'Market. Look for the exotic meat table. Ask for a Crocodile sandwich. And Anna...'

'Yes?'

'Better make it snappy.'

The kids are just the cheeky monkeys I like, yellow reflective tabards hanging off their jiggling shoulders. When we reach the turnstile, my phone call is long-over but I keep the mobile clamped to my ear. The last two boys are dawdling, so I chivvy them along. Squeak and I'm through the barrier! Hurrah!

But, uh-oh, hold on. There are staff-members stamping everyone in. And there's a teacher. This is more organisation than I'm used to. I try to look inconspicuous behind the kids but they're only tiny. I try to move away from this kettling area but a lady stops me with her arm.

'I'm just going to the toilet!'

'Can you just wait with your class, Madam, until all the children are checked in?' The teacher frowns over at me. Oh no. The children all turn to stare at me. Oh no.

Suddenly I sense shame. They're looking at me as if I'm the sort of idiot that would break into a zoo. Then I realise that some criminal lunatic has taken over my body and I have actually broken into the zoo.

'She's not with us. That lady is not with the school.'

Instantly the staff lower their eyes and approach. A gorgeous guy in a London Zoo security jacket beckons me. 'Can you come with me please.'

My facial blood-vessels fill with lava. The kids sound like they're hissing but it's the effect of thirty-two children whispering 'Who's she?!'

I'm lead through the rambling pathways and bushes. I cannot bear to look at anything but my feet. Visitors turn as I plead my way through small-talk.

'I don't normally do this sort of thing!'

'Of course, Madam.' He keeps his eyes away from me.

'I just love animals. And I have no money!'

'Even Animals have to eat, Madam. This is a charity. We only just scrape even as it is.'

Now I feel worse. I'm an ignorant zoo-breaker who starves endangered animals. We go around the back of kiosk, through a locked gate and inside a black door, marked private.

60. At the Zoo

I can't help it. When I'm tense I involuntarily sing.

'Someone told me it's all happening at the zoo. I do believe it. I do believe it's true.'

The dishy guy asked me to sit. Then he shuffled around a bit. Then he popped his head out of the door and muttered to someone. There was on-going muttering. Then the Dish left me on my own.

'The monkey stands for honesty, giraffes are insincere.'

It's a small, white-walled room with one barred window. Apart from the desk it looks like a cell. A barred cell-like room in a zoo, who woulda thunk it?

At last an older zoo-security guy comes in. 'OK then. My colleague tells me you're ... an animal-lover?'

'I am I am. I used to nurse injured animals!'

'Well,'

'The neighbourhood kids used to bring me damaged squirrels and things with sickness!'

'Well, we're having a bit of a mad day as it happens. If you've got enough on you to make up the entry fee, we'll turn a blind eye to what just happened.'

'Oh.'

'You don't have any money?'

My shaking head makes him frown and back out.

Security Dish comes back in with a glass of water. He takes my name. He asks me to spell it. He takes my address. He comments that 'Signe' is a very unusual name. Dish takes the form away and I'm alone again. Outside, children shriek. Birds squawk. The room is airless. There are two posters on the wall. One has a picture of a crowd of penguins. One penguin says to another 'But which ones are the waiters?' The other poster says 'Intruders, thieves and vandals are always prosecuted.'

I drink my water. When I'm tense I make drinks involuntarily jump down my chin.

Nothing happens for an unbelievably long time. The strip-light hums. It almost seems to be humming 'Down By the Sally Gardens.' I sing along for a bit. The door is slightly ajar so I go and peep out. There's a fire-exit open at the end of a deserted corridor. I could just leave. Maybe they want me to leave? That humming is louder now, only the song's changed.

It's 'The Last Rose of Summer.' I take an echoing step out of my cell.
There are a number of identical doors, all identically ajar. 'The Last Rose
of Summer' is definitely coming from the room next door. The first thing
to appear are two conker-toed brogues. Then tweed legs. And the rest, a
broiled, starved, abused, parched, seated Prop.

'Prop!'

The leap I make on him lands a little too heavily. He seems to have
withered in the space of two days.

'Prop! Where've you been? Everyone's going crazy looking for you!'
His eyes are milky and unfocused. He doesn't know me. The door of the
cell opens and it's Dish. 'Madam, you shouldn't be in here. This man's
sick.'

'But I know him!'

'You do?'

'In fact, I came here looking for him.'

'Why didn't you tell us that then?'

'I thought...'

Well, actually I don't know what I thought. I just don't like telling the
truth, even when it's out there.

Dish bobs down and taps Prop's arm, enunciating at a precise pitch.
'Sir? Do you know this lady?'

Prop tilts his head at me, nonplussed. He's still in his tweed jacket, his
face is burnt and scratched. 'He is forgetful.' Dish purses his lips.

'Do you know her, Sir?'

No. The lights aren't on. There's definitely no-one at home. My face
explodes into a blush. Fate and Karma are pointing and laughing at me.

Prop's expression reminds me of an episode of The Sky at Night,
where the world spins very slowly in darkness. Then gently and very
gradually, light starts to creep until the planet shines at last.

'Oh Miriam!' Prop turns and laughs at Dish. 'It's Miriam, Marjory's
niece.'

Dish shakes his head. 'She's called Sheena.'

Oh shit.

'Oh dear, Prop! I did say that. I said I was Signe.'

Dish's jaw drops. 'Prop? You just called him Prop?'

'Yes!'

'He said his name was Prop but he was so confused. We couldn't trace
him.'

Dish takes me to the front office to fill in forms. Apparently Prop was
spotted on CCTV, leaning over the wall of the lion exhibit most of the
day but by night he seemed to have gone.

'But where did you find him?'

'Asleep in the shrubbery near the lion enclosure. In the undergrowth. He'd spent the night there.'

Oh. Poor old Prop.

'Was he in the long, tall grasses?'

'Er. Yes.'

With my scant nursing training, I'm able to convincingly call into question the zoo's level of primary care. In this heat, Prop's still wearing tweeds and deer-stalker. He's dehydrated. When I whip his hat off, a massive purple bruise beams from his forehead.

'Ah-ooo,' responds Dish.

They agree to call an ambulance and within half an hour, Prop and I are dashed (and gridlocked) through cloggy London streets, in the Sound of Sirens, to North-West London NHS Trust.

Later, my Nobel Prize speech.

'So, Wym. Any luck?'

'No, none. I'm really starting to worry, Miriam, especially if you've had no leads either.'

'Weelllll...'

I swagger theatrically outside A&E, feeling one million feet tall. 'I've... found...him!' Long drawn out silence. 'Wym? Are you there?'

'Yes!'

'And you're happy?'

'I'm amazed!'

From my high moral pedestal, I'm able to disseminate news of Prop's scan and the likelihood of a few night's stay in hospital. Wym sounds like he's pacing around. Then I think he's crying quietly, I think. It's hard to tell.

Prop's been taken to the ward candidly named 'Geriatrics.' I find him sitting at the side of his bed while a nurse moves his torso to a more 'institutionally-friendly' position.

'Hello Miriam! We're having such fun!' he waves. The nurse wrapped around his pelvis may beg to differ as she heaves Prop one good ol' imperial inch left. Suddenly the lightest and gentlest of crunches.

The pelvis nurse recoils. She scampers backwards, holding her face.

Oh. Shitting. God.

A load of slurry passes like a shock wave across the room, greeted with 'Urghhhhs!' and 'Yuuuuuuks!'.

'Ah!' says Prop.

He reaches into his tweed pocket and withdraws crumpled eggshell.

'Forgot I picked it up before I went to the station. Amazing really they can last so long. Eggs are clever!'

61. Leverage

The line hisses.

'Oh hello Anna. How was Shepherds Bush Market?'

'I know you've got him. You send me to that filthy place because you knew he was at the zoo!'

'No I didn't, it was a complete fluke...'

'Flukes don't happen, especially not in London. So why did you want to find him before me?'

'Why did you want to find him before me?'

'Because I don't consider him particularly safe in your care!' I drop my phone which has the duel benefit of ending the call and bursting Anna's eardrum.

To have leverage over Wym is satisfying. I can ration him with update nuggets but, truth is, there's only so much that can be got from sunburn, dehydration, topical bruising and late-onset dementia. Prop is to spend the night in one of the most sought-after hospital beds in North London. Meanwhile, I go home for the night, chivalrously accompanied by Prop's rancid tweed suit in a see-through bag. At North Acton tube, the officious-looking black lady guarding the gate is never going to let me slip past her. I have an uncanny sense that whatever serendipity mill I've been plugged into, it's run dry. I blame my unlucky knickers – I've been wearing them two days straight. My free- riding life is over. A long, long walk home follows.

Through Wormwood Scrubs Park, past Linford Christie Stadium, eventually cornering Hyde Park where a man stands on a box, lecturing through a loud-speaker to an audience of no-one. (It's funny how opining on your own means imminent sectioning but with another person for company, it's a debating team and dreams of political leadership).

After Hyde Park, my feet swell into hovercraft. In my ballet flats, with sweating tweeds polywrapped over my shoulder, I feel a direct connection with those who tracked herds across continents ten millennia ago. Tweed, after eight miles, is heavy. I pass a Sue Ryder shop in Notting Hill, then double back. As I open the plastic back, it burps at me. Quickly emptying the suit pockets in one breath, I dig out some papers, seven pounds in the form of change, a cake wrapper, a yellow comb, a train ticket, a hankie with a sucked toffee and finally, crumpled egg-shell. I deposit the bag and eggy condensation on the counter of Sue Ryder's, warning the lady that 'despite smell and colour, it's top quality Henry Poole winter tweed.' and then eggsit smartly.

Huntley Street still emits an oatcake silence of affluent austerity. My feet throb on the concrete-effect floor. My soles are pure endorphin. This going-back-to-basics may be emotionally grounding but it's going to kill me before I reach Nirvana.

The papers from Prop's inside pocket are sitting on the kitchen table in a hill of cake crumbs and lint. Over a dull cup of tea, I open up a folded paper and discover it's a letter. The paper is thin, the blue ink is faded, the writing very tightly spaced but I am an ace at quickly reading documents that are not meant for my eyes. I take it to the light and squint.

Dear Edward, Father,

I hope this letter finds you well.

It is with great sadness that I send you news that my mother, Lovelace has died. She suffered a great deal in the end and is now, thankfully, at peace. She had a long life, was a devoted mother and never took another husband. With your support we lived comfortably and received good Christian educations. My sisters Amelia and Delilah have married and have moved from Kiamatura. My youngest sister Edwina is a doctor in America. I myself am a nurse and trained in Nairobi. Now that mother has passed, there is nothing to keep me here. I am coming to England in September on holiday and would like to see you, to carry to you the immense love that my mother maintained all these many years, even when it became plain that you would not return to her. Although her body stayed well until her final years, her heart was broken and did not mend.

Please accept this letter of friendship from your obedient oldest daughter,

Victoria

62. Creatures of the Night

I put down the letter. My heart is hammering. I read the letter again.

Possible expanding storylines start to run away from this letter in all directions. I have been given a peep behind a curtain that hides an Oxford Circus of emotion and heartbreak. I'm not sure if it's a scene I want to watch so quietly close the metaphorical curtain and move away.

At 3:30pm North-West London Hospitals N.H.S. Trust (Geriatrics) ring to say they've found a consultant with a pen and now Prop is discharged. My hovercraft feet are forced back into the ballet-flats and walked the five miles to pick up Clio.

I don't knock on Dad's door.

Prop stands in a day room in a teal-green polyester suit. With his round-neck collar and braces, he looks like the saddest, most uncomfortable New Romantic in town. He shuffles slightly.

'They gave me a bed bath.'

I fold Prop into the front seat of Clio, then stop at a garage and fill her tank. I have to work hard to use the bankcard. I realise with a lurch I've not used it since Chap Previous, the pin is his date of birth. Prop continually shifts his arms uncomfortably. A philanthropic urge makes me want to buy him a new suit. I know just where to go.

Prop shines like glory as I help him into a beautiful Henry Poole tweed. He steps out of the changing room and inspects himself with a cluck of pleasure. Sue Ryder have done a great job. His old suit looks almost new, I doubt it's been steam cleaned before. The frayed sleeves are darned and the baggy trousers pressed. What a gentleman! Cheaper than dry cleaning, you know AND Sue Ryder got a teal-green suit out of it!

7 pm. Prop and I break through the M25 bubble and head North East. He snores his upper false teeth out of his mouth. I try to imagine him as the virile young man who captured the everlasting love of Lovelace. But that long nose, those ears, the dropping eyelids must have been there from the outset. As far as seeding goes, he was a poor specimens of the breed. As am I. This morning at Hammersmith, I removed Clio silently. This will make Vivien worry because she'll think the car's been stolen and that'll annoy Dad. I should have just taken a deep breath and gone to see him. But cut me in half and you'll see the words 'Coward' drilled

through me, as well as a PS of 'Hey, why did you cut me in half? And stop with the drilling already!'

I tried being a truthful person when Dad lived with Mum, back when I was five. But I discovered that if I told the truth, they tended to shout more.

One time, I came back from school to find the house empty. A man came to see Dad. I asked him to wait and placed myself in the role of 'elegant hostess'. I tied a pinny around my waist and poured him a tall glass of whisky. That's the kind of thing Dad did. Dad still didn't come back so I poured another. And another. Then Dad did come back but it seemed my hostessing had damaged the man. Dad shouted at him and the guy left, falling off the doorstep and crawling to his car. My mum came home and shouted at Dad for leaving me on my own. I confessed about the whisky. I thought that would redirect their anger but it didn't, it just made it worse.

Somehow my parents always seemed to bounce back. Then one morning we were going out for a nice day trip. My parents were having a low-level sniping match, so I took the lead and went out to sit in the car to wait. I sat there for a long time. At last, I felt something was wrong and sat immobile with terror for a while longer. At last, with a sense that the world was collapsing, I went back in.

The world had collapsed.

Dad charged out of the door with a bag over his shoulder, got into the car that I'd just got out of and left. If I had stayed in it, would he have taken me?

I found Mum in the utility area, folding towels. I went to my room, understanding nothing except that by going out to the car, I had made my parents split up.

Props wakes up and says 'I need to make water!'

In a pub on Pakenham High Street, Prop goes to make water.

In the pub snug, close to the fireplace, a letter and two half-pints of cider wait with me for his return.

He greets the drink like an old friend and is just about to start telling about the wartime airfields of Suffolk when I place the letter before him. The letter has almost no effect. Did I know there were nearly thirty RAF and US airfields in the county?

'Prop, I found the letter in your pocket.'

'Not including the decoy airstrips that were built on farmland.'

'PROP!'

I lean very close, speaking directly into his ear, as close to his temporal lobe as possible. 'I found a letter addressed to you, in your pocket. Shall I read it to you?'

I call the words and his hearing aid squeals back in reply but I don't know if the contents have hit home. In the end I just place the thin paper in front of him. He picks it up. I notice that the skin on his hands is similar to the paper, very crumpled, translucent, blue lined and fragile. His eyes are red; they look like they've had piping sewn onto their rims.

'Did I meet her?'

'I don't know, Prop. Can you remember?'

'I was going to meet her. I wrote her a letter and told her to come to the Arundel on Thursday at six. But she wasn't there.'

'Because the Arundel isn't there.'

'I was going to buy tickets for the zoo. Children like to see the zoo.'

He looks blankly at the letter. Poor Prop is shell-shocked. He has been through two recent wars, external and internal.

'Lovelace is dead it says here.'

'Yes. I'm sorry.'

'There was never a way to see her again.'

'No. I'm sorry.'

His cider goes untouched. In the end I drink his for him, and we go back to the car with the whole Lovelace subject buried in a mound of dementia.

I drive into the dusk, which brings out the zombie tractors of East Anglia. They comb the B-roads, looking for traffic to delay and drop poo on. It's after ten by the time I reach the winding, tree-shadowed, pot-holed drive of Toft Hall. The silhouettes at the front door are Wym and bloody Anna. For some reason, my heart is doing back-flips. Prop stares at his knees, sullenly. Wym doesn't look too pleased either. I wasn't expecting Little House on the Prairie but I was hoping someone would be happy to see someone.

Anna leads Prop directly inside; good, I didn't want to face her. I realise that I've been praying that my amazing act of kindness will leap me over the queue of waiting ladies if Wym ever frees himself from marital or proprietorial angst.

I bound out of Clio and hand him the letters from the hospital, but something makes me hold back the letter from Victoria, which stays in my jacket pocket. I want to be protect Prop, yet I'm not sure how to do this.

I note that Wym's jaw is grinding slightly.

'He's fine. He's had a wash and I dry-cleaned his suit.' I sparkle.

'Good-good. We'll take it from here.' He's avoiding eye-contact. Why?

'Wym. I'm sorry I left so suddenly. Are you upset because I know about...'

'No no. Everyone knows about Helena.'

'I was expecting...well, I thought you'd be happier to see me.'

'Oh, if you're looking for grateful, you'd better go and see Kit. He's in his room. Feel free.'

Wym steps to one peevish side.

'Why Kit?'

'But that's who you're trying to impress? Anna told me that Kit rang you about the Arundel Club; he gave you orders to run around there and you jumped to it. That's how you heard about the zoo visit and you've been able to find Prop. Because you want to please Kit. He's the one you really want.'

'Don't believe Anna!'

'Didn't Kit tell you about the club?'

'Yes.'

'And you didn't feel like sharing that information with me?'

'But I didn't do it for Kit, I did it, I did it for Prop!'

(Lame-lame-lame)

'Tell me something, Miriam. Do you care about Kit? Honestly?'

Big question. I can only be honest by pushing away the bear-traps I've put between me and honesty.

Kit is a player. He has a seduction manual with just two pages; self-pity and flattery. He may as well be reading directly from the page for all the individual attention he gives. His heart is pretty untroubled by love, unless you count self-adoration. Could I be lured back into bed by him? No. My heart and head are empty. Empty of him I mean. But wait, a tiny noise, there's a squeak from my pelvis.

'Hey! Not in our name, we think he's sexy!' Darn it. My pelvic region seems to run from some reserve brain, unconnected to the rest of me.

This thought process is unfortunate, and takes a bit too long for Wym. He gazes at me, his mouth a narrow, white line. He turns and walks in. I'm not invited.

63. Phobic

Here's a funny thing. I fully expected to come home in a blaze of glory. Instead, it's more of a pyre of shame.

Back onto the West Road and around to the lodge (because there is no way to get directly from the Big House to my place, unless me and Clio cut across the lawn. One day my precious, one day). But there's another car parked in front of the cottage. It's Mum's! But only George drives outside Basingstoke. I suddenly have a panic – I know I deleted about thirty messages on my phone from people who are not Wym. If George is here, that means I've ignored a crisis of some magnitude. I prepare my face with the 'serious' look and step into the sitting room.

There's something a bit grubby about coming into your own bulb-lit sitting-room to a wall of 'Lola, l-o-l-a, Lola' but with no apparent person in earshot. Luckily my imagination is saved by the appearance of Lizzie from the kitchen. 'Slap-Head! Where have you been?!'

'To London to see the Queen. Lots of queens, in fact. Where's George?'

'Don't you know? They're off to Cyprus for two weeks.'

'Oh. So what are you doing here?'

'My God, do you never look at your phone?'

'I have a recognised condition, which is a fear of mobile phones.'

'No you don't!'

'Yes I do.'

Now we spend twenty-five minutes looking for 'fear of mobile phones' on the internet, which turns into a fun-filled evening. Even Signe joins in. 'Glossophobia' is the fear of phones. Omphalophobia' is the fear of belly-buttons. The fear of dildos and vibrators is 'hexoponialphobia' (the fear of six-sided pony dildos?). Mediclorinaphobia is the 'fear of sour confectioneries' (but sounds more like something from Star Wars). 'Porphyrophobia' is a fear of the colour purple. (Take that, Alice Walker!)

Lizzie is here because Inga is worried about Signe and wants her well-being confirmed visually. By the number of wine bottles on top of the kitchen mantelpiece, I'd say Signe's health has taken a knock since Lizzie arrived.

But it's time for me to stake my place as pack leader.

'So where are you going to sleep, Lizzie Dearest?'

'Oh I brought the roll-up futon and my own sleeping-bag.' she grins.

'I came prepared.' (She always was an irrepressible, disgusting little Brownie Guide). 'So you can have the couch!'

'Heeeey! Now, wait a flippin' second. It's MY name on the sub-tenancy agreement! I can't help it if Signe gets herself knocked up and you decide to crash-land, but this is MY house!'

'No it's not!' This is Signe's now. 'It's Marjory Drummond's house. You're on a freebie!'

'I look after cats for her!'

'You killed one!'

'I didn't kill it!'

Lizzie steps in. 'Look Miriam, all we're saying is, you are a lovely lifelong ligger. So it's just a bit unfair to point out mild ligging in others.'

And so, the sofa it is. Climbing into my sleeping bag, I lie my brain down among the dog hairs. Before my eyes shut, my phone tries to trick me into answering bloody Tom's call – back in the UK I'm guessing, in London, in Bloomsbury, in his sitting-room, looking at the space where his bike was. No way am I answering. Honestly – if a robber wanted to steal his bike that badly, there's nothing I could have done to stop it. It's not like a window is going to deter a determined thief.

He tries again. I mean, the bike must be more than a year old. He should look at this as an opportunity to upgrade.

I switch my phone off. I try to straighten my head out before sleep but only end up feeling as if I'm inside a giant hamsterball, crashing around, thinking I know what's going on outside but in fact I'm simply trapped.

How does Wym really feel? Why won't he tell me what his problems are? Why does he even care if I have a theoretical thing for Kit? I could go and corner Wym, throw a net over him and force him to talk. But what if I've read him wrong? Maybe he thinks I'm a maniac, he might panic and head for the hills. At least it would be a clear sign. Maybe he does care? Maybe he cares very badly? I don't know. The idiot is incredibly hard to read. And what do I do with Prop's secret? Secrets are never left in my care; if they land on me by mistake, there must be a reason for it.

At last I dream. I dream I'm in Toft Hall. Every room has a different scene and as I run from floor to floor, I find ex-boyfriends hiding in different nooks. Chap First furtively offers me tiny tokens of our relationship, wrapped in tin-foil; an ear-ring, an old sweet, a ripped piece of fabric from an old shirt I once owned. Then Chap Previous tries to kill me, chasing me around with an old coat-hanger. Wym is in his room, tightening a belt on his trousers so fervently that I know he'll cut his blood off and strangle himself. Kit is bird and beeing it up with many and various faceless women. Prop sits at his window seat crying into a sock. Also, I'm accompanied by a massive polar bear.

Apart from the bear, the abiding memory is Prop. The sock I think contained his daughters and his marriage. Being trapped in Prop's sock must be Hell. I really think I should do something to help Prop but having learnt to my cost that helping Prop contravenes many Hebbindon family regulations. However, a family can't stay trapped in his sock like this. Something has to be done.

Dawn. I crawl out of my bag and go out in the road to allow my skin to breathe. I listen to the birds are doing their tweet chorus. The Good-Cat Historical is no more than a grease-spot. The leaves are yellowing, summer is fading. If ever a helpful girl should go see Prop, now is the time and I am she.

64. Care in the Community

Sneaking in to the Big House is not too difficult on account of the many points of entry. The easiest is usually the french window that opens onto the terrace. The Garden Room has two exits, a large official door with moulding and a brass handle which shuttles you to the large hall. But the second door is smaller, less gaudy and turfs you into a corridor. Creeping along and then pausing for a few seconds, bracing to jump behind bookshelves and then scuttling forward, means the journey of only fifty feet takes roughly ten minutes.

Prop's staircase is a service route, so narrow you could fit three of it inside the main hall staircase. The thought of this stairs creates images of servants with their calloused hands, and Prop, and his family, and his deserted family, and his narrow staircase. Everything combines into a fur-ball of unfairness that sticks in my throat. I wouldn't be able to explain my views in an argument but I reach Prop's room with the all rattiness of a Bastille stormer.

He's brandishing a double-edged razor against his neck. Prop gives a crow-like croak as he sees me.

'Hello, dear Miriam, hello.'

'Hello! Stop!'

'I'm shaving.' Prop nods charmingly with a set of bloody weals on his face. The dressing table is scattered with rusty double-sided razors blades and blotted hankies.

'Can I help.'

'Well you can, I suppose.'

On the sideboard is a bottle of witch hazel and a hankie. He was obviously expecting trouble. I spread the skin of Prop's cheek and blot the fresh blood away. The repairing of Prop is the first step of my helping regime.

'I brought your letter back.'

'Thank you. My letter?'

'From Victoria your daughter.'

'Victoria.'

Prop blinks as if distant lenses were being dropped over his eyes.

'I have many letters. In my...'

He leans over at the dresser and opens the narrow bottom left drawer. He brings out a sealed freezer bag and I would think it was the bodily remains of a favourite terrier if it didn't have 'Letters' written in large, loopy writing. Not his own, I feel.

'Who packed these?'

'Oh, Molly Perry. She occasionally gives them a dust.'

I make an involuntary shrugging flapping gesture with my hands as the sandwich bag of turmoil sits on my lap. Prop reads my dance of disbelief.

'Shouldn't she dust them?'

The paper is neatly stacked, edges slightly torn, some with grease spots. And the writing, so neat and tiny and restrained.

"May the grace and the love of God be with you, your wife in Christ, Lovelace."

'All these replies.'

'Oh no, not replies. My wife made her feelings known to me straight away. I made a promise never to write to her or speak to her again. But Lovelace continued to write and I'm glad she did.'

I wonder how he got the correspondence across the threshold, but when I turn the package over, I spot a blue air-mail envelope with the address of Mr Francis Perry. So, Prop schemed as far as he could, considering a dusting from Miss Perry as preferable to a dusting for fingerprints from the Marchese.

Suddenly my one-sided attachment to Chap One seems to fade compared to a lifetime of waiting. I imagine faithful Lovelace, not knowing, but hoping and dreaming all the same. Did she know that he did exactly the same thing, three thousand miles away?

'It must have felt wrong to leave her when you loved her?'

Prop shrugs an exhalation of half a dozen harmonics.

'Love is important.' I protest.

'People treat love in a different manner these days. Apparently love is sacred. Back then, the heart was irrelevant. And of course, love to you young people is a sexual thing. It doesn't mean faithfulness or comradeship. These days, people swap religion with love and one wears one's heart on a sleeve like bloody Camino pilgrims with shells. Except Kit. He wears his cock on his sleeve.'

Gosh. I've never spoken to Prop like this, and never ever about sex. He pronounces it 'six-yewl.'

'Love is a conceit and so is youth. Youth is just a mask that grows thinner and thinner until at last it falls off.'

The last tract is said in one breath that blows away and it feels like there's no inhalation. Prop's eyes glaze, the philosopher is on safari.

A burst of our bubble; Wym enters the room, elbows first. He's carrying a bin bag. When he sees me, he starts and stops at the same time.

'Miriam!'

'I came to see Prop'.

'Social Work are here in twenty minutes!'

There's panic in Wym's eyes. He takes an empty bottle of cognac from Prop's side table and drops it in the bottle and scrapes socks from the floor.

'Social Work are not the Panzer Division! You don't need to worry!'

'What would Social Work make of this room?'

I glance around, the lampshade is scorched black, on the point of burning the house down. Prop's African knife and spear collection is lagging off the wall but he'd probably reach for his shotgun first, that's in the corner. The razor blades and Prop's chin and shirt front are speckled with blood.

Wym hands me the bag. 'Could you just prime him? Mother's stalking the hall, I'm scared she's going to thump somebody.'

He leaves before I can explain that thumping hasn't really happened for about forty years.

A few minutes later with a clinking black bag, I follow down to the hall. It also contains a freezer bag stuffed with letters. I wink at Wym as I stuff the bag in the Garden Room.

Young Miss Perry motors around with dusters, sprays and a plastic bag tucked into her belt. She's taking this visit as personally as her employers are. The Marchese is doing a figure of eight.

'This is ridiculous.'

'It's their job, Mother.' says Wym.

At 11.12, two bland-looking women arrive. At least, their car does. They sit inside it for some while. Then they get out and gawp.

'For pity's sake. They're not even coming in.' The Marchese spreads the etch-glassed inner doors and barks. This makes the ladies scuttle dutifully, one being an anaemic social worker and the other, a occupational therapist in a uniform that fashionistas might call 'mal-wear'.

The Marchese repeats her views on the necessity of this visit.

Wym reaffirms the irksome nature of their job and the two ladies go into a well-worn double act, which only falters when they stare up at the hall, the grand split staircase, the turkey-red Axminster and the stuffed polar-bear shot by an ancestor and now discretely placed in an alcove where David Attenborough will never find it.

The ladies are here to check that their 'client', Mr Hebbindon, is able to carry out daily life-tasks around his home. At the end, he will be given a 'care plan' which will be actioned by a local team.

'How jolly!' spits the Marchese.

We troop up the stairs with Miss Perry polishing in our wake.

'A lot of stairs.'

'Oh, he doesn't use this one', says the Marchese. 'He has his own staircase.'

I was unable to hide the spear or the gun. Luckily, both ladies are already suffering from shock by the time they enter Prop's rooms. They crane at the suite. The ceiling stands at eleven feet. There is nicotine-yellow silk wallpaper, brass wall brackets, complicated, dust-coated cornicing, ceiling rose and a pendulous art deco light. Massive hardwood doors lead to changing room and bathroom. Paintings, tarnished gilt frames, holed recliner, sun-bleached cherry wood desk, ripped Edwardian cushions with escaping Edwardian wadding. At last the Health Pros spy something they recognise; a confused, lacerated, knock-kneed elderly gentleman.

Social Worker brings out her clip board. 'Hello Edward.'

'LORD HEBBINDON.' barks the Marchese.

'PROP!' says Prop.

'We're here to assess your CARE NEEDS.' says Health Pro Number One. 'First Edward. We'd like to see you RUN A BATH.'

Prop stares at me for confirmation.

Health Pro Number Two repeats 'Could you just run a BATH as you would NORMALLY?'

'Right-ho!' shrugs Prop. He goes over to the fireplace. There's a brass button on the wall. He glances at me before pressing it. Young Miss Perry bursts through the door.

'Moi Lrrrd?'

'Um.' says Prop. He's never done this for an audience I guess. 'Could you draw me a bath?'

In the kitchen Prop is asked to make himself a hot drink. Young Miss Perry virtually throws herself bodily between him and the kettle because it's 'Benaith 'is Larrdship's dignity to moike 'is own cuppa toy!'

For the Health Pros, it's like viewing an educational diorama of how foreign or ancient (or in this case, an entirely alien race of) people live their lives.

Meanwhile, Prop frets.

'Are they sending me to Carlton Court? Don't let them send me back to Carlton Court.'

'Where's Carlton Court?'

'Horrid place. People dying left right and centre, it's worse than the Congo.'

'But why?'

'When the Marchese pushed me down the stairs. When I broke my hip.'

What?! I turn and stare at the Health Pros, who surely must have view on this. I repeat what I've just heard out loud so as to give people a second chance to spot the clue.

The Occupational Therapist says, 'Carlton Court is a convalescent home. It's very good.'

'It's not where he's convalescing, it's WHY he's convalescing!'

'I did wonder about the stairs.' says the OT to her colleague.

Close but no cigar on this occasion, so I turn to face the Marchese and go for broke. 'Just 'cause you live on a country estate and not a sink estate doesn't erase your family's dysfunction! You know, if you didn't have a big house, you'd have all been in court facing charges of neglect a decade ago! I've never come across a worse set of relatives.'

Wym looks like he's about to offer an opinion but I get there first. 'And he's your father. You and Kit, Tweedle-Dum and Tweedle-Dee, fighting while your own father needs protecting. And you're so obsessed with who I'm sleeping with! Well I'm not sleeping with Kit, you pervert. I wouldn't sleep with him, your or any other person who shares at least half a genome with the Hebbindons!'

My rant dries, curtails and flops to the floor like a pancake. Wym tugs at his ear and says, 'Prop, tell Miriam why you fell down the stairs. Were you pushed?'

'Your mother was shouting.'

'Were you pushed?'

Prop adjusts the hem of his pants and mumbles, 'Don't recall.'

'You were carrying the virginal downstairs, weren't you!'

I gasp 'The virginal what?'

'It's a clavichord, like a spinet but smaller.'

'Hello?' I wave.

'Imagine a Yamaha keyboard, only painted with cherubs and incredibly old. A priceless heirloom that no-one would decide to lug down two flights of stairs from the attic on their own.'

'She pushed me.' growls Prop.

'She was trying to save your life! You were on carpeted stairs in your socks. You're lucky you broke just the hip. The virginal was a write-off.'

'People only cared about that virginal once I fell on it.'

The mute Health Pros watch the scene as viewers of a tennis match stare at a rally. They simply do not have the tick-boxes available to deal with Prop's situation. The thing is, there was always a care-plan for Prop from the moment he was born. If he looked like he was about to make his own decision, someone else swooped in to save him from himself.

65. Microscopic Love

The Health Pros are finally shown the exit, having rotated their heads off their necks. The Marchese swipes a wipe of her hands and returns straight back indoors. Wym gives the car a grim wave as it grinds away over the gravel. As the last blue puffs of exhaust disperse, he says 'I know it's not obvious but we're all very grateful you found Prop.'

'Not obvious? It's even not visible under microscope.'

'I know. I was feeling wary. You see, you Short girls are quite the man eaters.

'What?'

Wym's face shuffles a bit. I am not affronted, let's get that clear. I have heard some pretty disgusting misinformation about myself and my family and that's nothing compared to the truth.

'Your other sister was doing her best to reel in Kit last weekend.'

'I know Signe, she doesn't do that sort of thing. Anyway, Kit comes pre-reeled.'

Wym gives a slightly worrying George Bushesque blink. 'I met her tip-toeing out of Kit's bedroom on Sunday morning.'

'Oh.'

'Sometimes I ask myself, what brought you both here? Two attractive single women arrive at a place they have no connection with, and discover Kit and I, two single men!'

'What?'

'And it works. Before the month is over, apparently you've slept with him, so has Signe and I've kissed you.'

'WHAT?!' Oh God, he thinks we're a band of ninja gold diggers.

I see him back-peddling from mouth cul-de-sac. 'If you think we're rich, we're not. You might think that living in a twenty-one bedroom house is romantic, well, to own the truth it's a lead weight. The amount of badly-designed extensions and stupid guttering solutions; our roof has more valleys than the Himalayas. They even stuck one down pipe through the heart of the building, so imagine trying to fix that.'

My hand involuntarily bats my forehead.

'Wow! Talk about fucking first world problems, Wym! Have you actually heard yourself?'

'You don't have to empty the buckets in the attic when the rain's coming in. You haven't seen the scaffolding that holds up the laundry and the chipboard we use to cover the mould. If I sink a screw into the wall of the scullery, green slime seeps in through the hole.'

'And for this, you're warning me off, me the man-hunter? I should be flattered I guess, you're dressing me in organisation skills I've never had! If I did, I wouldn't be homeless, I'd have a legitimate bloody career! And I wouldn't even think about attaching myself to a Hebbindon when one of them's a twirling dick on a stick and the other one's an anal cavity in a hairshirt!'

My voice echoes back to me, I'm whooping like a wading bird. Anger always brings out my inner Joyce Grenfell. I've gone too far, but then so has he. I turn and go, conscious that Wym is watching me. My toes scuff together. I pass the stinking courtyard, green climbing its drainpipes, ferns rising from gutters. A pat-pat-pat of a leaking overflow, a squish of soaking moss on the ground. Yes, of all this I could be mistress.

Back to my lodge, I open the door to see blue-eyes and artful curls and a shockingly-expensive canvas utilitarian courier-bag from Muji. These visual clues all point to the fact that Tom is standing in my hall.

'What?'

'Hello to you too. I've come to see Lizzie.' I can see that, as she's attached to his body. Ugh ugh ugh. They are snogging. In front of me.

Tom is tall and rangy. This cottage is small, it was designed for people stooped from centuries of forelock tugging. Having every single sibling here, unprecedented as this might be, is impossible. We may as well try and cram into a Sylvanian Bunny Nest.

In looks, Tom's actually closer to Signe than myself, both being at the blonder end of the spectrum and sharing a lizard-like circulatory system. Signe is polite; friendly even. She has nearly no relationship with him. It was me, the uncomfortable middle child, who spent years straddling the gap, like a bridge between two separating continents. All I got was psychological hip-strain.

'What are you doing here?!' I cut in. 'You can't stay! We've got no room as it is.'

Chirrups Lizzie, 'He can sleep in my sleeping bag!'

Oh God alive, please no, no, no.

'You are joking, young lady!' I squawk

'Don't talk to Lizzie like that,' says Tom.

'I can talk to my sister any way I like!'

'No you can't,' yaps Lizzie.

'Anyway,' says Tom, 'I've got a bone to pick with you.'

'Look. The bike. It was left in a perfectly safe location.'

'What?'

Huh?' (Oops) 'OK so what were you telling me off for?'

'I said I'd be back on Sunday? Well today is Monday and you didn't leave the key with the porter.'

'Ah.'

'I rang you about ten times! What's up with your phone?'

Lizzie says, 'Miriam has tele-phoney-phobia.'

'What's this about the bike?'

'Hey! I know, let's all go to the pub. I've got money so I'll pay!'

That's me in the corner. That's me in the spotlight, feeling dumb, self-conscious and all the other things that my siblings do to me. The Red Lion is as full as I've ever seen it with a couple of old guys in one corner and some young ones in the other. The Darkness pipes on the CD player. Fat Terry leans walrus-like on the bar, nodding his chins at me.

'Awreighy?'

Conversation is punctuated by what can only be described as geographic tongue. Tom's not the sort of person to be emotional in public but he's making up for lost time now. Lizzie is soon drunk on love. Tom is drunk on jet-lag. I am drunk on vodka and sambuca.

Signe and I take up positions at the bar. I reason with her that Kit was not a man to play emotional footsie with, even if your feet were shod in steel-toed boots with cyanide on the tips.

'I'm not interested in Kit.'

'You were seen coming out of Kit's bedroom!'

'That doesn't mean I'm interested.'

'But every signal you're giving him translates as 'interest'.'

Signe shrugs my argument. Terry the barman joins in.

'Tha'at Chrih-stopher? Yew know what the joke is. That they'av blew plaahsters in th'office at Thurlton Proimary School, 'cos of the amoun o' blew blood in the playgroun.'

I notice the blond tips of Signe's eyelashes spread slightly. While she chews on the news, I ask Terry about the skeletons, especially the ones that litter the ground between Kit and Wym.

'Oh thaat. S'old news really. Just after Will'erm got maarried, Kit gets 'is end awoiy, loike, with the new missis, squired 'er on the very weddin' noight! Horny little shit. We niver thoughteed do that to 'is own brother. Not suurproisin'ly, they don talk much.'

'No wonder this family's fucked up.'

'Oh it were fuuhrked long afor. Bin fuuhrked santoories now.'

66. The Bail Out

I had a bad night's sleep.

I'm not going to tell you why because I'm traumatised and I don't want to take anyone else down with me. It's an ill wind that blows no good but I seem to be in a tornado of rubbish. I am itchy in my skin. My skin is clammy against the sleeping bag. My cottage is grubby. And finally, I am the Toft Hall blow-in, bringing no good to beast nor man. So these are the facts as I see them. Kit slept with Wym's wife. The Hebbindon's of Toft will never have a happy ending no matter how many Pimms parties, barbecues, croquet matches or barn dances they throw. Wym will not trust a single girlfriend while Kit lives in the UK, attached to his own gonads. And no matter what, if all else fell in my favour, he would always wonder if I was just a lousy gold digger.

Anyway, Lizzie and Tom 'slept' in the kitchen in front of the AGA. The sitting-room shares a wall with the kitchen. A speedy a.m. conference takes place in the bathroom between me and Signe. We're both leery of going into the kitchen to make tea, just.in.case. Signe's less repulsed than me. I can't help mentioning dueling banjos and the habits of small isolated fishing communities near Cape Wrath.

'Look. You're the only one who thinks of them as brother and sister. To everyone else, they're two unrelated kids who've managed to find love in this shit-encrusted pigsty of a family. You need to get over it. And by the way, you've got a massive zit on your chin.'

So, to summarise. Instead of me pointing out a situation that clearly stinks, I am part of the stink. The spotty part.

The news of the morning is that the Tom/ Lizzie mutual appreciation society is going back to London. I've decided I'm going to travel with them. Signe is content to to be the Short incumbent, our own 'local housing Shortage'.

This time I pack up all my things, which is about four things more than normal. The fridge bag of letters is also coming with me, only because I don't want to be caught slipping back into Toft Hall with them. I give the good cat and the bad cat a cuddle, and even pat the AGA. Once stowed in the back of Lizzie's car with the luggage, I watch as chocolate box East Lodge and insanely yellow Clio finally succumb to distance.

'This wasn't really the place for you, was it?' Lizzie smiles. 'I see you more as a city girl.'

'Yup, lots of new territory out there for Miriam,' says the back of Tom's head.

'You'll be glad to be home though.' Chirrups the driver.

Home. If she can find one, I hope she drops me at the door.

When I left the rectory, aged about seven, I wrote my name on every wall and inside every cupboard of the house. It felt like leaving a beloved womb. I did actually return a few times once I'd passed my test. I noticed that my wall scrawling meant an entire redecoration of the house, which saddened me. It covered over that lovely smell, like a vegetarian's fart. Those were puffs of gas from the blocked drains. The two farts I've never objected to were my own and this house's. But apparently the odour wasn't good enough for the new owners; they fixed the drains. They apologised for painting over my height measurements at the back door, and asked me never to come back.

I mentally farewell everything I see. The roundabout with its hidden church and McDonald's drive-thru, then past Gillingham and its car boot acreage. Now over the bridge to Beccles, the living Gainsburgh film set. I sit in the back of the car outside the supermarket while Tom and Lizzie buy car journey food. The market square is already in motion; pink, chubby, affable Beccessians are pushing prams and buying veg and sitting under trees. The safety of a backwater is this, you do move but in slow circles, recapitulating to a life you recognise. Why shouldn't this be the place for me?

Back en route, I try to navigate Lizzie around the one-way system but Tom is unwilling to let me give any advice, even with reason on my side. We pass the train station. My attention is caught by a lady waiting for a taxi. She is large and black. The ethnic diversity of Suffolk falls well below the UK average. A bold-looking black women does draw the eye.

My perfectly good back-seat driving is thrown slightly by an inability to tell left from right. Tom advises me to stay silent.

Although autumn is very much on the cards in Beccles, the warmth and dust in the air is a summer byproduct. We sweep past the station for a second time. The black lady is still there. I notice she is wearing a coat. Even when England does its best turn at 'Wot a scorcher,' she's chilly.

Round and round we go. I give up making farewells as it seems I'll be seeing Beccles church and market square and its jolly locals for the rest of my life. We approach the train station for the third time. So the black lady isn't a local, and she just got off the London train.

My heart and brain lurch me to attention. She had a long dress and headwrap, she was African! I throw my hands to the car window. As we pass the station square, the woman is just climbing into the back of a taxi.

It's Victoria – the certainty presses in on me. A scene of devastation is about to land in Toft Hall. I have the letters, there's nothing to explain the woman's presence. Prop...

Lizzie has decided to leave Beccles by any route. She goes back out onto the bypass to find a connection south.

'Oh shit!' I hiss.

'No, we can do this and go via Diss.' says Lizzie.

'Shit shit shit shit!' I need to get back to Toft Hall. Victoria's taxi must be behind us still.

'I need to get back to Toft Hall.'

'Jesus Christ! We're not taking you to Toft Hall!' roars Tom.

'I have to get out.'

'Stay in the fucking car and shut the fuck up!'

'Tom!' Lizzie stares at him.

'She drives me insane!' says Tom.

We're approaching the Gillingham roundabout. I'm just two miles from Toft Monks.

'I've got to go!' I say

'But...' Lizzie's voice quavers. 'Your things!'

'It doesn't matter. Keep my things!'

The car slows and I reach for the door.

'For fuck's sake!...' is the last thing I hear.

Suddenly I'm out on the road. I run on to the verge as Lizzie does a panicking circle of the roundabout with her window open. 'Miriam! Get back in the car.'

'No!'

I start down the Toft Monks road and see Lizzie's car doing a few more circles. She is having a wide-mouthed conversation with Tom. I can imagine what is being said. She wants to drive me back, Tom is telling her what a useful education a long walk home will be for me. Another car joins the circular dance, a taxi. It exits on to my road and passes by. Victoria's silhouette is statue-like in the back seat.

Shit! I am going to have to aggressively hitchhike.

Running in the manner of a fifties damsel in distress, while staring over my shoulder and swearing is not the best way to invite myself into a stranger's car. One van actually slows, takes a second look and drives away again. I throw my arms frantically at vehicles, screaming abuse at their backs. But the more anxiety I exhibit, the more invisible I become.

Now covered in sweat and dust, twenty minutes feels like ten hours of panic, of swearing and self-generated images of Prop in peril. I am nearing Toft Monks. It's another five miles to the hall.

A stringy figure looms in the Fiat Forecourt. His name...his name...
'JUMBO!'

Jumbo does a double take. He's trying to fix a sign on top of a car.
'JUMBO! HELP ME!'

I have never previously used these three words in conjunction in my life.

As lanky as he is, poor Jumbo has nowhere to hide. I try to explain. I wish I had been nicer to him the the first time he offered me a lift.

'Please, Jumbo, it's an emergency. Do you remember you helped me once? Well, do it again! Now it's really important.'

He coils his forehead.

'Oi'ave to stow moi tools n stuff first. Moi carrs out front loike.'

He takes so long, so long, I dance my feet down to my knees. And he drives so very gently. I lean against the dashboard, rocking gently.

'You loikin livin 'ere then?'

'Oh god, Jumbo. I don't know. It's fine, can you drive a bit faster?'

'Moi mum says "People don't say much 'roun 'ere but they mean a lot." That's what she says anyow.'

He's going to take me to my cottage.

'Front! Front! Take me to the Big House.'

My yelling has no effect on his composure. 'Roight.'

Jesus, he's so slow. Pot holes schmott holes. Finally he stops avoiding them and we crunch onto thickening gravel.

'Ok ok ok. I have to run! Jumbo, you're the best, my hero!'

'Roight then.' He grimaces.

I feel a bit bad.

'Tell your mum Hi. I agree about what she said!'

I can't remember what she said.

I know the layout of Toft Hall enough to know the quickest way is a side door, down the corridor, through the green baize...

Screaming! Good proper screaming! Women screaming! I burst through the baize swing door.

The woman is massive, not only in stature but in fury. She is a good foot taller than the Marchese. Her eyes are wide and her nostrils flared. The Marchese has one hand on her hip and her other flies like a whipping electrical cable.

I can't even hear what the Marchese is saying, it's a gobbledy-gook of white noise and Italian. Wym and Kit are both present. Kit leans uncomfortably on the study door with one finger scratching his ear. Wym shadows the Marchese with his arms puppeted out like a boxing referee. He's making mild, placating noises. This situation is a slurry lagoon and he's way out of his depth.

The only option is to throw an even bigger bomb into the room. I jump between the two women like an oestrogen circuit breaker. I turn my back to the Marchese, a dangerous move at any time.

'Victoria!'

That stalls her. She focuses on me as a bull on the last piece of china in the shop.

'Victoria, you have every reason to be upset but this is the latest in a long line of misunderstanding. If you'll just listen for a second.'

The hall is silent. My knees are shaking, my heart actually wants to vomit. No one can help me, I'm on my own.

'Prop tried to meet you last week. He went to London on his own initiative but he's frail and old, he gets confused. The fact that he missed you upset him very much.'

Victoria's mouth is tight and pursed. 'Then why.' Her voice is strident with confidence. 'Why didn't he call me at the hotel I was staying in?'

'He became ill in London, he ended up in hospital.'

Now the Hebbidons find their voices.

Marchese crows over my shoulder 'How do you know this woman? Did you bring her here?'

And Wym is beside my ear. 'Why didn't you tell me about this?'

He sounds hurt and this catches me out for a moment.

'I didn't know about it until we were returning home. Prop had a letter.'

'And you still didn't tell me?'

Victoria tips her head back to look at Wym. The silence rushes from my feet like a preparing tidal wave.

'I have come to see Edward Hebbindon.'

I feel the Marchese's hot breath scorch my back. 'You are NOT going to see my husband! You are going to leave my house! You are an intruder!'

The Marchese stomps to the office, wagging her finger and clattering bracelets. 'Call the police, Christopher! The police!'

Kit doesn't move, he simply looks cool-ly at Victoria.

'What do you want from Father?'

'It is none of your business. This is just something for he and I. I want to see my father.'

I can see from the movement of light around the office door, that the Marchese is pacing the room. She gives a hoot and a shriek and a 'Get her out of the house! Out!'

Kit says 'Oh god, it's all true then.'

Wym is motionless and pale.

'What do you mean, your father?'

The Marchese peddles out, high heels clunking. She places both her hands on Victoria's broad back and shoves her. 'Out! Out!'

Victoria's eyes widen, I see her shoulders rise. Oh dear, there is a good chance that the Marchese is about to receive a right hook.

'What's all this?'

Standing half way down the staircase, Prop wobbles slightly.

'What's going on?'

This would be a bad moment for his lordship to fall to his death. I go to steady him.

'Prop,' I whisper 'This is Victoria, your daughter from Kiamutura.'

67. Hubris

The house in Kiamutura was nothing special. Built in the same style as its neighbours, you might notice that the grass in the lawn was slightly greener, and the trees were taller and lush. The plaster on the walls was pink and the small windows were patterned.

Prop's photo albums are out on display on the kitchen table. Prop and Victoria hunch over the tiny black and white squares. Kit occasionally squints and discards an image. Wym is hunched, sipping his tea as if drinking a flu remedy.

The arrival of his first born had sent Prop into an boundary-free span of incomprehension. Even Victoria's anger subsides when she sees that the vessel of her bitterness is not a ocean-going liner but a crusty old coracle. The Marchese found her view on things was not universally supported, and seeing the party would not walk her line, announced she was going to Norwich for the day.

Prop (and I think this is an aristo thing) has a button that he can push in his brain that replicates grace, manners, alertness and informed interest for a finite period of time. He nods and sparkles and reminisces. The exotic names of people we have never met are shared by he and Victoria, proof of his other life. But at last the effort exhausts him. He has still not made a connection between the lady in his kitchen and the tiny daughters he said goodbye to in 1965, but he can certainly reminisce and affirm with alacrity. But when his cheeks go grey, Miss Perry guides him to his bedroom.

Victoria tidies up the photos with efficiency, making self-conscious tuts on seeing familiar images. She is utterly in control of the room and she knows it. Wym clears his throat and finds his voice.

'In terms of our father, what do you want?'

Victoria has a look of headmistresses inspecting an errant pupil.

'No money and I don't need anything in his will.'

There is a strained hush. The AGA pilot relights, a clock chimes, a distant phone rings.

Victoria pushes the album stack away.

'I am in the UK for two weeks. I'm applying for British Citizenship. As my father's name is not on my birth certificate, I will need his help.'

I try to imagine the kind of help Prop could give in an official capacity, and somehow picture burnt out cars, sounding alarms and approaching sirens.

'Why didn't he sign your birth certificate?' asks Wym. Kit and I stare back at her.

'My parents were not married in the law.'

'Ah.'

'They were married in the sight of God.'

'But you can't take God to a tribunal.'

'It is all very complex. Many acts of nationality that have been passed here since Kenyan independence in 1963. I have a lawyer looking into my case. I am British by descent but I have to prove that Edward Hebbindon is my father.'

Wym puts his hands in his hair. 'Our father has memory lapses.'

Kit mutters 'The guvnor has dementia. In my opinion.'

Wym gives the table a serious look. 'It's not dementia until a doctor diagnosis it as such.'

'Your call.'

The sedate warfare is interrupted by a soft tap at the kitchen door.

Young Miss Perry comes in, pink in the cheek with her mouth sucked in like a drawstring purse. Her eyes swivel around the room, not daring to rest on anything.

'That were her Ladyship. She says she's on 'er way baack.'

That focuses minds pretty sharply. Both Wym and Kit automatically stiffen in their chairs. Miss Perry, who has decided to retake the kitchen, huffs into the room, banging kettles and slamming oven doors.

Victoria stands. She is neat and conservatively dressed but has a green wrap, coiled like a thick rope around her head. She is as tall as Wym and shares the same serious, brow-laden look of her brothers. Every tentative feeler of friendship she quickly bats away. She will not stay the night as she has many meetings and appointments in London tomorrow. In order to catch the 15:25 train to London, she has already booked a taxi. She will not accept a lift. She's not interested in small talk while we wait and doesn't wave when she leaves.

I don't want to be around for the Marchese when she returns so I try to find a crack in space/time to slip through. Wym and Kit are having a tete-a-tete, the first time I've seen them engage each other in non-spiteful conversation. I've almost backed myself around the corner when Wym spots me.

'Miriam!'

He jogs over, calling back to his brother. 'I'll be a few minutes.'

'For God's sake, don't be long.'

We walk across the lawn to the faded grass that becomes pathway that turns into rut that eventually leads back to the cottage that's not my home anymore. I'm aware that I smell quite rank, probably the worst stench ever emitted. Under duress, toxic compounds head straight out of my pores, tickertaping the evidence of recent panic out of my armpits. I keep my distance from Wym even though his years in cow sheds have probably erased the receptors in his nose. But he's too busy trying to make the first move in conversation.

'You were one ahead of us there.'

'I should have warned you.'

'Well, I didn't make things easy. I'm sorry, I've been a pompous prat of the highest degree.'

Wym is a pompous prat, but I don't think I'd have it any other way. Compared to other possible male frailties, a bit of hubris is fine; a loss leader in this case.

'No Wym, really you're not. I mean, I've spent my whole life being reprimanded. My entire life has been a failure from the moment I popped out and disappointed my father in his hopes of a son. Whatever you felt was pretty much par for the course.'

'Your sister is still in Marjory's cottage isn't she?'

'Yes. She has a very good foot-hold. There'll be a fight before Marjory gets it back.'

'Then please do collect your things and stay at my house.'

'Er. I don't have any things.'

Wym points his brow at me.

'My things are in the back of Lizzie's car, on their way to London. I jumped out at Gillingham when I saw Victoria coming. I ran most of the way here to catch her, which is why I smell so ... manly.'

'Sorry, you say you jumped?'

'From a car.'

'And ran?'

'I got a lift from Toft Monks.'

'To warn us?'

'To, well, I didn't know what I was going to do.'

Oh god, he's stopped. I may have done too much of a reveal. He's just seen the mess behind the shower curtain of my brain. The magic circle would never have me as a member.

But no, he approaches and puts his arms very tightly around my shoulders. Very tight.

'But I'm all manly,' I squeak.

'You are such a good, kind person.' I feel his lungs do a complete exhale and inhale. 'If you'll take a compliment from me, and believe it, and think it's valuable, then please do. I've never met anyone who goes as far as you, Miriam.'

Then he kisses me, through an updraft of musk.

My bedroom has not changed since I left Wym's house. A phone-call from Kit reminds us that the second act is still to play out. Before Wym leaves, he unlocks the dressing room and takes a root around in it. Then he comes out with two bin liners of clothing.

'These were Helena's. All clean, maybe a little old-fashioned but she liked good quality. There will be things that fit you. Please...'

He tosses the bags on the bed, kisses me and leaves.

68. Gravity

Prop and I sit in front of his dressing table mirror, a steaming bowl of hot water in front of us. His last shave's injuries are healing. He hums an Irish air as I press a hot towel to his chin. It feels like I'm preparing him for a wedding.

My brief period of employment in a care-home gave me experience in shaving elderly gentlemen (you have to spread the skin until it's taut, even if that takes two hands) but this is no quick bic-trick. Prop has products. The Muhle double-edged razor, the Cyril R. Salter Badger Bristle Brush, Mitchell's Wool Fat Shaving Soap and the No. 74 Victorian Lime Cologne.

His suits live in his dressing-room. If there is a war against moths, this part of the battlefront has already capitulated. Prop choses a 'Thresher & Glenny' suit circa 1938. Unlike the rags and stains that divide and rule his other outfits, this one has just one neat little keyhole chewed in the shoulder. Getting dressed pre-war style is very tactile. It's part performance art, part ceremony and is a good example of a colonial determination to fight gravity without the help of velcro, nylon or lycra. I straighten his tie (tweed) and brush away stray hairs.

'How do I look?'

'You look fine.'

'Will it do well?'

'Victoria wants to see you, not your suit. But yes, you look fab.'

In the three days after Victoria's taxi left, Toft Hall became gunpowder keg. Nothing on God's earth was going to tempt me to get even a step closer to Toft Hall than the shrubbery. I was there to greet Wym every time he returned, looking crumpled and worn. The Marchese used every emotional weapon she had at hand and flung it. There is shattered recrimination, torn-up convictions and betrayal piled in heaps around the building. I'm not sure if it helped Wym by coming home to the Hichcockian experience of me sitting in his ex-wife's clothes.

The best way of clearing up this situation was to lead him to his bedroom, and allow him to the remove the clothing, until I was a pristine Miriam again. The bed in his darkened room was like a little boat with the world pushed away. The love-making was a break between the talking and was a bit clunky like new love-making can be. But being smitten again;

I love love. It's like being slotted into a soda stream and feeling bubbles being forced through your body. This time, for the first time since Chap First, I have someone I can believe in; my very own pompous, special-needs prat. I looked across the landscape of his chest. He was smiling. I'm pretty certain. His teeth showed at least twice.

The next morning, I did take an early morning take a dash to the cottage to charge my phone but found the door locked and the Bad Cat languishing outside. On the return journey, I spied Signe padding barefoot away from the Big House. Poor, dogged Kit. Like Captain Scott, he thinks he's made it over the icy waste-land of my sister and is now in with a chance. Idiot.

I waited until she met me on the track. She put her hands on her waist like a gunslinger about to draw.

'Hello.'

'Hello.'

'So, you're still here.'

'Yes.'

Eying my jumper and shirt, she felt the edge of my sleeve.

'Nice clothes. Why didn't you tell me you were still here?'

'I didn't think you would be interested.'

'You're so self-centered. It would have been good manners, don't you think?'

'And Kit must have told you already.'

Her head twitched slightly.

'Why would he tell me?'

'Because you're sleeping with him. I can tell, you're covered in love-bites. Mine are just fading. If you keep a beady eye out, it's the tell-tale mark on most local ladies aged between sixteen and fifty.'

I have been blessed with a mouth that is braver than the rest of me. My feet turned and frisked back to White Rabbit Garden before Signe could singe me with her icy breath.

By now I have adjusted Prop's braces for the third time, cleaned his dentures, re-tied his laces, brushed his featherlike hair and slipped him into a great coat but procrastination and the 10:25 train are in conflict with each other and we have to get across the battlefront in the hall.

The storming from downstairs is making the china shake. Prop raises his shaggy eyebrows.

'What's that?'

'The Marchese is a little in doubt over your trip to London.'

'Oh well!'

She's been expressing doubts for over two hours this morning. The screeching, crying and yodelling run in turn, and if the Marchese's like me, she'll use the floodgates as a tactic for winning even the most hopeless of fights. As Prop and I come gingerly down the stairs, she turns. Her face is a revelation; without the use of make-up, her face gleaming and carnation and her eyelids, puffed spheres.

'I forbid! I forbid!'

Kit and Wym move around the hall, keeping good space between themselves and their mother.

'Prop just wants to meet his daughter. It's perfectly reasonable,' says Kit.

'DON'T call her a daughter!'

'She is his daughter, and she's our sister. I want to meet her too.' Wym dares.

Prop adds his logic. 'We're off up to London.'

'And you want to have the bastard child of a house girl as your sister, you're going to invite them into our home?'

The Marchese towers up to at least five foot four.

'I expected claptrap from Christopher, but not you, William.'

Wym looks down at his mother with a mixture of disdain and sympathy.

'Apparently, I have four sisters.'

Prop hears this, his lips clamp together. The Marchese continues, heedless and headstrong.

'Your house girl! Dirty little tramp! Lovelace was a slut!'

Prop spins in his great coat with an agility I have never seen before. He raises his walking still high in the air and his other arm out. Suddenly in his outsized coat, he looks formidable.

'LOVELACE was my WIFE!'

Kit takes the stick and lowers it, then turns his father and guides him out of the glass door.

'I have SUBLIMATED MY WHOLE LIFE FOR YOU, WOMAN!'

The Marchese looks like a burst football, the stitching is coming away from beneath her chin. I actually feel a portion of sympathy for her. Her lifelong battle to win the love of her husband has finally ended in defeat.

69. Dude

We take Kit's work car to the station. It's a smoky old Audi, and must double as his filing cabinet, because every cup holder and door pocket is stuffed with official-looking documents, receipts and invoices. Sticky squares on windows point to a to-and-fro conversation with traffic wardens from two counties.

Silence holds sway against the engine's rattle. I pick at the sleeves of my cashmere jumper and silk shirt. I seem to be acquiring by stealth the whole Upper Class containment of good honest emotion inside fancy threads.

Prop falls asleep pretty much as soon as his head hits the train. The carriage is almost empty and it gives me ample opportunity to mess with Wym's innocence and do all kinds of things that aren't usually allowed by British Rail. It's not really him I'm communicating with, but two of his subliminal settings; social coyness versus desire. If I carry on, all the electrical substations in his brain will explode.

When more people get on at Woodbridge, I resume my seat. Wym looks pink, ruffled and smug. Smug? Hmmmm. Eve must have also wondered if giving that Adam dude the apple was such a good idea after all, especially as he then seemed a lot more horny than she was. However, I didn't think Wym's 'fresh from the box' persona would so quickly give way to corruption.

We both gaze at Prop, securely asleep, his dentures are lagging from his mouth.

'Did you know nothing about all this?'

'There were always rumours, used to overhear my parents arguing about it. We knew enough to get the basics. There was another woman somewhere, with children. The fights were always about maintenance payments but, really, Mother was insecure. She needed Father's love and this has always troubled her. And then, there was the way they met.'

'I don't know how they met.'

'You don't? Prop usually tells people within five minutes of meeting them.'

Wym's teeth clamp together slightly.

'When my father was in London in the sixties, he and his old school friends had a game they played, a sort of paper chase across the city. It was a list of things, just random things that they had to find you know; a tartan sock, someone's glasses, a fig leaf and a book signed by the author.'

'This is not a game I've ever played.'

'It was childish. Basically it's an invitation to be as be as pushy and annoying as you like; those who have a natural sense of entitlement do well at it. Well, Prop was good at bending the rules. One of these lists, the last item, was 'Bring something Italian for supper.' So he went to the Italian embassy in Mayfair and my mother was one of those on reception. She was a pretty little thing and accordingly, came home for supper.'

Oh gosh, the poor Marchese was part of a game. It's just the sort of move Kit would make.

'Prop started dating her to placate his mother. Things were getting messy in Kenya before independence and life there was uncertain. My grandparents were led to believe that the Marchese was wealthy. Prop was dragged to Venice and he married my mother there. In fact, her brothers threatened to drag him through every canal in the city if he didn't. They're quite bullish, her brothers.'

Prop snorts a little, his nostrils like two caves in a sea cliff. I have to shake my head to confirm to myself that what I heard was not quite the most fantastical cock and bull, because who on earth would throw their lives away on such inadvisable marriages? I do a quick count on my fingers. Everyone, it seems.

Even through the darkened windows, I can see the sky is grey. Rain skitters sideways on the glass. It feels like decades since I've seen British weather. The enchanted summer is over. All the Hebbindon skeletons have fallen in a pile from the wardrobe. Wym looks out at the plains of Stowmarket. He must have felt he alone had a duty to carry on the family role of misfortune in love. I hold his hand and kiss the back of it.

A whine of a hearing aid. Prop sits up, blinks his teeth back into place and says 'flowers.'

Liverpool Street. Victoria is plainly visible in the middle of the station concourse. Her headwrap is larger, her dress and jacket top are nattier. Who greets us is a smiling, warm, pleased-to-see-us sister. She puts her hands out and grips each by the arm. Prop looks flushed. The last few weeks of crises have fuzzed his memory; he thinks Victoria is Lovelace.

Wym and I offer to accompany her to the private clinic where the paternity test is to take place but she's adamant.

'I am a nurse. I am the best person to take my father to this appointment.'

Wym and I are both useless in the face of strong personalities. With a bit of shuffling and throat clearing, he lets go of his father, and then wrings his hands as the old man disappears into the city. It's raining and leaden outside. The British Museum is where I suggest we all agree to meet, as no weather can wither her nor custom stale her infinite variety.

Especially as it takes two weeks to see every exhibit from end to end.

Novelty unfurls in front of me and it's the little things between Wym and I. This is our first time together on the Underground; nothing is automatic yet, our behavior has yet to knit. It's a logarithm still to be computed so everything is choice a) or b). Whether he goes ahead at the barriers, or lag behind to let me through? Does he wait at the escalator or guide me from behind? Does he watch the end of the stairs approaching fixedly or does he turn and talk to me? The answers are b), b), and a).

We face to face on the hanging straps, bumping and smiling. I glance around to get some visual feedback from other people but no-one can see us hidden in our bubble.

At Goodge Street my phone rings. It's Tom. He's probably less that a hundred yards away in Huntley Street. The idea of Tom meeting Wym is a scene I have acted out in my imagination with pride and pleasure.

'Hello?'

'Where's my fucking bike?!'

'Ah. Oh.'

The line is very bad, I think, because Tom's head is swiveling like a police light.

'My bike has gone and the window's open! Open like I said it shouldn't ever be!'

I stick my finger in my free ear in case this conversation should leak out to Wym but he can tell from my expression that I'm getting ready to reel.

'You're the most God almighty freaking hash-brained moronic sieve, you're a bloody cluster-bomb, you just go around blowing stuff to bits don't you!? For f....' and his voice tails off. The phone is passed to another hand. Lizzie's, I'm hoping. I let my guard down.

'Miriam, it's Tateh.'

My stomach clamps. My father and my brother at this very moment are at one end Huntley Street and I'm at the other. If I drop my phone from my ear, I might actually be able to hear Tom screaming. The line crackles and an ambulance goes past. I hear the same ambulance half a second later on the mobile.

'Miriam, where is Tom's bike? Have you lent it to someone, darling? It's very important to him, it's...'

'The fucking parts alone cost more than the bike itself!' screams the background.

'Customised,' says Dad.

I stop and place my head on a lamp post. Shit.

Wym stops too.

Tom is still hogging the line, which comes and goes. What I'm getting is 'Stupid...think-incapable....thinkless cow!'

'What's wrong?' whispers Wym?

'My brother's bike's been stolen, and it's my fault. I left a window open. Slightly.'

'So, do you need to buy him a new one?'

'I can't possibly afford to buy him a bike, he's all special saddles and alloy wheels.'

Dad tries to talk but at the moment, it seems the national collection of emergency sirens is going past. We have the whoo-whoos, the weep weeps and even good old nee-nahs.

When silence returns, the phone is silent.

'Dad?'

'Miriam, where are you?'

'Why?'

'Tell me where you are?'

'London.'

'Are you anywhere near here?'

'Yes, I'm going to the British Museum.'

'Then I think you should come here and speak to Tom in person.'

This was not how the imaginary scene of my true love and my family was planned.

'Sorry Dad, I'm waiting for an appointment.'

'What? What appointment?'

Another siren. A police car races past.

'I'm helping someone do a paternity test.'

There's a crackle and white noise. My father seems poleaxed.

'You? A paternity test?'

'Yes! And I'm meeting them at the British Museum. Now. So, gotta go.'

'Fucking hell!'

Dad doesn't normally swear. This makes me less inclined to backtrack for a boyfriend/father interface. I take Wym by the hand and canter him skittishly away.

70. Culture Vultures

The British Museum; the beautiful tessellated palace of plunder. Whenever I feel bad about my kleptomaniac streak, I think of all the stuff the Victorian Upper Class schlepped back in their rucksacks from Greece et al and don't feel so guilty.

It's busy on account of the rain. Knife and fork and coffee machines echo off Egyptian busts and Navaho totem poles. All human culture is represented and fun to observe from a corner table. Wym asks me more about Tom's bike. Then he asks me about Tom and then about my father and before I can help it, I blink and my lips turn down like a fat banana. The three year old who I tried so hard to protect the last time I was in London is out and crying, and not a delicate single Sinead O'Connor tear either. It's a big baby snot tornado that I'm pouring. I lean into Wym to let him cuddle me and inadvertently smash my head off a tray shelf that is just behind him. In the woozy, crying, giggling, owing interlude I hear a growl from some way away.

'There she is!'

I lean up and there is my father, barrel-chested and striding across to me with his finger out.

'YOU!'

Tom is running in Dad's wake. Tom looks anxious. I might be reading it wrong, but it feels like I'm still in trouble but the dog house has moved.

Dad still approaches, he's not slowing down at all. 'What is THIS?'

Onwards, onwards. He leans into me and grabs the lapels of my ex-Helena lime green Boden macintosh. Then I feel myself being wrenched upright.

'WHAT IS THIS?!'

'I'm sorry!' I splutter 'I'll try and get a new one!'

'WHAT? A NEW WHAT?' Dad is actually spitting in my face. He's crimson and shaking with fury.

'A bike?' I whimper

Wym's arm comes over my shoulder and forces my father by the chest backwards.

'I'll buy Tom a new bike. We can get one today, whichever one he wants.' Wym says.

'And who the Hell is this tosser?'

My Dad is so small compared to Wym. I don't know what I feel any more.

'I'm her boyfriend! I'm Wym and I love Miriam and I'll buy you a new bike.' He says this over my father's shoulder, to Tom.

'I DON'T CARE ABOUT THE FUCKING BIKE!' screams Dad.

I think I feel a trickle of pee run down my leg.

'I care about my fucking bike,' says Tom.

The Great Court has quietened. A security guard is muttering into a walkie-walkie. Dad has not noticed.

'You, GIRL, tell me right now what this BULLSHIT is about this test? What the HELL is happening?'

I have no idea what he means. My mouth drops, I am dizzy with ignorance.

'Don't give me you stupid, little-girl, bovine stare! For once in your spoilt shit life tell me about the PATERNITY TEST!'

And there it is; a wave of relief curls in slow motion and rushes over me. A simple mistake. I am about to laugh. Wym, who is now so white that his freckles look magenta, lurches forward and throws his arms out between myself and my family.

'Don't talk to Miriam like that! When I came to London, I was accompanied by a confident woman. In the last hour she's been turned into a frightened child by you and her brother. She is an adult and I'd appreciate it if you dealt with her on that basis.'

'Ok then, Country Boy! YOU tell me why she's getting a paternity test?!'

'She's helping me. To get my father, that's my father, to London for *his* paternity test, to confirm he is the father of my sister, Victoria.'

And then there's a long break. I hear a spoon drop. The British Museum has never had a living anthropological study such as this inside its walls.

'Your dad?' Dad shrinks away slightly.

'Mine. Somehow you've rather too quickly placed yourself at the middle of this drama, jumped to the wrong conclusion and in doing so, humiliated Miriam and embarrassed me.'

Dad looks at Tom, Tom looks at Dad. Tom then looks at Wym with a kind of lazy bravura.

'You must be crazy to date Miriam. In our family, she comes with a health warning.'

'All I've seen is the way she feels demoralized whenever she comes into contact with you. I love Miriam and I don't like to see her upset.'

Dad's smoothness is returning. He gives a dry chuckle.

'With your hair, who the Hell could you belong to if it wasn't me?'

'Quite.' I mumble.

'You gave your Tateh quite a turn.'

I don't know what to think. My heart is spiraling around my body and somehow, he takes the prize for being upset. At that moment, the jade-bright figure of Victoria is towering at our backs, with Prop walking as sprightly as I've seen for a while.

'What is this?' Victoria has noticed an atmosphere.

'My family.' I give a low moan.

'Family?' Victoria widens her eyes and looks down at my father, almost half a foot smaller than her. 'When I came in, you looked as if you were being attacked.'

'Yes, that's my family.'

'It is not how we treat family in Kenya.'

'Well, well, well!' grins heedless Prop. 'It takes more than a blood test to be a father, is what I say! Don't you think, Miriam?'

'Oh! Gosh! Didn't it...?'

Victoria quickly steps in. 'The results will take at least a week.'

'But the fathering game is in the service of your loved-ones. It has bally-all to do with a certificate.'

'Don't you think, Dad?' I throw pointedly.

Prop hasn't finished. He arcs his arms gracefully at Victoria '"And with no less nobility of love, than that which dearest father bears his daughter, do I impart toward you." Of course, Shakespeare said "son" but the meaning's the same.'

My father is just about to say something ingratiating when Wym shuffles himself into action.

'Sorry, excuse me. Er, you are?'

'Philip Short.'

'Philip, Tom, let me introduce my father, Edward Hebbindon.'

Odd hand shaking, glazed eyes, funneled smiles.

'And my sister, Victoria.'

More blank-faced greetings. At last the security guard who was summoned some minutes ago to assess the action. He scans what, on the face of it, is a jovial group. He taps his chin.

'I got a report of an argument. Is everything alright here?'

'Oh quite alright, thank you!' beams Prop.

We all of us nod; I nod the hardest. The security guard clicks with approval. Then gives me a second look.

'You!'

This gangly young man points his finger at me.

'You, here again! We had to do emergency conservation work on that Limestone Drum Stone in 33! You've been barred.'

And so, that's how we all end up on street, outside the British Museum.

71. Chap Last

Ten things I know now I didn't know before:

1. A pig is for Christmas, not for life.

2. Silage smells exactly like a posh cheese cheese counter. Sometimes I stand in the cow barn and pretend I'm in Planet Organic.

3. Pigeons taste like crap. No matter how you cook them.

4. Wym likes Bob Dylan.

5. I've discovered that the song 'Tiger Lovin' Blues' is actually called 'Tangled up in Blue.' I've been singing it wrong in public for a very, very long time.

6. Never take the path less travelled. Chances are it's actually just a deer track and you're only going to end up trapped between a fence and a pine tree with your hair knitted by twig-ends.

7. If your dairy herd gets diarrhea, you're up shit creek.

8. UK Dairy prices are, frankly, a joke. We pay the smallest amount for milk in the whole of the EU when ours tastes the best. Things would only improve if our cows produced cider OR Balti OR cable TV.

9. Referencing modern culture while discussing local place names (i.e. Mentioning 'Steyning' and alluding to the film *The Shining*) may go over people's heads and cause the sort of offense that's tricky to back out of.

10. The company who supply the farm's sheds is called 'Shufflebottom'. Ah-hahahaha!

Signe is still in Marjory's cottage and is now 18 weeks pregnant. She looks like an exotic wading bird who is constantly worrying about tax returns. I've passed the job of finding Good Cat One to her. She's a very thorough person. If anyone can find it, she will. For the Marchese, Signe has now taken on the role of hoary little gold digger in my stead. (Perhaps I've mixed the words up.) Signe is definitely pregnant and she is definitely sleeping with Kit. The Marchese is convinced he's going to marry her and the bastard child will run away with the 'neritance. Anyway, we're safe for now because she's been called to Italy to go into battle against her brothers over a will. We plan to greet her return with 'How very well Miriam has done as Prop's carer'. I might be the only person who openly does care for Prop. Last week, we received a letter to Victoria-Dalila Oseyo or Hebbindon of Kiamutura, Central State, Kenya, telling us that her application had been approved. She would be moving to the UK in the near future. We haven't told the Marchese. 'Long tall grasses' as they say.

December. Dad and Vivien choose to marry in Totnes. Defining features of this town are distance and the middle-class. Neither my father nor his bride-to-be have any connection with Devon, but must feel that a six-hour journey into the setting winter sun is the best way to bind a family harmoniously together.

Wym and I have been sharing the same house for seven weeks and two days. I worried for a while that he might have placed me on a pedestal. As my balance is poor, I'm very badly designed for this. It requires daily de-epilating to a whisker and hiding in the bathroom to fart. I truly hold that a fart from a lover is a sign of pure commitment. Without sphincter relaxation, as any Freud will point out, an engagement ring will never emerge. As it were. Wym has never farted within a mile of me, but I'm not sweating it yet (I'm wearing way too much antiperspirant for that).

This is the first time we've driven any distance together. With me behind Clio's steering wheel and him slung in the passenger seat, I feel like a victorious cave-girl home from the hunt. I'm secretly very proud to be able to show him off. The only cloud on the South Western horizon is that my whole family will be on show to him. Images of likely Hebbindon/Short/Bosun interfaces click before my eyes like that slide viewer Uncle Owen used to exhibit his creepy photos on.

We're running late. I get lost in Totnes, a ramshackle cobweb of a place that proves that a toddler with a thing for crenellations must never be put in charge of the planning office.

The venue is a rustic family idiot-pile called Dartington Hall, chosen for its a cathedral-like lounge and a celebrant who's happy to turn a blind eye and an open purse to wedding number four for nominally Jewish Dad and wedding number two for ex-Mormon Vivien. This is their combined 6th attempt at marital bliss. Let's hope practice makes perfect because I refuse to attend any more of what I now consider a complicated and expensive neurotic tic, what my father calls marriage. Afterall, I can't develop a phobia of handmade lace before my own nuptials, can I?

Dartington Hall is reached by a long driveway through mature woodland. Oh God. The panic is rising. I pull over, open the door a fraction and open the door for some air beside a stone Buddha. That was how it all started. A cold stone Buddha.

If the summer of 2003 hadn't been so hot, I would still be in the city, living five miles from my father the stranger, and even further from my brother and sister. There would be no Wym, no Kit, no Prop and no Marchese. I now have two dysfunctional families where previously I had none.

'Miriam, are you still feeling sick?'

'Yes. I'm also reviewing my life.'

'Do you want go ahead with this?'

Everyone's now seated inside, except for Sheila (wife number three) who's having a last minute fag under the arch of the huge door. I've always loved Sheila every since she took me to my first pantomime aged fourteen; an eye-opening transgender feminist re-working of Cinderella.

'Jesus, Miriam. If you weren't such a peach you'd drive us all to bloody murder. Hi there!' (This is Sheila waving her cigarette at Wym as we hurry in). Sheila's brilliant, I wish my Dad was still married to her.

The only seats left are extra chairs placed in front of the official chairs, we're up in the cock-pit with the marriage pilots. As Wym and I de-coat in front of my entire family, I note my mother and George blinking me morse code distress messages. Ahead of them are the conjoined twins, Tom and Lizzie. Does he ever let go of her hand? How does she go to the loo?

A few rows closer sit Icy Signe and the dogged Kit. The sight makes me feel just a little rancid – Kit here! Even for Signe, it's cheap; she's using him as a pregnancy validation Kit. What can Wym be thinking? I blush at the thought. Wym turns and whispers

'I'm sorry, I had no idea Kit was coming. If I'd known I'd have warned you.'

I love this guy. He always knows what I'm thinking.

To the straining ponce of a hired student string quartet, Vivien steps between the seats, blushing her spray-tan maroon. She has been mummified inhalingly in a tube bandage as far as the hips and multitiered duster to the floor. She looks radiantly happy. And, perhaps, just a little pregnant? Nooo surely not.

I have seen weddings before, mostly those of my own father. Sometimes I need to slip into fantasy to survive the experience.

I look to the future. One day Wym and I will be standing in front of a red-bricked registrars in Bloomsbury. Honeymoon will be an old cottage in Dorset. There won't be a three-layered cake or a six-course meal. Uncle Clive will not 'Get Disorientated' among the staff bedrooms. My very drunk cousins will not let off Chinese lanterns which float amok through the grounds setting light to, among other things, the thatch of a historic gazebo.

We will marry secretly and then slip, silently, into the night.

Acknowledgements

I would like to take the opportunity to thank all those who were there at the very birth of this book, when it was called 'tinychaptersontherun'. I started this project as a challenge to myself, to write a novel by publishing a one-thousand word chapter every day online. These people kept me going by demanding to know where the daily chapter was, on the numerous occasions I didn't publish it on time. They didn't know I was sitting at home, gently rocking and muttering 'words, too many words!'

Much love and thanks go to my husband and children who have been patient with this project, especially as they were the ones who were most effected by its production. Also, many thanks to my parents and my extended family, all of whom are clever, sweet, patient and supportive and are nothing like the family depicted in these pages.

During the publishing of the novel, I am very grateful to the good-humoured support of Bobby Nayyar and all the talented staff of Limehouse Press.

My story is only half-written. Thank you for adding to the content of my own personal novel. I hope we all have happy endings.

A Limehouse Books Publication

All characters and events in this publication, other than those clearly in the public domain, are fictitious and any resemblance to real persons, living or dead, is purely coincidental.

The moral rights of the author have been asserted. All rights reserved.

No part of this publication may be reproduced, stored in a retrieval system, or transmitted, in any form or by any means, without the prior permission in writing of the publisher, nor be otherwise circulated in any form.

First published 4/09/2014

© Sophie McCook 2014

Typset in Arno Pro, Ugly Qua, Trajan Pro and Dakota.

978-1-907536-17-5

Limehouse Books
Flat 30,
58 Glasshouse Fields
London
E1W 3AB

Printed at TJ International Ltd.

Distributed in North America by SCB Distributors and in UK and EU by Turnaround.

sophiemccook.com

limehousebooks.co.uk